"Perfect title. Perfect setting. Perfectly [...]
it down. This one goes on your keep[...]
read it again and again. Can't wait for the next one!"

LYNETTE EASON, best-selling and award-winning author of the
Extreme Measures series

"A thrill ride that kept me flipping the pages as fast as I could! With a
premise as current as today's front-page news, readers will be hooked
from the first paragraph. Highly recommended!"

COLLEEN COBLE, USA Today best-selling author of Edge of Dusk
and the Pelican Harbor series

"Just when you think it's coming together, it all unravels! Kimberley
Woodhouse shows off her suspenseful side with a villainous twist!
For readers who love Dani Pettrey or Lynette Eason, you're going to
want to have this book on your shelf ASAP!"

JAIME JO WRIGHT, author of The Premonition at Withers Farm
and Christy Award–winning The House on Foster Hill

"26 Below is an action-packed page-turner that I couldn't put down.
I've always enjoyed Kimberley Woodhouse's writings, but this one
blew me away. If you like stories of intrigue, action, romance, and
biblical hope, this is the story for you. I can hardly wait for the rest
of the series."

TRACIE PETERSON, ECPA and USA Today best-selling author of
over 100 books

"This book holds you in its clutches as the terrifyingly real scenario ticks down to a cold-blooded ending. Who will survive the arctic dark shadow and who will die in its frozen grip?"

JANYRE TROMP, best-selling author of *Shadows in the Mind's Eye*

"In *26 Below*, Kimberley Woodhouse plunges readers into a chilling scenario that will keep them flipping the pages and turning up the thermostat. Highly recommended."

NANCY MEHL, award-winning author of the Quantico Files series

26 BELOW

ALASKAN CYBER HUNTERS

26 Below
8 Down
70 North

ALASKAN CYBER HUNTERS | BOOK ONE

26 BELOW

KIMBERLEY WOODHOUSE

KREGEL
PUBLICATIONS

26 Below
© 2023 by Kimberley Woodhouse

Published by Kregel Publications, a division of Kregel Inc., 2450 Oak Industrial Dr. NE, Grand Rapids, MI 49505. www.kregel.com.

The persons and events portrayed in this work are the creations of the author, and any resemblance to persons living or dead is purely coincidental.

The "Airman's Creed" is in public domain.

Lyrics to "Amazing Grace" by John Newton, 1779. Public domain.

Lyrics to "O Safe to the Rock That Is Higher Than I" by W. O. Cushing, 1876. Public domain.

Library of Congress Cataloging-in-Publication Data
Names: Woodhouse, Kimberley, author.
Title: 26 below / Kimberley Woodhouse.
Other titles: Twenty-six below
Identifiers: LCCN 2022049916 (print) | LCCN 2022049917 (ebook)
Subjects: LCGFT: Thrillers (Fiction) | Novels.
Classification: LCC PS3623.O665 T94 2023 (print) | LCC PS3623.O665
  (ebook) | DDC 813/.6--dc23/eng/20221019

ISBN 978-0-8254-4772-3, print
ISBN 978-0-8254-7015-8, epub
ISBN 978-0-8254-7110-0, Kindle

Printed in the United States of America
23 24 25 26 27 28 29 30 31 32 / 5 4 3 2 1

This book is lovingly dedicated to
my husband of thirty-one years,
JEREMY.
Without you, this book wouldn't be here.
You are my best friend.
You are my very own Superman.
You are an inspiration, encourager, brainstormer,
life partner, and so much more.
I could write a million words about you,
and it wouldn't be enough.
I love you more.

TO GOD BE THE GLORY!

PREFACE

DEAR READER,

This series started in my mind back in December of 2009. My husband said, "Here's an idea . . . what if when the temperature hits twenty-six below, all the power goes out." From there, my mind took off. A thousand different scenarios were hashed out and brainstormed. But it all goes back to Jeremy's original thought. He even titled the book—which I love.

Never would I have guessed that a decade later, I would have a conversation with the man who would become my son-in-love and that he would assist me in adding the final element. Steven helped me to make this story what it is.

I don't know how well versed you are in all things cybersecurity, but the more I learn, the more I am grateful for men and women like him who work to keep our country safe. Steven is a West Point graduate who, at the writing of this book, has been posted at the ACI—Army Cyber Institute—at West Point for a few years. He has faithfully served his country in many postings and deployments around the world. But seeing him back at West Point, where he got engaged and then married to our daughter, has been a joy. The Cyber Research Project that he's had the opportunity to work on is brilliant. Again, I'm so thankful for the people who work so diligently to protect us. For more information on the project, please check out the "Note from the Author" at the end of the story.

Preface

You'll see the Fairbanks Police and Alaska State Troopers mentioned a lot in the story. The city of Fairbanks has an incredible police department as well as an established presence of the state troopers. These two work separately and together. I don't go into great detail explaining who does what because that isn't necessary for you to follow the story, but please join me in respecting and honoring these two agencies and the men and women who keep Alaskans safe.

Emergency Managers and Emergency Operations Centers are valuable mainstays of our cities. They work behind the scenes to save lives every day. They prepare for disasters, try to prevent the ones they can, and respond whenever needed. I was shocked to learn that so many people have no idea these positions even exist—until they go through a disaster and then are thankful for the foresight of the authorities.

One thing I learned doing research for this series is that most attacks and disasters (especially natural ones) *can't* be prevented. That's why we need people who know how to respond and how to get us through.

As you read, please know I have done a tremendous amount of research to ensure the story is accurate and applicable. Our technology is always rapidly changing, so differences will occur over time. Any mistakes/differences are my own or intentional for the story.

If you have been one of my readers for a while, you understand that I am a research junkie. I love it. Sadly, 95 percent of the cool tidbits I find don't get used, but I still love it. For security purposes, I intentionally fictionalized a lot of the protocols in this book. Names of schools are also intentionally fictionalized.

For more details on what is real and what is fictionalized, see the "Note from the Author" at the end.

Finally, Alaska is my favorite state. After living there for several years—on a remote island in the Aleutian chain (what some people would consider the bush) and then also in Anchorage (the big city)—it has been my goal to accurately portray the largest state in the United States. I have more than a dozen books that take place there.

Alaskans are amazing people. They are tough. They are loyal.

They love their state. And they really dislike when people don't get things about Alaska or their way of life accurate.

So here's to all my Alaskan friends, family, and readers. *26 Below.*

Enjoy the journey,
Kimberley Woodhouse

TERMINOLOGY

the mountain is out—Denali is allowing himself to be seen and is not covered in clouds. Since the High One is so massive, he creates his own weather. All mountains do that a little bit, but Denali does it in a much more dramatic way. Probably because his rise is so abrupt and high.

chasing the mountain—Denali is out and people will "chase" him up and down the Parks Highway to try to get the best photos before he shrouds himself again in clouds.

moose—These guys are everywhere. There are more moose than people. In Anchorage it was a normal occurrence to have a huge bull moose walk across five lanes of traffic without a care in the world. Oh, and they ate my shrubs. All. The. Time. Sigh.

reindeer (caribou)—They are prevalent. There's even a reindeer farm you can visit, and many of them live up at the Santa Clause House in North Pole. And yes, Alaskan restaurants serve reindeer sausage.

snowmachine—If you call it a snowmobile in Alaska, they might kick you out.

PROLOGUE

75 Degrees Above Zero
August 12—7:00 p.m.
Fairbanks, Alaska

THE WARMTH OF THE SUMMER wouldn't last. After all, this was Alaska. Termination dust was sure to fly soon. That first dusting of snow on the mountaintops was almost always by the end of August. And when the heat faded and the snow flew, then everything would be in motion.

For devastation. Destruction. The end of the power of the government.

And he couldn't wait.

They would be that much closer to the culmination of all his efforts. Years of investment. But it would be worth it. His plan was brilliant. His boss respected him now. Brought him into the inner circle. They were a team. And their future plans were much bigger than just this one strike. But *this* would show those responsible that they were serious.

He paced a trail of flower petals. Back and forth. The couple getting married across the field was focused on love and happiness. When they should be focused on the plan. His plan. But he could let them have their day. They were useful. For now.

Genius, really. How he'd gotten all the different members on board. What they didn't know wouldn't hurt them. At least not at this moment.

To think that his family thought he was crazy. Needed help. Wanted him on controlling medications. Wait until they heard. No one would call him that anymore. They'd see how powerful he'd become. How he'd overcome the illness, banishing it by the sheer force of his will.

It was time for people to listen to what he had to say.

Only one way to get a point across. Take away what people thought they needed to survive.

Men and women alike crumbled at their own mortality.

The time was coming.

They'd do whatever he said for the simple chance to stay alive.

* * *

62 Above Zero
August 21—7:34 a.m.
Somewhere Along the Chena River

Natalie ran through a field of magenta fireweed, just as she had when she was young.

Wait . . . Her feet stilled, and she studied the sky. White clouds moved across the blue background as if the world was spinning faster and faster. She closed her eyes and opened them once more. She *was* young again. Glancing down at her hands, she watched them transform from wrinkled and aged back to smooth and firm. Young for now. Wherever she was.

Thump, thump, thump.

The field changed. Fireweed and blue sky morphed into floor and walls. Her home. The one where she'd raised six children and buried Tito. The home she lost after he died.

Thump, thump.

With a blink, she now fought the Alaskan wind. Struggled against the blinding snow. A small part of her brain recognized she was dreaming. The people at the clinic in Anchorage had warned her the disease would ravage her brain. The most frustrating part was not always recognizing what was real and what was a dream or a memory. The dreams and memories were places she begged to stay. Reality much harder to swallow.

Where would her mind take her now? The wind bit through her sweater and sent a chill up her arms.

Shelter. That's what she needed. Before she froze. Shelter . . . Where had she found shelter? A glimpse of hope at the tip of her mind wouldn't materialize. What could she do? Where could she go?

Cold. So cold.

Thump, scrape.

A little jolt took her breath away. She blinked several times. Where was she now? Wait . . . she wasn't cold anymore.

Her favorite blanket was around her. A soft pillow under her head. Blinking several times, she looked at the wood planks above her head.

That's right—she'd found shelter in a tiny cabin about three miles from Fairbanks.

Slivers of light through the floorboards above where she lay didn't help her concentrate. Her breathing was shallow. Then the fog at the edges of her mind cleared away. That's right. She'd found the cabin early yesterday—wasn't it yesterday?—before the diminishing sun had faded behind the mountains in the distance. Before the sky went black. After that moose tore a hole in her old tent. This shelter was better and would last her through winter too. That would save her the trouble of finding another place and working so hard to remember where it was.

What month was it? July? But the sun went down around 10:00 p.m. Couldn't be July. This was August. Wasn't it? Was this real?

She touched the dirt floor beneath her. It was real.

Details from the day before floated into her mind's eye and pieced back into memory.

Yesterday she'd walked the length of the cabin looking for signs of habitation. She'd made the mistake thinking an abandoned cabin would stay that way once before and couldn't risk it again.

When she heard the echoing emptiness by the small table, she'd smiled. Moving aside a few chairs, she'd intended to pry up a loose floorboard to see if the space underneath was large enough, only to find an actual hatch a few inches over. That made things much easier. It creaked and groaned from disuse, which meant she should be safe to take shelter beneath. It was a large area. Perhaps it had been a cellar at one point. No matter. It suited her just fine.

"Welcome, men."

The voice. Where was it coming from? Where was she?

Oh, that's right. The cabin. The hatch. She was safe.

They couldn't see her . . . could they? Natalie closed her eyes, as though her lack of sight would hide her better. Men didn't like her. *People* didn't like her. Not anymore. Sometimes she couldn't remember her own name let alone what happened five minutes ago. Sometimes things were clear, like they seemed to be now, but those moments were becoming more and more rare.

"It's time to ramp things up. Time for everyone to pay attention. We are not the government's pawns. We will not go quietly. They need to listen to what we have to say. And to do that . . . Well, they will know we are serious." That voice. Commanding. Decisive.

It made her open her eyes again and drew her gaze to the sliver of light. Natalie dared to peek through the slats.

Something in the man's words and the way the others agreed with him made her skin crawl. It wasn't right. It was dark. Frightening.

Whatever they were speaking of was important. She felt it in her bones. But all she could see were blobs of darkness where feet or chairs blocked the light. The fog edged its way in again. No! She couldn't let it take her away. Not when there was something significant happening above her.

Significant . . . What did that word mean again?

"Time to put our plan into action."

She squinted. A plan. There was a plan. Remember the plan. *God, please help me to focus. To remember.*

"We only have a few more weeks of summer, so use this time to get everything in place before the snow flies. Every contingency has been covered, so there is no room for mistakes. Double-check and triple-check to make sure you leave no signature."

Plan. Before snow. Remember! The rest confused her.

"Once it hits twenty-six below . . ." Laughter. The mean kind. From more than one throat. More harsh words. Ugly words. Hateful words. Words that made her want to curl into a ball and hide. They scared her.

She shook her head against the fear. No—she wouldn't hide. She could do something. She could.

Plan. Twenty-six below. *Remember, Natalie. Remember!*

"Any questions?"

"Yeah."

This voice had a deeper timbre. Like Tito's voice. How she'd loved that man. He was a good man, not like the ones above her now.

"What are we going to do about that new chick they hired? Someone needs to get rid of her."

Chicks were fluffy and cute. Once, a long time ago, she'd held one in her hand. Fluffy. She liked fluffy things. They were soft.

Soft.

She had a soft bed back at home where Tito waited for her. He was a good man.

"Don't worry about her. Just because the media is praising the governor for his new appointees doesn't mean we should go into a panic. I'll take care of it."

The commanding voice kept talking, but she couldn't grab onto the words. Everything faded.

She was so tired.

. . . take care of it . . .

Take care. Yes, taking care was good. Tito always took good care of her. The fog surrounded her now, and she laid back on the ground, pulled her blanket around her, and curled into a ball.

Natalie closed her eyes and sighed. The blue sky filled with warm sunlight beckoned her.

She reached a hand toward it. The wrinkled, bent, arthritic fingers transformed before her eyes.

Home. This was where she longed to be. Forever.

Her young legs ran through the tall grass, magenta fireweed greeting her fingertips.

CHAPTER ONE

50 Above Zero
October 1—2:00 p.m.
Fairbanks

FIRST OFFICIAL DAY ON THE job as Emergency Operations Center director, and Darcie Phillips found herself wanting to play hooky. At least to skip the meeting ahead of her. The environmentalists and preservationists were known for droning on and on about every detail of every animal and its habitat, every issue about global warming and greenhouse gases, and so forth and so on. Not that she didn't believe in taking care of the planet and animals. She *did*.

She recycled. She had even looked into a new hybrid vehicle.

But saving the environment wasn't her job. Wasn't her passion. Her job was keeping the communities safe and also resilient to emergency and disaster hazards.

Back in Juneau there were others who handled the different groups that wanted to be heard. Here though? She'd have to deal with all of it. By herself. Which had lost any and all appeal about an hour after she took the position.

No. Stop it. She needed to look at the positive side of things. So maybe she wasn't always the greatest at handling people, but this was an opportunity to share about the important work she was doing. She should think of this as a practice run . . . because she'd have to come across as convincing to far more influential people—

Wait. Was that yelling?

Light filtered through the wood blinds on the conference room's windows as she stepped through the door. Words were tossed about the room in sharp bursts and brought her feet to a halt.

With a step back, she checked the number beside the doorjamb. Yep. This was the right place. She glanced down at the folder in her hand. She'd set up this room at city hall for her presentation a half hour ago. She was supposed to be briefing a group of concerned citizens on her new position—people concerned about making sure that animals and wildlife were taken into consideration during any disasters, natural or man-made. No one wanted another *Exxon Valdez* mess on their hands. It was supposed to be a walk in the park. Easy. Right?

Apparently it was tougher than she'd thought. She certainly hadn't expected to walk into World War III. As she approached the podium, the tension increased. It sounded like the most argumentative group of people she'd ever met. And in her time working for the government, she'd dealt with a *lot* of groups. Even the gorgeous view of the southern mountains couldn't help her now.

Scanning the room for any sense of welcome or even a slight offering of a smile, she took a deep breath.

Not a warm glance among them.

The task in front of her loomed like a giant tornado ready to suck her up into its belly of dark, swirling clouds. But that's what she did best, wasn't it? Faced the beast? Six years in the Air Force as a weather specialist had given her experience after experience in that arena.

She pasted on a smile and leaned closer to the microphone. "Good morning."

All eyes darted toward her. Like hawks on prey. A few raised eyebrows, along with numerous frowns, greeted her. No introductions. Nothing. Just silence. The proverbial pin could drop and everyone would hear it.

She reached for her clicker to advance the PowerPoint presentation to her first slide. "My name is Darcie Phillips, and I'm the new Emergency Operations director for our economic region. The governor has put together a plan for our great state to prepare for any impending disasters. It is my job to make sure that all areas work together to ensure that government, utilities, emergency services, health care, and everything in between are able to continue serving our community in light of any potential natural disaster or terrorist threat. In this age of technology, there's a lot of updating we need to do to keep our people safe, but rest assured, I am prepared for the challenge ahead." With a nod, she clicked to the next slide.

"Excuse me, Ms. Phillips, but I think we've had enough of the political mumbo jumbo. We want to know how you—and the governor's office—are going to work with us and meet our needs. Our *demands.*" The steely eyes behind wire-rimmed glasses challenged her.

Political mumbo jumbo? She hadn't even said anything important yet. That was just her introduction. "Exactly what needs—"

"Get real, Ms. Phillips. Why do you think we asked to meet with you?" Another sneer, this time from the other side of the room.

A man in a cowboy hat must have thought it was time to throw in his two cents. He stood, arms crossed. "We've had enough of the small talk and rehearsed speeches, of having people spoon-feed us what they think we want to hear. It's apparent you're up to the same game as everyone else who has talked to us. You may say you're the manager or whatever, but we know that the governor has ulterior motives—he's wanting to open ANWR now that the leasing programs are in place." He flicked his head toward the screen.

The Arctic National Wildlife Refuge? Her pulse kicked up a notch. Why did it always have to go back to oil and gas being the bad guys for these people? "I have no information about drilling or leasing in ANWR—"

"Yeah, right. Like we can't see right through this little facade of *emergency manager.*"

The misuse of her title and the snide tone made her skin crawl. The room erupted into sarcastic remarks about her position.

Who was this group again? These people didn't care about what she had to say. Darcie couldn't think straight for all the interruptions. Why on earth did they think she was here for ANWR? While it was true that the Alaska pipeline was a huge part of her project, no one had mentioned anything about new oil drilling in the refuge or the new proposed gas pipeline. It wasn't even under construction yet. She pulled out her folio to look at her meticulous notes. But words departed her brain.

"Gentlemen, gentlemen." The sugary-sweet voice that broke through the angry noise belonged to a large woman seated in the corner. "Let's not run over Ms. Phillips and the government in Juneau just yet. She's supposed to be here for *us*, now isn't she?" The woman turned her gaze to Darcie—then narrowed it. "Please. Tell us exactly how you are here for our benefit and not just for the moneymakers in Washington."

"I . . . I . . ." Never had she struggled to put her words into coherent order . . . Well, not since high school. What was wrong with her? "I'm here for the benefit of everyone within our economic region. As you know, the governor has put a plan in place that protects all areas of our great state. The cyber threat has become very real to every one of the city infrastructures." What was she supposed to say that would resonate with these people? It was like she was caught up in an episode of *The Twilight Zone*. But she had to create some semblance of order. She furrowed her brow and fixed her gaze on the podium. "While the protection of the existing pipeline is of utmost importance and a large piece of my duties, I am not here in any capacity about ANWR. You . . . you must have your information . . ." She made the mistake of looking up.

Cowboy hat shook his head and grimaced. The sharp bursts of anger and questions vaulted at her once again. One voice in particular stabbed at her.

All of a sudden she was back in high school. Being heckled by Mr. Oliver, her speech and debate teacher. The man was horrid. Had killed any confidence she had for almost two years.

Where was that voice coming from? Searching the room, she wanted to make sure Mr. Oliver hadn't suddenly appeared. No, he wasn't there. This was all her imagination. She wasn't that person anymore. That horrid man was *not* in the room. Maybe if she said it five more times, it would make it true.

She was confident. Controlled. A professional.

Then the questions firing at her came back into focus.

Time to answer the questions. This was her meeting. She was in charge.

But her mind went blank. Did her boss *know* he had thrown her to the wolves by arranging this? This was supposed to be a meeting, not an attack. And as to their demands? What were they? Who were these people really?

Wire-rimmed steel eyes spoke again. "Yes? We're waiting." He gestured around the large room. "But please spare us the political jargon. We just want someone to be honest with us."

Her temper flared. "Excuse me, but I haven't used any political jargon. You haven't even given me the courtesy of listening to what I have to say—"

"Here." Large lady plopped a folder on the podium as she glided by. "This is what we want. Tell your boss. Tell the governor. And you might want to work on that stutter."

A mass exodus happened in what seemed to be fast-forward. Before she could form a coherent reply, the room emptied. It smelled of too much cologne, stale nacho chips, and permanent markers.

What had just happened?

She blinked several times. Looked down at the clicker in her hand and then to the door. Stutter? She didn't stutter. They hadn't even given her a chance to speak. "Nice to meet all of you too," she spoke to the now-empty chairs mocking her. When she got back to the office, she'd put in a call to the governor about this group. Good grief.

As she packed her satchel, she shook her head. In all her thirty-two years, she couldn't remember meeting a group as angry as those people. How dare they accuse her of not being honest with them. She *was* honest. And reliable. And good at her job. That's why she got the director position to begin with. Lots of people had wanted the coveted job, and yet it was given to her. Okay, so she wasn't prepared for whatever *this* was supposed to be, but that didn't mean she wasn't honest! Or that she should be tormented by a group of bullies who wouldn't let her get a word in edgewise. Whatever was in the folder could be handled by someone else. She'd done the meet and greet, so to speak. They knew who she was. Her assistant could deal with them now. This was ridiculous.

If they would have simply listened to what she had to say, they would know what she was here to do. How it would benefit their community and the entire region. She was one of the good guys.

"And why yes, thank you for allowing me to share with you all." With every ounce of aggravation she had, she flung the sarcastic words out to the room.

"Who ya talkin' to, Darcie?" A vaguely familiar voice came from behind her.

She whipped around. "Um, what?"

A man in a suit sat in the corner, his legs crossed, a slight smile on his lips. A second of silence passed. Then he stood and walked toward her. "Darrell. Darrell Collins." He stuck out his hand.

Darcie shook it. "I'm sorry, Darrell. I didn't recognize you at first." Heat crept up her neck. He was from Juneau too. He'd vied for the director position and lost. To *her*. "What are you doing all the way up in Fairbanks?"

"Oh, I'm just here to help."

"Help?" Darcie went back to her bag and tossed the last computer cord in. "Who sent you to help?"

"Oh, it's nothing like that. Don't get yourself tied up in knots." He slid his hands into his pockets as if he had all the time in the world.

He offered nothing else. Great. "Oh, well, I'm sure I can find a job for you. There's a lot to be done."

"That won't be necessary. I'm not here for a job."

Then why *was* he here? Darcie studied him for a moment. Why was he being so vague? She didn't have time to play games. Best to just end the conversation and move on. "It was nice to see you again. I have a lot of work to do, as you can imagine. Especially after . . . that." She waved her hand to the room.

"Unfortunately, yes, I must agree. That will be quite the mess to clean up." He crossed his arms across his broad chest and leaned against the wall. "Especially when the press gets wind of it."

Even better. Her embarrassment deepened with his dig. Had there been a reporter or two in that group? She hadn't seen any badges, but that didn't mean much. For all she knew, Darrell was blowing smoke.

As much as she wanted to give him a piece of her mind—in her current temperament, something she wished she could have done with the whole group—she bit her tongue and pretended his words had no effect on her. Calm facade. No rash movements. She was a professional.

"That's the thing about being the person in charge. You have to know how to handle these kinds of people and situations that just pop up."

What was he implying? Heat radiated through her abdomen and shot up her neck. No. Stay calm. He just wanted to rile her. Why— she had no idea. But that seemed to be the signature of the day. Wait a minute . . . just pop up? Darrell hadn't instigated this group and their meeting . . . had he?

"Well, you're clearly busy and have a lot on your mind. I'll leave you to it." He opened the door and took a step but turned and looked back at her. "You really might want to work on that stutter. And brush up your résumé while you're at it." He gave her a fake smile and a wink. "See ya."

Warmth rushed her face. Of all the arrogant, egotistical, competitive pigs! So that's why he was here.

To torment her. Belittle her. Make her life miserable.

Who in their right mind said *see ya* anyway? Acid burned in her stomach.

She walked to the window, raised the blinds, and pressed her forehead to the glass, angry and frustrated. Which made the whole thing that much worse. The biggest annoyance of all this? It was nice to *feel* something. Something other than numb. Anger and frustration were better than nothing, right? She let out a long sigh. This job was supposed to be a fresh start. A way to get her life back and figure out what plagued her.

Nothing back in Juneau had been right for a while. That's why she'd left.

Mom and Dad were off gallivanting with their own lives. Didn't even bother checking on her anymore. And her fiancé was long gone.

No. She wasn't going there. All of that was in the past.

She took a long inhale, counted to seven and held her breath, and then released it while counting once again. The glass fogged in front of her, and she went through the whole process four more times.

In. Hold. Out.

That was better.

As the storm within her calmed a touch, the typical deadness returned. Numb. She hated that feeling.

But if she wasn't numb, she was mad. About whatever was happening on the news, about her neighbors being too loud, about the grocery store not carrying her favorite yogurt.

Was anger the only emotion she was capable of feeling anymore? That couldn't be healthy. It had been months since anything else had touched her. That's why she'd left. Her counselor said it was the only way to let go of the hurt. And she had. Hadn't she?

But numbness took its place.

When that voice had pierced through her mind during her briefing . . . the memories she'd worked so diligently to squash threatened to resurface. Every inadequacy from her past begged for an audience.

If the meeting hadn't been bad enough, Darrell's appearance had gotten under her skin. Why was he here?

No. There was no use dwelling on any of this. She rubbed her temples. It was just a bad day. Darrell didn't matter. The angry whatever-they-were activist group didn't matter. She had a job to focus on. And a report to make to the governor.

She grabbed her things off the podium and lifted her shoulders. Numb she could deal with.

But she slammed the conference room door behind her. A fitting end to that so-called meeting. It felt good.

Closing her eyes, she leaned against the wall.

As the events of the past hour ran through her mind, she let out a groan. So much for making a good first impression. She'd looked forward to the new position because she assumed people would welcome the idea of having someone take on the job. It should make them feel more secure. She was the good guy, the one who would make sure that everyone had power and water and access to emergency services in the face of disaster.

So much for that idea.

She couldn't allow whatever this was to take over. She had a job to do. A job that was all about saving people's lives.

With every ounce of pent-up energy she had, she headed for the stairs. Might as well run down the three flights and get some stomping out of her system. By the time she reached the bottom, she was ready to wash her hands of the entire meeting.

With a huff, she looped her satchel strap over her head, then tightened her ponytail, preparing to face the record-breaking fifty-degree heat. What she wouldn't give to get away from this mess. Whenever she got worked up, she put off enough heat to warm her whole house. Warmth filled her face. As if everything inside of her came to a boil. Whatever possessed her to take this crazy job anyway?

Good grief. She was a mess. This was what she'd worked for. She wanted this position.

Maybe if she repeated that five hundred stinkin' times, she'd believe it.

At least her truck had air-conditioning. She could crank it up and freeze out all this anger energy. Her thoughts went straight to Amanda—her friend for a decade—who enjoyed the warm climate of the South in the lower forty-eight. If she told her friend that she was burning up at fifty degrees, Amanda would laugh hysterically and tell Darcie that was winter weather for her hometown in south Alabama.

That thought gave her a moment of relief as she left the building—until she rounded the corner.

Two of her tires were slashed. And she bet when she checked the other side, she'd find the same.

Maybe she should just give up now and go home.

CHAPTER TWO

51 Above Zero
October 12—11:01 a.m.
Fairbanks

THE MORNING WAS GLORIOUS AND sunny, not a cloud in the sky. And the record-high fifty-one-degree temp at this time of the morning was a bit more welcome than Darcie had anticipated. Every Alaskan understood that Fairbanks experienced the most extreme of temperatures. Anywhere from forty below zero to the high eighties above zero could be the norm. But she'd never experienced it. Until now. Her Juneau-acclimated body would simply have to find a way to adjust somehow. Fifty degrees in sunshine was a whole lot different than fifty degrees in cloudy, rainy conditions.

Juneau had been her home for as long as she could remember. And it was located in a rain forest. Lots of rain. Lots of snow. *Much* milder temperatures all year compared with Fairbanks.

Sweat poured from her brow as she walked back to her office. She definitely hadn't needed her sweater today. The kids at the Starbucks that morning had given her weird expressions as they all sat in their shorts and flip-flops.

Regular Alaskan attire. Even with snow on the ground, most teens back home would simply don a hoodie to show their admittance that it was cold. Darcie bet they didn't wander around in Fairbanks like that after it was below zero. "Nose-hair-freezing weather," her dad used to say. And then he'd proceed to state over and over that was why they lived in Juneau and he'd never want to live anywhere else. Because he was an Alaskan. But just because he was proud of being Alaska grown didn't mean he wanted to deal with a Fairbanks winter. *"Juneau is the best place on the planet to live. You'll have to bury me here."*

The memory of her dad turned her stomach. Not now. She couldn't let her thoughts go there. So she forced them back to her troubles at hand. She and her assistant still needed to deal with the group's folder of demands on top of everything else they needed to do to get their office up and running. But she'd been fortunate that another news story had redirected the attention of the press away from that disastrous meeting almost two weeks ago.

Apparently an older, native woman held everyone's interest. From what Darcie understood, the woman had made small waves all summer with her dire predictions. But she appeared in random locations and disappeared without a trace. Most people had said she was superstitious or crazy. Then a news crew just happened to be in the right place at the right time and had caught her on video. That's when it went viral. Everyone was talking about it now.

As long as the woman kept people's attention elsewhere, Darcie was content to let them talk. It was nice to not be in the limelight. Not that she wanted to sweep anything under the carpet, but she needed control—to have all the answers to all the questions—before anything was printed about her new position.

A blast of cold air greeted her as she swung open the door. The heating and cooling system in the building probably didn't know what to do with these temps that were crazy for this time of year. Thank God she didn't have to program the thermostat.

The words filled her mind before she even realized it. That sounded like her mom. Praise God for this and thank God for that . . .

Faith in an almighty creator was from her past. She'd gone to church until her parents split up when she was twelve. Yeah, she'd been sincere when she'd given her life to Christ. But she'd been a child. As an adult, she was all too aware that the world's blows were far stronger than whatever faith she'd once had.

First thoughts of her dad. Now her mom. Ugh. She didn't need this right now.

"Darcie, you've got to see this." Misty—her assistant and resident miracle worker—stepped over with her iPad. She tapped the Play button in the middle of the screen.

A petite woman with long black hair peppered with gray was dressed in traditional Athabaskan garb. The mystery woman. Her long dress was either caribou or moose hide, tanned and then decorated with beadwork. It was lovely.

"Turn up the volume. I can't hear what she's saying." Darcie leaned closer to the screen.

"Sorry. I turned it down when the phone rang." Misty pressed a button on the side.

The camera zoomed in on the woman. Beautiful even in her older years, the woman was lifting her arms high, and a deep frown filled her face. "The end is near. It is coming. We must prepare. We must!" She stared into the camera and then turned to the people gawking at her in the street—many of them with their cell phones raised, videoing her most likely. "When it hits twenty-six below, all will be lost. People will die. The end is near!"

More people gathered, and she grew louder as the video went on, repeating the same thing over and over until her voice strained.

Darcie reached over and tapped the screen to pause it and then played it again.

After the third time, Misty tapped her shoulder. "Something catch your eye?"

Darcie came out of her stupor and shook her head. "No." She'd seen her share of superstitious people in her time. But this was . . . different. Something in the woman's eyes drew Darcie. It wasn't harried craziness there. More of a desperation to get people to listen. For the first time in a long time, she felt emotion clog her throat. She wanted—no, *needed*—to help this person. She stared at the captured image of the woman. Those eyes. It was like they pierced through to Darcie's very soul.

"Darcie?"

"Sorry." She shook her head again, trying to clear it. The woman was old. Not her problem. "Does anyone know who she is?"

Misty's smooth, straight hair swung back and forth in a shiny sheath as she shook her head. "Nope. No one has any idea who she is or where she came from. The news crews tried finding her later and there's no sign of her."

"Huh." Darcie pushed covetous thoughts about tamable hair away. Something about the woman on the screen begged for her attention. What was it? Her whole life she'd been surrounded by beautiful native Alaskans of different tribes and traditions. Sure she'd seen her share of superstitious people, and surely this woman was just another one of them. Why did she find it so hard to look away?

Misty flipped the cover over the iPad. "Want me to do anything?"

It wasn't her job to make sure people didn't spout off in the streets. Nor was it her job to keep the community from believing the end-is-near predictions that could escalate into chaos or all-out panic.

It was if the chaos or all-out panic *hit* that she would be expected to deal with it. "Keep an eye on it. That's for sure. And if we find out anything else about the woman. Who she is, where she lives, why she thinks the end is near . . ." She waved off her own words and headed to her desk. There were many other things to keep her occupied. "You've got the file from the group I met with a couple weeks ago—that's enough to keep you busy in any spare time for a while."

"Ugh. Don't remind me." Misty's laugh filled the office as she walked toward her cubicle.

Darcie sat and inhaled the scent of the huge bouquet of fresh Alaska wildflowers the governor's office had sent over. They mingled with the rich scent of her mocha and washed over her. This job was going to be a challenge. But she thrived on challenge.

When the governor ordered for every economic region within

Alaska with more than twenty-five thousand people to put an Emergency Operations Center in place, Darcie had applauded. That was exactly what they needed. The larger towns already had emergency management services in place, but with the escalation of terrorism since 9/11, technology advancing at increasingly fast rates, and the war on terror, it was more important than ever to prepare for the continuity of services in light of disasters. Whether they were a result of a natural disaster, terrorists, or equipment failure—it didn't matter.

Alaska was huge. Full of resources for the country and the world. It was about time people understood what it took to protect it. The largest state in the United States wasn't just about tourists venturing to it to fulfill a bucket list as they chased down the highest mountain in North America, took pictures of moose and caribou, and visited Santa's workshop.

No. Alaska was the most amazing place in the world. Which was why she loved having the opportunity to be in charge of the Emergency Operations Center for her region. Her Interior Economic Region encompassed the Denali Borough, Fairbanks North Star Borough, Southeast Fairbanks Census Area, and the Yukon-Koyukuk Census Area. A large and vitally important region. It covered tens of millions of acres. Larger than most states in the lower forty-eight.

Threat assessment was where she excelled. Not only had she served proudly in the United States Air Force as a weather specialist, but she had spent years studying and training in the fields of health care administration and emergency management. This *should* be her dream job.

So why did that incident with the group the other day get to her?

Why did Mr. Oliver's words of the past get to her?

Why did a woman touting that the end was near get to her?

As she sat behind her desk, she stared out the window. Giving herself a mental pep talk wasn't doing any good.

Action was needed.

A lot of action, actually. Because the biggest threat around the world nowadays was a cyberattack.

Power, phone, water, hospitals, emergency services—police, fire, ambulance—government offices, cell towers, the pipeline, all management. They had one major thing they all relied upon: the computer systems that ran them and connected them.

Even more concerning, an attacker could be anywhere with myriad motivations.

One cyberattack could essentially shut down *everything*. Making chaos king of the day, with no communication. No way to help people. No way to turn things back on.

Just the thought of it made her cringe. But that's what she had to prepare for. Had to have every emergency service prepared for it. All utilities. All hospitals. Everything.

It wasn't an easy job. But she hadn't signed up for easy.

Easy wouldn't take away the numbness she'd felt since Dad had taken off with his physical therapist and moved to Italy. It wouldn't take away the fact that Mom had moved to Hawaii and the only communication was a card on Darcie's birthdays. It couldn't reverse time and stop that horrid teacher from saying, "Darcie isn't one of the gifted people."

No. Easy was for *other* people. Not her.

* * *

50 Above Zero
October 14—10:07 a.m.
Trans-Alaska Pipeline System (TAPS), South of Fairbanks

Jason Myers's radio crackled as he strode up to the office at Pump Station 4. "Jason—sorry for the interruption—the new Emergency director-something-or-other just pulled through the gate, and she's looking for you."

Great. He let out a long sigh. While technically his job had brought him to Fairbanks to train the new ops center in all things cybersecurity, he was in the middle of a programming mess at the moment. An extra project added to his plate by his boss and the governor. Since he had background in oil and had helped TAPS with their industrial control systems over the years, he couldn't say no. The pipeline was too important. But now he didn't have time to fraternize and make the new director feel better about what he was doing.

He cringed at his own attitude. Either he had woken up on the wrong side of the bed this morning, or he needed more coffee. This was definitely not the way nor the mindset with which he wanted to greet her.

Swinging the door open, he mentally prepared to be nice and pushed his frustrations to the side.

"It's about time."

The all-too-familiar voice of his brother hit Jason like a slap in the face. The main source of his frustrations for the past eight days.

"I've been waiting for over twenty minutes."

Jason watched his long-lost, drug-addled brother pace the room. To think he'd been looking for Kirk for years—even took this job in hopes of finding him—and little brother just showed up on his own. Every day for the past week. With a new haircut, clean clothes, and a fresh shave. At least he appeared a touch normal rather than the crazed, glassy-eyed look he'd boasted in the past.

But today was not a good day for this interruption. Especially not with the new bigwig on the premises.

"What are you doing here?" Jason walked to the desk and tried to keep his tone casual. Kirk had always been easily spooked.

"Nice to see you too, but I think you know why I'm here." His brother's eyes were red rimmed. He reached into his pocket and then popped a pill into his mouth. "And then you kept me waiting."

"I'm sorry you had to wait, Kirk, but I didn't know you were here. You can't just barge in and demand my time whenever it's best for you. We've already talked about this. In case you haven't noticed, I'm kinda in the middle of something." Jason let his phone drop onto the desk. If he could just stay calm, be a good example to his hotheaded brother . . . *Lord, give me patience. Keep me from killing him. That's gonna take divine intervention.*

"Well, you know what I think about your job, Mr. Know-It-All. That's why I'm here." Spit flew out of Kirk's mouth with the words.

"Give it a rest, Kirk. I've read the papers. You and your little environmental group have nothing to protest here. The company has been working on this for years, and now this project—this *approved* project—is what's best for Alaska. For our country. The land won't be impacted. The animals won't be impacted. It's all in the computers. There's nothing for you to protest."

Kirk's fists balled at his side.

Great. The volcano was about to erupt. Jason wiped a hand down his face and sighed.

"My *little* environmental group and I are not to be trifled with, big brother. This expansion can't be completed. It won't. We'll stop it."

"You can't." The brotherly rebuttal was out before he realized what Kirk had said. Expansion? What had Kirk been smoking? What exactly were they trying to stop?

"Oh yes we can. And we will. We have power." Kirk crossed his arms, looking more like a petulant toddler with each passing moment. "ANWR should never be open for the gas pipeline. Never. No more drilling. No more of this." He gestured around him.

"Whatever. TAPS has been here for almost fifty years. The Trans-Alaskan Pipeline System is here to stay. And ANWR is an entirely different subject. I don't have anything to do with that. I'm a cybersecurity specialist, remember?" He growled out the last part. Shot a prayer to heaven for help. "Look, I love you. You're my brother. But I've got work to do. I don't have time to argue. Why don't we get together later and have dinner? Catch up? Maybe call Mom and Dad?" Jason struggled to let go of the anger building in his gut.

"Call Mom and Dad?" His brother sneered. "Why would I want to do that?"

It wasn't worth it. He picked up his phone and his laptop. Maybe if he just ignored Kirk, he'd leave.

Yeah, right. That hadn't worked for the thirty-plus years Kirk had been alive.

But Jason could always hope for the impossible.

Kirk leaned over the desk and got in his face. The unmistakable scent of marijuana washed over Jason. The least of his brother's vices. "You've got a choice to make, brother. You either start listening to me, or you'll have to face the consequences."

"Consequences?" His brother had gone too far. Pushed too many of Jason's buttons. He struggled to keep from laughing. "You mean, like one of your little stunts in North Dakota?"

Kirk's eyes narrowed. "Don't make fun of me, Jason. I mean it."

Jason had to force himself not to roll his eyes. Kirk could be so irrational sometimes. "I'm not making fun—"

Knock, knock, knock!

The door flew open. "Good morning, Mr. Myers." A slight smile greeted him from underneath a mass of curls. The woman ran a hand through her brown hair and pulled it off her face. "Sorry for the entrance. The wind is kicking up a notch, isn't it?" Vibrant blue eyes drilled into Jason's. Taking a coiled band from her wrist, she tied her hair up into a knot on top of her head. The curls exploded out of it like a fountain.

"Not a problem." He found his manners and thrust out a hand in greeting. "It's been rattling the windows all morning."

"Well, if you haven't guessed, I'm Darcie Phillips. The new Emergency Operations Center director."

"Nice to meet you." He winced as he glanced over at Kirk's angry face. Hopefully, his brother could keep his mouth shut for a few minutes. "I'm sorry I haven't made it to your office yet."

"No apology necessary. The work that's being done here is important and paramount to our discussion anyway." She shoved her hands into the back pockets of her jeans. "I heard you'd been asked to assist over here, so I came to you." She looked at the schematics on the desk. "Why don't you explain all this?"

"One of the valves failed late last night, and since the plan was to put in new valves and reprogram all the systems with heightened security anyway, Alyeska requested that we assist with that and tackle it all during a planned shutdown. We just bumped the timeline up. Sorry my boss took me away from our project before we even started, but this shouldn't take up more than two weeks. It's the programming that takes the most time. The urgent part is the pipeline getting back online as swiftly as possible." He darted a glance at Kirk. The tension in the room was palpable. But Kirk stepped back into the corner. What was he up to?

"Hm." Ms. Phillips's voice brought his attention back around. She nodded and studied the plans. "It was wise to take care of it now." Movement in the corner made her look at Kirk. "My apologies. I didn't mean to interrupt."

"It's not a problem. Kirk was just leaving." Jason couldn't let his brother bend the new director's ear. She'd never hear the end of it.

She stuck out her hand again and smiled. "Well, I really just came so we could meet face-to-face. I appreciate you giving me a moment. I'm introducing myself to everyone in person so that we can start eating this elephant together. I'd like to have everything in place before the new year."

He tilted his head to the right and lifted his eyebrows. Not that he wanted to burst her bubble, but that was asking a lot. Jason shook her hand. "That's a lofty goal, Ms. Phillips. But I will do my best to help."

"Perhaps later this afternoon you could stop by my office for a more in-depth chat?"

Checking his watch, he thought through his day. "I could swing that, Ms. Phillips. Around four o'clock?"

"Please. Call me Darcie. Four will be great. Sorry to interrupt and take up your time. I appreciate you working it into your schedule. I know we have a lot to cover the next few months, and I'm anxious to get things moving."

"Alright, Darcie. Feel free to call me Jason, and I'll be there." Something citrusy filled his nose. She smelled good.

He gave her a smile and sneaked a peek at his brother.

Kirk's gaze narrowed. The glare he sent them both was anything but friendly.

Ms. Phillips—Darcie—glanced to the corner and dipped her chin. "My apologies again. I didn't realize I'd interrupted."

Kirk stepped out of the corner in a flash. "Yes, you did."

"Kirk!" Jason couldn't believe the lack of social skills in his brother.

"But I'm sure he will fill you in on the great importance of our chat . . . won't you, Jason?" Kirk's eyes widened, which only made him look crazy.

She nodded and gave a gracious smile. "I'll look forward to it. If you will excuse me, gentlemen?"

Carl—the head of Pump Station 4's crew—burst through the door and blocked her exit. "Jason, I need your help. We've got a problem."

"Great." Jason would take any problem other than his brother at the moment. But he really didn't need Darcie to see any of this. What a mess. "What can I do?"

Carl took off his hard hat and ran a hand over his balding head. "We've got to get that failed valve replaced ASAP, but our computer seems to be down. Could you come take a look?"

Jason narrowed his eyes at Kirk and then let out a sigh. "I'll be right there."

"Carl!" A hulk of a man filled the doorway behind the head of the crew. "I've got guys on the clock and no equipment for them to run."

"What?"

"What?" Darcie's voice echoed Jason's.

"Every piece of heavy machinery is gone."

Carl shook his head, the shock of the words settling onto his face. "You have got to be kidding me, right?"

Jason blinked several times. "Tons of machinery doesn't walk off by itself." Or just disappear into thin air. What a nightmare. Then a sinking feeling hit his gut. First the computer? Now this? He glanced over at Kirk.

A smug smile lifted his brother's lips.

No. It had to be a coincidence. Kirk wasn't capable of pulling off something of this magnitude.

Words tumbled out of his mouth. "You better not—"

"Carl! Carl!" Their radios crackled at the same time. "We need you down at the relief pipe right now!"

Carl ripped the radio off his belt and lifted it to his mouth. "Can't you guys take care of anything?" His frustration filled the room.

The door burst open again as another man tried to stack himself into the tiny space. This time it was Carl's assistant who leaned around the hulk. "Boss, we've got a problem." But this man's face was ashen, his voice low.

Jason pinched the bridge of his nose. "Why don't we get out of your hair, Carl?" He motioned to Darcie and Kirk.

But the new kid didn't move. "They found something in one of the pipes." His voice shook, and he looked ready to topple over.

Carl's temper blew. "Are you telling me the guys can't even clear a pipe on their own? What's the matter with th—"

"Boss. They found a body."

CHAPTER THREE

45 Above Zero
October 15—12:35 p.m.
Emergency Operations Center, Fairbanks

THE CRAZY WIND FROM YESTERDAY helped the temperature drop out of the record-hitting zone from the past few days. Darcie found it much more tolerable as she walked back to her office after lunch. Winter would probably be even more of a shock to her system since Fairbanks experienced brutal winters compared with Alaska's capital. But cold was cold, wasn't it? She'd be fine.

All morning long she'd worked on her lists for the organization of all emergency systems. She'd met the heads of almost every department face-to-face and had meetings on the calendar to go over every aspect of security. The biggest piece of the puzzle would be the computer systems. Not only had the governor sent Jason Myers, who was supposed to be the best of the best, to train her in all the new cyber-security features that needed to be programmed and implemented, but now she would have to become conversant—know enough so no one could blow smoke past her—and pass on that training to everyone else.

Settling back in at her desk, she perused all her hard work. When she'd been given the position and the directives, the governor told her she would have a year to get her office up and running. There was plenty of funding since the price of oil was up. It would also help the PFD—the permanent fund dividend—which would make Alaskan citizens happy.

Her personal goal for the project to be in place by the first of January didn't seem attainable at this moment. Each list held at least fifty items. And there were twenty-two lists spread out in front of her.

She loved organizing. Loved the feeling when she checked off each item. It was what kept her grounded. Made her feel normal. But this massive amount was overwhelming even for her chart-and-planner-loving brain.

Why hadn't they given her an entire team to work with? Maybe she should send her boss a note and find out if her budget could be increased for more staff. Or was it too soon for that? Would he think she was incapable of doing the job?

One way to find out without calling her boss. Picking up her cell, she dialed Amanda's office. If anyone had answers, it'd be someone who did the job herself.

"Amanda Knight." Her friend's steady voice washed over her like a balm.

"Hey, Amanda. It's Darcie. This a bad time?"

"Darc! Not at all. It's perfect. I have about fifteen minutes before I leave for a dinner meeting. How's the new job?"

She glanced at the time on her computer—it was almost 5:00 p.m. Eastern Time. "That's why I'm calling. It's a bit overwhelming now that I look at the big picture. Things happened so fast when I took this position. I'm wondering if you mind if I ask you a couple professional questions?"

"Not a bit."

Out of all the people she'd ever known, Amanda always made her feel comfortable being herself. "You know me. I'm independent and hate asking for advice or help."

Amanda's laughter filled the phone. "Man, we are two peas in a pod."

"But I was so excited about this job that I'm beginning to think I didn't start off asking the right questions."

"I hear ya. Whatcha got?"

"Right now it's just me and my full-time assistant. How many staff members do you have? Is it okay for me to ask for more? This job is so huge, I'm not sure I can tackle all that needs to be addressed."

"What you need to remember is that every state and city is different. Alaska is overwhelming for me to even think about because it's so massive. My town has nine executive offices that all work together. So give yourself freedom and time to figure it out. Didn't you say they had some emergency management already in place?"

"Yes. Which is great, but there's so many areas that haven't been addressed, and I'm hoping to streamline it all."

"Good luck with that." Her friend laughed. "Keep reminding yourself that government often moves at a snail's pace—which doesn't exactly help us to deal with the real-world speed of gigs per second."

Oh, it was so great to talk to someone who understood. Why didn't she do this more often? Their conversation continued for several minutes as Darcie asked all her pertinent questions as quick as possible, trying to be respectful of Amanda's time.

"I'd say go ahead and ask for more funding if you can. You've got a huge area to cover. That's a lot of people if it's all within a few square miles, but you're talking about thousands of square miles, aren't you?"

"Yep." She let out an exaggerated sigh. "Like I said, I probably bit off more than I can chew, but at least now I feel it's a little more doable."

"Doable is good." Amanda laughed. "Alright, friend. So how are you really?"

The question cut her to the quick. No one had asked her that in a while. Probably no one was close enough to her to be willing to ask it. She took another deep breath. "Other than overwhelmed, I think I'm okay. The numbness is still my constant companion. I've begun to wonder if it will ever go away."

"There's a ton to process through, Darcie. You've done a lot of work, I know. Maybe it's time to find a new counselor in your area. Maybe you and I need to schedule regular chats. Would that help? I didn't mean to drop off the face of the planet in all my busyness."

The thought of opening herself up to someone new made her cringe. Why couldn't she just get better and be done with it? "I'd love to chat more, but I know how busy you are. I'm sure I will be swamped for a while myself."

"Hey, look, I'm so sorry to cut you off, but my IT guy is here. We've got some work to do on the computers."

"Not a problem. Thanks for all your help, Amanda. I really appreciate it."

"Anytime. Seriously. Call me if you need me. Gotta run!"

"Bye." Darcie swiped End. The call boosted her. But her wheels were constantly spinning. As soon as Amanda had said the word *computers*, Darcie's mind shifted back to the work at hand.

Leaning back in her desk chair, she stretched. So much depended on the computer systems. And that was not her area of expertise. That was why the powers-that-be sent Jason. Of course, he'd already been snagged for other things. What if the work out at the pipeline took longer than expected? That would throw off her schedule even more. Especially since she'd postponed their meeting from yesterday until today.

She ran a hand through her wayward curls. When they didn't cooperate, she pulled them back into a ponytail.

Yesterday . . . had been eye-opening.

The pipeline was a source of great pride and financial security for Alaska. It had also been involved in many a debate. But to discover a dead body there? That was something she never wanted to lay eyes on. Just thinking about it made her stomach queasy. Here she was, the person in charge of ensuring everyone was safe in an emergency, and she couldn't handle the sight of blood. After all the years she'd spent in the Air Force and all the training she'd had in emergency management, that was still her Achilles' heel.

At least the troopers had taken over since it was in their jurisdiction and told her not to worry. They would investigate and figure out what happened.

Darcie had hightailed it out of there after that, hoping and praying the press wouldn't get wind of the murder and her presence at the scene, then come to her office for a statement. Because she couldn't respond the way most people did. She knew she came across cold and unfeeling. And that didn't exactly convey peace and calm.

These kinds of situations were the ones she wanted to avoid. The random tragedies that demanded emotional responses. Events that rallied the public's attention but that she had no answers for. It had nothing to do with her work and was completely out of her control. But her boss had warned her that once people found out her position was in place, they would turn to her for *everything*. Just like that group that had blindsided her.

It would be better if she could have her own press conference soon, once she spoke to Jason and they had all their ducks in a row. If she had to lay low until then, she would. Perhaps her friend Amanda's advice of seeking a new counselor was the wise thing to do.

Because her job was to take care of people. To do that, they probably needed someone who actually cared.

She reached for her water bottle. Taking a long chug, she sat back up and leaned over the papers on her desk. She definitely needed to hire more staff. And soon.

Misty tapped on her doorframe later that afternoon.

Darcie worked out a kink in her back. Once again she'd gotten sucked into the work. When would she learn to get up and move around more often? She glanced at her watch. "What's up?"

"You're not going to like this, but I knew you'd want to see it ASAP."

"Has our mysterious woman been on the news again?"

"No." Misty brought the iPad to Darcie. "But this was a few minutes ago." She tapped the Play icon.

The screen filled with a view of the pipeline and then zoomed in on a woman reporter chasing down Jason. The banner at the bottom scrolled: *Dead body found at pipeline.* "Mr. Myers, a moment of your time, please?"

The man took long strides toward his truck. His expression clearly conveyed *leave me alone—don't ask me any questions.* But the woman caught up to him, and he was cornered with a camera in his face. "I suggest you speak with the state troopers. They are handling the situation." He turned, but the woman laid a hand on his shoulder.

She faced the camera with what looked like a death grip on Jason. Poor guy. "We're live at the Trans-Alaska Pipeline operated by Alyeska Pipeline Service with cybersecurity specialist Jason Myers, where they've discovered a body. Mr. Myers, we understand you were sent here by the governor?"

Another sigh. "That is correct." His almost jet-black hair in stark contrast to her overbleached tresses.

"And what does the governor have to say about the body that was found today?" She shoved the microphone in his face.

Jason crossed his arms over his chest and narrowed his eyes. It seemed he was about as comfortable with the press as Darcie. "My job isn't to speak for the governor. Like I said, you should speak with the state troopers."

"You were working on the pipeline when the body was found?" The woman was a bulldog.

"On the computers, yes." The longer he stood there, the more his jaw clenched.

"Why did the governor send you here? Is there a problem? A spill?"

Jason's shoulders lifted with a breath, and he straightened to his full height. The reporter had to tilt her head up. "No, there are no spills. My work is as a cyber specialist. I'm here to work with the new Emergency Operations Center for the region and was called in to help with a computer issue. It has nothing to do with the body." With that, he turned and opened the door to his truck.

"Mr. Myers, what about—"

"If you have questions about any problems at the pipeline, I suggest you call the Alyeska Pipeline Service Company." Shifting to his vehicle, he leaned away from the microphone.

But the woman wouldn't budge and shoved it closer. "Why did the governor send you here for the Emergency Operations Center? Are our emergency services at risk?"

A huff left his mouth. "You should direct your questions to Ms. Darcie Phillips. That's all I have to say." He placed his hands on her shoulders and physically moved the woman out of his way. He climbed into his truck, slammed the door shut, and gave a half-hearted wave.

Darcie couldn't blame the man for hightailing it out of there, but she wasn't happy with how it played out. Just what she needed, for her name to be all over the news about a problem that wasn't even hers. How did it turn into her name getting thrown out there?

The reporter turned and prattled on as Jason's truck pulled away, then Misty stopped the recording. She winced. "Sorry."

"No, don't apologize. I needed to see it." That didn't mean she had to like it. In fact, she was furious he'd given her name without answering the woman's question about the ops center having problems. They didn't have any problems. But she'd have to keep her temper in check. Misty didn't need to get the brunt of her wrath. "I thought Mr. Myers was a decent enough guy when I met him. But now? Well, if he was willing to throw me under the bus so quickly, the next few months working with him might be more of a challenge than I anticipated."

"Not that I'm excusing what he did, but the reporter put him on the spot. Maybe he didn't know what else to say?" Her assistant's nose crinkled up as she threw out the suggestion. With a shrug, she closed the cover over the iPad. "He didn't seem like he wanted to be interviewed."

"Who does?" The incredulous question had her grimacing. "Definitely not me."

Misty shook her head and leaned against the doorframe. "Hate to tell you this, but that's part of your job."

"Don't remind me. It wouldn't be so bad if reporters simply wanted facts. The truth. I'm good at that. But *no* . . . they're always looking to sensationalize whatever they can for dramatic effect." Darcie looked back down at the papers across her desk. "I better write a statement for you to share, because I'm sure they'll start calling soon."

"Yeah. As soon as they can't go any further with the body at the pipeline story, they're sure to turn their attention here." Her assistant shrugged. "But I don't mind talking to them. Whip up whatever response you want me to give, and I'll handle it."

"Thanks. Now I just have to figure out a way to be civil with Mr. Myers and not bite his head off when he gets here in a bit for our meeting."

"Ouch. Glad I'm not him." Misty let out a light laugh. "I'll pray for you. And maybe him too."

With a roll of her eyes, Darcie waved her assistant off. "No praying for him. Right now he's the enemy." Not that she believed much in the power of prayer anymore. Those muscles had gone unused for a long time.

Her assistant sent her a conspiratorial glance. "Want me to give him a glare when he arrives? Maybe put salt in his coffee rather than sugar?"

Darcie laughed at the antics of the other woman. The opposite of herself—bubbly, tiny, an optimist—Misty was exactly what Darcie needed. Even though she was just a teeny bit jealous of the perfectly straight and silky hair that always looked amazing and the fact that Misty could eat five cheeseburgers and not gain an ounce. Other than that, the woman was a perfect asset and knew what Darcie needed to make it through today. "You need to be paid your weight in gold."

"I'll remind you of that when my annual evaluation is due." The phone rang at Misty's desk. She winked and turned to leave. "I'll be back when your nemesis arrives."

Her nemesis. Ha! She doubted Jason would appreciate that title, but for now he deserved it. Darcie rolled her shoulders to release the kinks and tension and allowed herself to laugh. Misty was a godsend.

Now if she had about ten clones of her, that would be perfect. Listening to her assistant's side of the phone conversation, Darcie typed faster. She'd better send this email fast.

After shooting off her press response, Darcie went back to her lists to prepare for her meeting with Mr. Myers. No matter what she did, she couldn't let go of the anger she grappled with toward him and that little stunt he'd pulled. This wasn't how she'd hoped to start off, but she was going to have to let him know the protocol. That she was the one in charge, yes. But he couldn't just drop her name every time it was uncomfortable for him to answer questions. He was a big boy, and he should be able to speak for himself. He *was* in a position of authority, after all.

An hour later the phones hadn't stopped ringing. All thanks to Mr. Myers and his big mouth. Misty handled it all with grace and ease, but it frayed Darcie's nerves. After the umpteenth request for an interview, Darcie instructed Misty to schedule a press conference for tomorrow. Much sooner than she'd wanted. And after Mr. Myers left today, she'd have to work on what she wanted to say. Take control immediately and show her confidence and expertise. Perhaps Misty could be the one to take questions after she laid it all out? No—Darcie wasn't that much of a bigwig to get away with handing it over like that.

A deviation in her plans didn't set well.

But everyone wanted to know about what the government had set up. What she intended to do with the position. How all of it would affect and help the individuals in their economic region.

It was her job to provide answers.

And she needed to do it well.

The elevator's ding signaled her guest's arrival, and she straightened her desk, placing the simple list she'd created for this meeting on top. Even though things hadn't started off the best, she had to steer the ship back in the correct direction. Whether he intentionally riled her up or not, she would have to make sure he understood the ramifications of his actions.

It all sounded well and good in her mind, but that didn't defuse the animosity that grew in her mind every time she thought of how he'd made her life more difficult. The last thing she needed to do was lose her temper. Breathe. In. Out.

Watching through the large window that looked over their office area, Darcie folded her hands on her desk and studied the cyber expert the governor had sent her way. His easy stride as he followed Misty told her that he was comfortable with himself—and not at all nervous about their meeting. He either had no idea that he'd released the wolves on her or didn't care. The question was, which was it?

When she'd first met him, she'd liked him. As a professional, she should go with her gut instinct, right?

A little voice—which sounded remarkably like her last counselor—in her mind told her to calm down and give him a chance.

All right. She breathed deep. His brown eyes were serious underneath a brooding brow, but his dark-green golf shirt and jeans said he was more casual than his clean-cut appearance might suggest. Even though he'd made a serious faux pas with the press, she shouldn't hold it against him. Maybe.

At least, not yet. Breathe. Nice and easy.

Maybe Misty was rubbing off on her a little bit.

"Good afternoon, Ms. Phillips." He nodded and held out a hand.

She stood, took his hand, and gave a hearty shake. "Darcie. No need for the formalities since we'll be working together a lot. Thank you for coming." Taking her chair again, she inhaled another deep breath. Why couldn't she be as comfortable in her own skin as he appeared to be? This was her office. Her turf. Her meeting.

He set his computer bag in one of the chairs and took a seat in the other. Leaning forward, he ran a hand over his short-cropped hair and then leaned his elbows on his knees. "Look. I need to apologize to you. I'm not sure if you saw the news or not, but I was frustrated on a number of levels and didn't want to answer questions. I told them to direct questions to you. I'm sorry for doing that. I didn't even think before the words flew out, and I'm sure that has probably caused all kinds of grief for you today. That was not my intention."

After the rush of words, he sighed. His eyes connected with hers. There was no guile. No fake remorse. The man simply appeared . . . honest. To the point.

It wasn't what she had been expecting. She clamped her lips against the scolding she had planned and studied him for several more seconds. "Thank you for your apology." Why did she sound so stiff? "It did indeed cause a bit of chaos, but Misty and I have it under control. If we—you and I—are going to work together, I hope that moving forward, we can communicate better with the press and trust that we won't throw each other under the bus." Inwardly, she felt shaky, but at least her voice stayed firm.

He winced at her words. "I agree. Again, I offer my apologies. That was unprofessional on my part."

Those dark brown eyes of his sucked her into their depths. He seemed sincere.

Darcie gave a nod and swallowed as she gathered her thoughts and regrouped. She had to work with this man. He would be her right hand for a while—she needed him. But what did she say? She smoothed her hand across the pages on her desk. The paper crinkled and drew her eye. Her list. That's where she should start. "I've made a list of the major tasks we need to complete. Of course, I'm sure we will have to break it all down into smaller categories, but I was hoping to go over this today and see if the plan will work with the ideas you bring to the table." She turned the paper to face him.

After he studied it for a few moments, he ran a hand over his jaw. "I'm impressed, Ms. Phillips—"

"Darcie."

"Darcie." He glanced at her with the hint of a smile. "Most people don't think about all the ways implementing stricter security for their cyber world affects their plans and business. You've done your homework."

Letting the compliment wash over her, she pulled out another file folder. "That's my job. I know it's paramount to have contingency plans for everything. How soon do you think we can get started?"

"I'll need at least two more weeks to finish up what they've asked me to do out at the pipeline. Someone didn't know what they were doing and made a mess out of one of the systems. By the end of the month? The governor's office assured me that wouldn't be a problem for you, but I know you're probably anxious to get your action plan in place as soon as possible."

Darcie flipped through her paper planner, her daily to-do list, and then the calendar on her laptop. Catching a glimpse of him out of the corner of her eye, she couldn't ignore the quizzical expression on his face. She raised an eyebrow and waited for him to speak.

"How many calendars do you have?" Jason's eyes crinkled at the corners with his grin.

"Apparently, more than you think necessary." So he was one of *those* kinds of people. She allowed a smirk to lift her lips. "May I ask—as a cyber guy—what you use to keep yourself on track?"

He returned her smirk. "Control F."

She couldn't help but laugh. "The search function. Seriously? Don't you keep a calendar?"

"Sure, I do. But it's priority only. Deadlines, meetings, appointments, etc." He shrugged.

"And you just have to remember the rest?"

Another shrug. "I judge the quality of my day by whether my to-do list gets shorter or longer." He pointed at her. "And I have copious reminders."

With a shake of her head, Darcie went back to her computer. "You probably think it's overkill, but I have a planner for my planners. Organization is my greatest strength."

"I admire that. I do. My computer keeps me organized. For the most part. But I could always get better at it." The look he sent her was indecipherable, but it made her stomach flip.

Which meant she needed things back on stable ground. "I can deal with two weeks. That will give me time to do a bit more of the research for a couple of areas. But you'll let me know if it is going to be delayed any further?"

He raised a hand. "I promise."

Picking up her pen, she pulled her green leather notebook toward her. "In the meantime, do you have any suggestions for what we could be reading up on—working on—that would make the process more efficient?"

He blinked a few times, and a wide smile filled his face.

It did funny things to her stomach again. Or maybe that was just lunch misbehaving in there.

"You are the first person to ever ask me anything like that." A small chuckle.

But his laugh and the way his eyes were so full of life made her want to smile and laugh along. Maybe it wasn't lunch after all.

He reached into his bag and pulled out a laptop. "Let me send you a few links that will highlight a project I've been working on the past few years. It's a lot of dense reading, but if you can make it through, it will give you a strong outline for what we'll be working on."

Back to business. Right. Pay attention. "Perfect. I'm a bit of a nerd, so dense reading is right up my alley."

"A nerd after my own heart." His voice had a bit more enthusiasm than when he'd apologized.

And just like that, she relaxed with Jason Myers. When she'd first been told the governor was sending a specialist, she had balked and dreaded having to work with some know-it-all. But now it didn't seem so bad. They shared information, confirmed she received the links, and chatted about books they'd read recently.

By the time he left, her misgivings had melted away.

She stared at the door until Misty filled it.

"Well?" Her assistant quirked one eyebrow at her.

"Well, what?"

"You didn't bite his head off . . . so that's a good thing, right?"

Darcie laughed and leaned back in her chair. "Right. I think we will work together just fine."

"Good to know I won't have to break up any fights. My tae kwon do skills are a little rusty." Misty winked, approached Darcie's desk, and handed her a letter-sized poly zip envelope. "A messenger dropped this off during your meeting."

"Thanks." She took the packet and flipped it over. "No return address?"

"Nope."

"No receipt either?"

"None. It wasn't one of the usual messengers I've seen."

"Huh." But on the outside the label read *Urgent.* Unzipping the envelope, the smell hit her in the face.

"Ew. That's awful." Misty covered her nose.

Darcie hated that rotten-egg smell. But she peered in anyway and spied the single sheet of paper.

A deep dread filled her stomach. There were only a few typed words:

Go back to Juneau. We don't want you here.

CHAPTER FOUR

38 Above Zero
October 17—2:30 p.m.
Along the Chena River

SITTING ON THE GROUND, NATALIE ran her hand over the tall, thick grass.

Here, she was hidden. No one could see her because the fireweed was so tall. It gave her time to think.

It had been weeks—months maybe—since she'd had this much clarity. All afternoon she'd walked barefoot in the field. Relishing the good memories and so thankful they were still there. She wasn't crazy, but sometimes she felt that way. Because this disease was taking everything from her. Even her identity.

Tito . . . her precious Tito. What she wouldn't give to have a few more hours with him. Raymond, April, Ivy, Nikita, Sarah, and Kuzi. Oh, how she missed her children. Where were they? Why had it been so long since she'd seen them?

At least she had the memories. And today—for right now—they weren't confused or muddled.

But the fear at the back of her mind wouldn't go away.

The knowledge of the plan she'd overheard weighed her down. Every time she thought of it, she recited the few things she knew. The urgency growing each time. It was her calling to let people know.

If only they would listen.

Every few weeks, the angry men met in her cabin. Last time they said they were going to meet more often because things were about to get interesting.

But no matter how hard she tried, each time she only remembered snippets of what they said. If she remembered anything at all.

"Twenty-six below," she repeated to herself.

Was it enough?

*   *   *

32 Above Zero
October 20—6:30 p.m.
Fairbanks

Pushing the door shut with his boot, Jason let out a long sigh. His arms full of takeout, his mail, and research, it was a miracle he hadn't dumped everything trying to unlock the door. The apartment they'd put him up in for the next few months was nice enough, but it was small and didn't give him what he really needed . . . a sanctuary. A word his band of accountability brothers had adopted recently. One of the wives used it all the time, and the guys decided they liked it as well. At least it sounded a bit more mature than man cave.

A place to escape all the pressures of his job here. Wide-open spaces for him to hike and climb and work out all the upheaval. Most importantly, it lacked a way for him to work out his personal frustrations—mainly, Kirk.

The apartment complex had a fitness center, but Jason missed his own equipment. Especially his punching bag and speed bag. While he had never been a fan of actual fighting, his trainer in Anchorage had taught him the benefits of boxing workouts for his whole body. It provided an intense exercise regimen. And right now he could use a few minutes with the heavy bag. Maybe it would take away the urge to knock some sense into his brother.

For years Jason had prayed to find his brother, and now that he had?

Jason was acting like a toddler who finally got the toy he demanded but it wasn't doing what he wanted.

I don't know what Your plan is, God, but I could really use a heads-up. I don't know how to feel about this. I want to be angry. And I want it to be righteous anger. Because I feel like I'm owed that. After all the sacrifices I've made. Mom and Dad have made. He cringed. Yep. Typical toddler right there. *God, You're going to have to do some major work here, because I've had it.*

With a swallow, he inhaled the aromas of the meal waiting for him. It calmed him a little. Should've thanked God for the food. Then out of the blue, a graphic his mom had texted him years ago came to mind. Something about Elijah crying out to God that he wanted to die and God offering food and some sleep—so we should never underestimate the spiritual power of a nap and a snack. Mom had called him, giggling like a little girl because it was "so Jason." Apparently, when he was little and got out of sorts, she gave him a snack and made him take a nap. Fixed him every time.

All right, God, I get the hint.

Parking himself at the raised breakfast bar, Jason opened up the bag of food from The Pump House. It had become his new favorite place, and tonight he'd desperately needed the pick-me-up of good food. The birch-syrup-glazed bacon-wrapped Alaskan scallops and crab mac and cheese would definitely fit the bill.

With a quick prayer of thanks for the food, he dove in to his dinner. But his thoughts drifted straight back to his brother. Kirk was far worse than any of his family realized. Off the deep end was a more accurate description, but Jason couldn't tell his family that. Not yet. But what his brother was involved with, he couldn't say for sure. It put an ounce or two of fear into his mind, that's for certain. But there wasn't anything concrete. No proof of Jason's suspicions. He hadn't even told his parents that he'd found Kirk. Afraid that it would hurt Mom and Dad more if he told them and then his brother took off again without a trace.

During the years he'd searched for Kirk, Jason had seen glimpses of him in blurry newspaper images and on the fringes of videos. With an unkempt look and wild eyes, Kirk had always been involved with extremist groups that tried to get attention but didn't accomplish much. With members probably too strung out on drugs to pull off anything of any magnitude, the groups had made a few small headlines.

But something about Kirk's appearance of late didn't sit well with Jason. Even though it was good to see his younger brother cleaned up and looking like he wasn't living among a pack of wolves, the determined look in his eyes was scarier than the sloven-addict version.

The question was, what was Jason going to do about it? Was it time to tell Mom and Dad that he'd found their long-lost son? That thought was the one that scared him the most. It was a lose-lose situation. On the one hand, if he told them, Kirk would probably bolt as soon as they confronted him and possibly get into something even worse. At least right now he seemed to be clean and staying in one place. The only positives. On the other hand, if Jason's instincts were on track, Kirk might do something radical and hurt people. That might just kill his parents.

Of course, if he didn't tell them and they found out that Jason had been seeing his brother on a regular basis—no matter what Kirk was up to—his parents would be angry that they didn't have the chance to try to reconcile.

The conundrum had kept him up every night since Kirk first appeared. Over the years, the toll of a missing and sick son had made his parents fragile. Jason had prayed more for his brother in the past few weeks than he had in a long time. Asking the Almighty for guidance, wisdom, and the control to not beat the snot out of his little brother for putting their family through the past decade of heartache.

So far there hadn't been any divine answers. He was a patient man. But after ten years of frustration had passed since Kirk refused treatment and rehab, Jason's patience grew smaller than the latest microprocessor. Especially now that his brother was around on a regular basis. At least he appeared to be taken care of. *Who* was doing the caregiving was a question for another day.

Jason rolled his shoulders and neck as his mind raced over the time. He would be thirty-five this year. A lot had happened the last few years, but what he'd hoped to accomplish and be by this stage hadn't happened. Mainly on the personal level. Marriage and a family of his own had been at the top of his list. All these years, he'd planned, saved, and prepared for it. But he'd always pushed aside his own wants and needs, telling himself that once he got Kirk squared away, he could focus on himself.

As Jason shoved another bite into his mouth, the sweet and savory scallops were the perfect accompaniment to the hearty and rich mac. Yeah, it was a lot of calories, but he'd go running later and pound the pavement to get his endorphins pumping and prayerfully release a lot of the tension that made everything inside of him tight and stressed.

Running was a better choice than drugs. Watching what addictive substances had done to his younger brother had been the best drug-prevention program he could have gone through as a young adult.

The only thing he allowed himself was coffee each morning. And there were days he'd considered getting rid of that—but it would be a stretch for him. Who was he kidding? More than a stretch, coffee—strong, highly caffeinated coffee—in the cyber world was a must. Pretty sure it was part of the written rules somewhere.

With all the thoughts of Kirk raging through his mind, no wonder he was stressed out. God had a plan . . . otherwise He wouldn't have brought Jason here at the very time when Kirk was here.

Jason would need to rest in God's promises. He needed to stop obsessing over his brother—where he was, what he was doing, if he was okay. Needed to learn how to overcome his desire to control and fix the situation.

How to accomplish that was another thing entirely.

After dumping the empty plastic trays, he forced himself to refocus his thoughts. There was an end in sight to the mess with the computers at the pipeline. In fact, with the new security measures, it should make programming easier to streamline procedures for the new emergency measures the governor was putting into place. Which meant his job with Darcie Phillips should be fairly easy. Smoothing the bumps in the road for her should help her forgive him for sticking his foot in his mouth with that reporter. Something that he still kicked himself for every time the news blared.

Hopefully, the time passing since he'd last seen Darcie would help ease the rift he'd created. Even though he'd apologized, he'd seen the fire in her eyes. He was pretty sure she had been ready to give him quite the lecture. But to her credit, she'd handled the situation with grace.

Leaning back, his mind wandered to the woman who used her work to build a big wall around her. Couldn't help but notice that the first time they'd met. But behind the professional facade, there was a hint of vulnerability. She intrigued him. Something not many women did. There was no doubt she was intelligent, talented, and quite a beauty with those huge blue eyes.

He shook his head. The attraction he felt needed to be put aside. Because his gut threw up a red flag. He couldn't put his finger on it, but she didn't seem comfortable in her own skin. Was she simply trying to prove herself with the job? Or was she hiding something?

Only time would tell. Especially since a security network of this magnitude had never been attempted up here. Most people didn't understand what it would take . . . how *long* it would take to get the programming and computer systems in place.

Most regular citizens were spoiled by technology and the instantaneous world they lived in. They quickly voiced their frustrations when something didn't work right away, or when the internet went out, or when the little wheel spun on their phones, tablets, or computers. Because it was expected to work. Perfectly. All the time.

But all it took was one tiny miscalculation, one slip, and the systems no longer functioned together.

And if there were an emergency? An earthquake that knocked out cell towers and internet? Or, God forbid, a terrorist attack? People would want that instantaneous communication to operate properly. But they didn't realize that the future of terrorism wasn't nearly as much bombings and physical attacks as it was in the cyber world. Because everything—absolutely *everything*—depended on computers nowadays.

If people actually thought about it and the ramifications, they'd be more cautious online. Do things differently. Yep, even prep for a world without technology.

But the majority of people didn't want to think about that. Couldn't even bear to acknowledge that they were addicted to their phones, the internet, and instant access. In fact, Jason doubted that 90 percent of the population would even know what to do in the face of a crisis of that magnitude.

Which was why he was here. Having trained with a group from the Army Cyber Institute who'd developed a program and project over the years to instruct and inform major cities how to prepare for such disasters, Jason was an expert in his field. The cyber team he worked with out of Anchorage had joined forces with the state to create the security desperately needed.

The weight on his shoulders for these projects got heavier with each passing day. People's lives were at stake.

His cell phone rang, and Jason stepped off the barstool and went to the coffee table, where he'd deposited his laptop bag.

The number was blocked. Probably one of the higher-ups in Juneau. "Myers."

"Jason, I need your help." Kirk's voice was breathless, agitated.

Closing his eyes, Jason took a deep breath. "Where are you?"

"Van Horn Road. There's an auto salvage place. I'm hiding behind some cars at the tree line."

"What's going on, Kirk? Are you in trouble—in danger?"

"Just come. Quick."

The line disconnected.

CHAPTER FIVE

31 Above Zero
October 20—6:55 p.m.
Undisclosed Location

"KELLER, YOU'VE LOST YOUR MIND if you think I'm going to give in to you." He spit the words. The idiot in front of him had taken one too many pills today.

Of course, that's what happened when you associated with addicts. He should know.

"I'm tired of playing your games, Griz." The shortened nickname echoed in the air. "Letting you call all the shots. You're not in charge. Not really. Now hand it over." Keller waved a revolver around with a shaky hand, pointing it at everything and showing his inexperience with the weapon.

"I can't do that." Griz kept his voice steady. Firm. "You need to sleep it off, Keller, or you'll find out why they call me Grizzly. Come back tomorrow, and we'll chat. I'll talk to the boss and get you what you want. You're not finished with your job."

The man shook his head. "Nope. Not gonna fall for that again. I did what you asked. Now it's time you coughed up what you promised. I'm tired of taking orders from you. Besides, the boss needs me and you know it."

"That's where you're wrong. You don't think he would rest the entire plan on just you, now do you? You're disposable. A duplicate. Just like all the others."

Keller's face fell as fear filled his bloodshot eyes.

Griz lifted his Glock and fired twice.

The other man dropped to the ground.

Picking up his brass, he shook his head at the moron. "*I* don't need anyone either." He reached into his pocket and popped a pill. It would take the edge off. At least for now.

Too bad the others didn't know how to control their addictions. He walked backward away from the body. In the last vestiges of light after sunset, he used his right boot to sweep away his footprints as he left.

Time to call up another rookie from the trenches.

* * *

28 Above Zero
October 20—10:00 p.m.
Fairbanks

Darcie clicked over to the news, her mind still reeling from the day. Ever since her press conference, she'd had meeting after meeting with everyone from the hospital administrator to utilities directors to Joey's grandma who ran a preschool. It seemed like all she and Misty had accomplished the past week was attempting to answer the public's questions.

Thankfully, the governor's office had approved a budget for more staff. But she was having a difficult time finding two qualified people. And neither she nor Misty had the time to put into the hunt. Her boss sent her résumés of a few people he thought would be good fits, but none of them lived in Fairbanks. And Darrell Collins—the sniveling instigator—was completely out of the question. No matter how many times he submitted his résumé. After he'd gloated about that horrible meeting her first day on the job, she wanted to avoid him like ten-day-old salmon.

As the meteorologist came on for the quick preview at the beginning of the newscast, Darcie shivered hearing the coming winter was predicted to hit record lows just like they hit record highs this summer. Pulling her notebook onto her lap, she made a note to talk to Misty about what else they could do for emergency preparedness in case of a severe cold snap and loss of any services.

Which reminded her . . . she still had to venture out to see the recent upgrade to BESS 2.0—the backup battery system for the electric association. Ever since 2003 it had helped keep the power on and prevent more than fifteen hundred outages. Which in Alaska could mean life or death, especially in the dead of winter. BESS was one of the few things that actually made her job easier. Unlike everything else, it seemed.

During the commercial break, she tossed a bag of popcorn into the microwave and hit the Popcorn button. That was one of her prerequisites—a microwave that could pop the perfect bag of popcorn—and thankfully her new house had one of the best she'd ever used. Oh, the refrigerator, stove, and dishwasher were all equally impressive, but none of them saw as much use as the microwave.

One of these days, she really should learn how to cook herself a decent meal.

She lifted the remote to change it over to her streaming service so she could binge a few episodes of *NCIS*. But the news came back on with a "Breaking News" banner. "Violent crime on the rise" scrolled. She turned the volume up. And then it went to commercial. Good grief.

Why she thrived on crisis, crime, and chaos, she really couldn't say. Maybe that's why she felt an emergency management position was perfect for her. Or maybe because she was desperate to *feel* something.

She shoved that thought away. There was nothing wrong with her. She was just wired differently. Sure she loved *NCIS* and crime shows.

But she hated the sight of blood. Crises and catastrophes gave her a little thrill of excitement, but she couldn't bear to see a dead animal in the road.

It was time to face it—she was weird. A juxtaposition, to be sure.

The news returned, and the reporter appeared to be at some sort of junkyard.

Darcie tucked her legs up under her and tossed some of the buttery goodness into her mouth.

Her crunching covered up the beginning of the report, so she cranked up the volume.

". . . this latest murder in an ever-growing number of violent crimes in our fair city has many people worried about their safety." The reporter turned to a tall man beside her. "Trooper Lindsay, does this recent murder have anything to do with the body found at the pipeline? We were told that was a murder as well, but haven't been updated." She shoved a mic into the state trooper's face.

"It's too early to ascertain at this time. But there is no evidence that the two crimes are related."

"I hear you already have a suspect in custody?"

"Not a suspect. A person of interest." The man's radio crackled, and he reached to silence it. "If you'll excuse me."

The reporter did not seem pleased that the trooper walked away as she faced the camera—a bit of the wind knocked out of her sails. "As always, we will keep you up to date on this breaking news story."

The anchor started quoting statistics on violent crimes in the area, and Darcie scrunched her brow. When she'd moved here from Juneau, she didn't remember seeing the crime rate was that high. And she'd done a good deal of research. Was it only because of the two murders in the past few weeks? It's not like she lived in DC or Los Angeles.

She muted the television and went to check her doors. At the office, they had powerful electronic key-coded locks. Which—like all electronic keypad locks—were battery operated. Of course there was an alarm system and cameras too, but those fancy locks always made her feel safer. Turning the deadbolt on the front and then the door that led to the garage, she made a mental note to always set the alarm. Maybe a sticky note on the door would remind her and help her to make it a habit from now on. Then tomorrow she could check into changing her locks to the electronic ones.

Plopping back down on the couch, she pushed the popcorn bowl aside and pulled her laptop out. Her mind spun in a million different scenarios. Maybe she had been watching too much *NCIS* recently. Couple that with the daunting task of her job and her imagination could take off without her. Still, no harm in being prepared, right?

Her cell buzzed from the coffee table. She glanced at the screen—Misty.

Darcie set her laptop to the side and picked up the phone. "Hey, I thought you went to bed at ten?"

"Yeah . . . I do. But I just had a call from the state troopers' office."

That made Darcie frown. "Oh?"

"The calls from the office are forwarded to me."

"That's right. Do we need to change that protocol?"

"No. It's my job. Anyway, they're looking for you. Need you to call them back. Something about you verifying the identity of someone." Misty yawned.

"Give me the number." Darcie wrote down the information her assistant gave her. "Go back to bed, I'll take care of this."

Another yawn. "Okay. 'Night."

She stared at the paper for a few seconds and then dialed the number. Whose identity was she supposed to verify? She hadn't lived here long enough . . . unless it was one of the people she'd met recently? One of the government officials? Maybe this was their only way to save face.

The woman who answered the phone didn't give her any information. Simply asked her to come down to the department.

Darcie looked down at her yoga pants and T-shirt. This probably called for her to be dressed more professional, but she didn't care.

It was late, and it—hopefully—wouldn't take too long. Throwing on a lightweight jacket, she shoved her wallet, phone, and keys into her pockets. At the door to the garage, she disarmed her alarm and headed out.

Commanding Siri to give her directions to the address the woman had given her, she pulled out of her neighborhood. The drive to the troopers' headquarters was short, but that didn't stop her mind from whirling with potential candidates who would have her summoned.

At the station, she showed her ID and was led to a room down a long hall.

When the door opened, her eyes widened.

There sat Jason Myers in handcuffs. The trooper next to him frowning.

CHAPTER SIX

25 Above Zero
October 20—10:18 p.m.
State Trooper HQ, Fairbanks

UNCOMFORTABLE WAS TOO TAME A word for how Jason felt at that moment. The look on Darcie's face as she entered the room was one of shock that then took a quick turn to concern. Her blue eyes were wider than he'd ever seen.

The trooper at his left spoke first. "Ms. Phillips, do you know this man?"

She visibly swallowed. "Yes, sir. This is Jason Myers."

The man relaxed. "How long have you known him?"

"Not long, sir. We both moved to the area recently for our jobs."

"You're in charge of the new Emergency Ops Center?"

"Yes, sir." Darcie's brow dipped into a frown. "What is this about? And why is Mr. Myers in handcuffs?" She crossed her arms over her chest in a protective stance.

He held up a hand. "We've been briefed on your new position and appreciate you being here." The trooper stepped around the stainless-steel table and held out his hand to her.

She shook it, but her eyes narrowed. "Thank you. And I'm very grateful for the work all of you do as well."

"Thank you for coming down on such short notice. This man was found without any identification, and we haven't received the results of his fingerprints yet. Our computer systems seem to be down, and we can't check any of our databases online."

This man. That's what he was being called? Him! Wait a second. Their computers were down?

"That's the Jason Myers I've worked with."

Why did it sound like all of a sudden she doubted him? Of course, if he were in her shoes, he would probably question things too. Hopefully, the trooper didn't pick up on it.

The big man sighed and put his hands on his belt. "That's what we hoped you would say after we put in a call to his company and the governor's office."

"Did you say the computers were down?" Jason looked between the two, feeling like he was at a tennis match.

"Yes. IT has been working on the problem. It's happened three times this summer. The deputy commissioner is none too pleased." The tall trooper looked down at him.

"I can understand why. That's unacceptable." Jason shook his head. Something else to look into later. Once he was *out* of here. But the niggling at the back of his mind wouldn't relent. Something wasn't adding up. "I hate to be a complainer, but do you think we could remove these now?" He held up his cuffed hands. It wasn't his intention to sound so grumpy, but this evening had been nothing but one disaster after another. Anger at Kirk threatened to boil to the surface, and embarrassment at his current predicament made him want to run out the door as fast as he could. But he couldn't. He had to face this head-on. What would Ms. Phillips think of him now?

"My apologies, Mr. Myers, but you understand the gravity of the situation." The trooper came back toward him and unlocked the cuffs.

Jason nodded and rubbed at his wrists. "Does this mean I'm free to go?"

"Yes. We have your testimony and will call if we need you."

"Don't leave town?" He stood as he attempted to lighten the room with a joke.

The trooper's brows raised. "That would be correct. Sorry for the inconvenience, but we have procedures to follow—especially in a murder investigation." The man opened the door and motioned for them to exit.

Jason stepped out. "Understood." Best not to irk the man any further. This was not the kind of impression he wanted to make on the woman beside him.

"Wait. A murder investigation?" Darcie stopped in the hall.

Jason took her elbow. "I can explain."

The trooper's hands were on his belt. "Ms. Phillips, will you be able to give Mr. Myers a ride home?"

Her wide eyes went back and forth between the two of them. She blinked several times. Her gaze cut through Jason's.

"I can call an Uber." He kept walking toward the door. Couldn't get out of there fast enough.

"Good. I'll be in touch." The trooper opened the electronically locked door.

He glanced behind him to see if Darcie was following him or had decided to ask some questions of her own. Not that he could blame her. She'd been called down to the trooper station late at night. For him. In a murder investigation.

Darcie's lips pinched into a thin line, and she took swift strides to the exit.

Once they were outside, she turned to him with her hands on her hips. "You have some explaining to do, Mr. Myers."

So they were back to formality. He should have expected it. Especially under these circumstances. He held up his hands. "First, I don't need a ride home, but a ride back to my car would be great."

"Fine." One eyebrow lifted. "Explanation now?"

"My brother called and said he needed help. He was out on Van Horn Road behind the auto salvage place."

Her eyes narrowed. "Where the body was found tonight?"

"Yep. I drove out there to find him."

Darcie's face scrunched up. "So where is your brother? Why wasn't he in there too?"

"I don't know. I never saw him."

Her eyes were mere slits now as she chewed on her lip.

Distracted by the action, he blinked to change the direction of his thoughts. No. This was not the time for attraction. Not when she was looking at him like she wanted to see him trampled by a moose.

"Exactly *why* did they bring you in?" Her tone implied a whole family of moose should carry it out.

Wait until she heard the rest. "I was standing by the dead man when they drove up."

That made her eyebrows shoot back up to her hairline. "You're the person of interest they were talking about on the news?"

"Yep." He shoved his hands into his jeans pockets.

For several moments she studied him as if she could see right through him. She let out a long breath, and her face softened just a touch. "So what happened?"

"By some freak coincidence—and mind you, I don't believe in coincidences—I happened upon the dead man while I was looking for my brother. Whoever it was had been shot twice by what I could tell, and as I went to call 911, I was tackled to the ground. My phone and wallet were taken. Then not more than fifteen seconds later, I was getting to my feet when the troopers pulled up with their lights and sirens blaring. Said they'd been called with a tip about a murder."

She crossed her arms over her chest. "Yeah, that's a bit too much of a coincidence. And you haven't heard from your brother?"

With a long exhale, Jason swiped a hand down his face. "I don't know. My phone is gone."

"Do you think he had anything to do with this?"

He stared down at the pavement. "I hope not. But it doesn't look good."

"That doesn't help me, Jason." She shook her head and huffed at him.

Pressing his lips together, he did his best to keep his composure. "Look. I'm just as frustrated as you. Probably more so. The only reason they let me go was because they found another set of footprints that appeared to belong to whoever tackled me to the ground, and I didn't have a weapon on me." He stepped closer, willing her to believe him. The faint smell of something citrusy floated through his senses. Even in this awful moment, he couldn't deny there was something special about her. But at this point, he was still a suspect, even though someone at the governor's office had vouched for him—at least for the Jason Myers they knew. Who couldn't be verified because the computers were down? Too many things raised the hairs on the back of his neck. Once again he wanted to cringe at the thought of how much the world depended on technology. His own identity was up for debate.

A flicker of something—a moment of vulnerability?—flashed in her eyes. "I don't understand why you had them call my office . . . why you had to get me involved."

The hurt in her voice struck him in the gut. He hated that he was the one who put it there. He'd already involved her one too many times with the press . . .

Taming his tone so his own frustration didn't ooze out, he shoved his hands into his pockets again. "They needed someone of substance to identify me and quickly. My company and the governor's office corroborated that Jason Myers was a cybersecurity specialist working with the Emergency Ops Center, but I had no ID on me. You and I both know what's riding on our work here. It's paramount that we attain and keep the trust of the people. But if the press had gotten ahold of this, the governor's office, your office, the mayor's office would have all kinds of fallout."

"I take it you believe your brother wasn't ever there?"

She was smarter than he'd given her credit. "You're probably correct. But he's my brother, I had to go." Might as well tell her the whole truth. "You met him at the pipeline."

Her jaw dropped as realization dawned on her face. "The guy who was high?" She clearly schooled her expression. "I'm sorry. That was rude of me."

"No need to apologize. One and the same. Kirk has been the black sheep for a long time. We haven't known where he was until recently."

"So you think he set you up?"

While he hated to think it, it was most likely true. "I don't know what else to think." He searched her face. "I'm sorry to drag you down here. But the governor's office was livid about this. They're trying to do good work, and there's been too many roadblocks along the way. We don't need any negative press associated with the job you have to do. The job *I* have to do to help you. Do you mind if I borrow your phone and call an Uber?"

She scrutinized him for several seconds. "No need. I'll give you a ride. Besides, how are you going to pay with no wallet and no phone?"

She had a point. Why the woman didn't walk away then and there, he couldn't say. But this was a step in the right direction. He would be issuing constant apologies to her at this rate. Something he wasn't prone to do often. "I appreciate it."

"You owe me." No change in expression.

"Yeah . . . I had a feeling you would say that." As they walked through the parking lot, he winced. "Name your price."

"You may regret that. You interrupted my date with a bowl of popcorn and *NCIS*."

The hint of snark in her tone made him smile to himself. Perhaps there was more to Darcie Phillips after all.

"Oh, ouch. It will be a hefty price indeed." He wanted to keep it lighthearted now they'd found that footing, but he needed to eat humble pie for the unforeseen future. "Again. I'm sorry. But thank you for coming." He followed her to her vehicle.

Using the remote in her hand, she unlocked her truck. "Get in. It's late and I'm tired."

Yeah, he was definitely going to be in the doghouse for a while. He'd have to smooth things over somehow.

And throttle his brother next time he saw him.

If he saw him. But if the feeling in his gut was any indication, Kirk was long gone for now. Until the next time he wanted to use Jason as his scapegoat.

Any hope of his brother turning his life around had vanished when Jason saw that body.

Swallowing against the fury that threatened to creep up his throat, he had to face a hard truth.

His brother was most likely a murderer.

CHAPTER SEVEN

22 Above Zero
October 22—9:24 a.m.
Alyeska Pipeline, South of Fairbanks

NO ONE ELSE KNEW WHAT had transpired last night. Whoever had the power kept a lid on it. Jason would be eternally grateful for that.

But he couldn't quite forgive himself for falling for Kirk's scheme. Even after picking up a new phone first thing this morning and syncing it with the cloud, there wasn't a word from his brother. Which meant one of two things: something horrible had happened to him, or Jason had been played.

Had it all been a ruse? If so . . . That thought terrified him more than angered him. It meant Kirk was involved in something much worse than Jason had imagined. This went beyond an addicted sibling who wasn't in his right mind. A murder had taken place.

Grabbing his third cup of coffee for the morning, he sat back down at the computers and focused on the task at hand. But the systems mess that had been created at the pipeline didn't seem to be an accident.

It was intentional. He'd bet his job on it.

For now, he'd collect all the information he could and fix it. As soon as he finished, he'd schedule a secure call with his boss. Between what was happening here at the pipeline and then the suspicious computer problems at the troopers' office, Jason was pretty sure something much bigger was taking place behind the scenes. He just hadn't figured out what. Or who was behind it.

The phone beside him rang. *Please don't let it be the press.*

He picked up the receiver. "This is Myers."

"Mr. Myers, Trooper Lindsay. I just wanted to inform you that we caught the man who mugged you last night. So that part of your story has been confirmed."

His story. That meant he was still a person of interest. No matter what the governor's office said. "Thank you for letting me know. Did he know anything about the murder?" He desperately needed to know why all of the events of last night occurred. Whether to condemn his brother or prove him innocent, he didn't care. But this uncertainty was killing him.

"He was paid a hundred dollars to mug you, take your phone and wallet. He was strung out and didn't know which end was up when we found him."

"He didn't witness the murder? Or see anyone else?" Jason pushed.

"Mr. Myers, we are in the middle of an investigation. This call was a courtesy to you—"

"And I appreciate that. But I haven't heard from my brother, and I don't have to tell you that this has me more than a bit concerned."

The man cleared his throat. "We found your brother. He has an alibi for last night. He wasn't even in town. Said he never called you."

Wait . . . what? "But—"

"We traced the call to your cell that you allege was your brother. It was a burner phone."

"Which means a dead end, right?"

Trooper Lindsay released a breath. "Mr. Myers, it's an ongoing investigation. Your superiors have assured us that you will be cooperative. Get back to your normal life, but don't leave town. Have a good day." The line clicked.

Of course he would cooperate. He had nothing to do with the crime. Nothing to hide. He hated to play the part of a martyr, but he was a victim here. Jason stood up and stormed out of the building.

Kirk.

What was he involved in? To think that he didn't have any qualms involving Jason in a crime made the anger burn even hotter.

Jason hadn't imagined that phone call last night. It *was* his brother. Of that he was certain. But what kind of game was being played?

Stomping out to his truck, he wanted to find Kirk and knock some sense into him. The problem was, he had no idea where to find him.

As he grabbed the handle of the driver's door, the conviction to get ahold of his emotions flooded his mind. What was he doing? *God, I need Your help here. Kirk's reappearance has turned me inside out, and I'm angry enough to do something stupid.* It had been a long time since he'd felt so helpless and mad at the same time.

Closing his eyes, he took a deep breath. He hadn't been to church since he'd come to Fairbanks. Hadn't been in touch with his accountability brothers back in Anchorage. In fact, as soon as Kirk appeared, Jason had been trying to control and fix. On his own. Because that's what big brothers did, right?

Good grief. He knew better. No use spinning his wheels over this. It was completely out of his control. *Okay, Lord, I need to give this over to You and leave it there. I don't want to . . . but You know me. Give me wisdom to deal with this and to do my work to the best of my ability.*

Leaning against his truck, he pulled out his cell and texted the group of men at home who were closer than biological brothers. Asked them for a time where they could all hop on Zoom for a meeting. It was time to let everyone know what he was dealing with. That he wasn't superman and couldn't save the world all on his own—something he was prone to think he could do. Mac was in that group. His boss, mentor, and best friend. The man would want to skin him alive for not coming to them earlier.

Which also meant he needed to call his parents and tell them that he'd seen Kirk. A lot. And he'd have to figure out how to tell them his brother was in trouble—what had happened. He hated to break their hearts with the negative news and for them to hear of Kirk's lies, but they deserved to know.

Maybe once he got back to his apartment tonight, he'd give them a call.

He shoved his phone into his pocket and headed back to the office. He had plenty of work to do so that he could finally get to the job he was originally supposed to tackle.

Just the thought of working with Darcie made him cringe. Not one to be embarrassed easily, Jason was filled with it every time he remembered seeing her face when he was in handcuffs. Like he'd been asked to speak at MIT to thousands of computer science majors and then couldn't boot up his own computer in front of the crowd. Not the greatest way to build a solid working relationship.

When they'd first met, he had to admit that deep down he'd thought she appeared a little lost and had doubted her abilities for the position. His own arrogance thinking he was the leader, the strong one, the moral one.

So much for that. Now he'd have to earn back her trust and respect before they even started. No longer was his résumé and assignment from the governor good enough. Not after that debacle at the trooper station.

She would be calling all the shots. He'd seen the doubt in her eyes.

As he went back to the computers, he prayed for his attitude. Humility wasn't one of his strengths.

His cell buzzed in his pocket.

Looking at the screen, Jason knew he couldn't ignore this one.

Mom.

He answered.

"Jason, are you alright?" Her voice was breathless.

"Of course."

"Oh good. You had us worried." She whispered something— probably to Dad. He must be sitting beside her.

"Worried? Why?"

"Well, you won't believe it. Kirk called! After all these years. He sounded so good, Jason. *So* good. But at the end of his call, he told us you had been arrested for murder! Is this true?"

* * *

17 Above Zero
October 22—8:12 p.m.
Somewhere Along the Chena River

Curling up in her cozy space, Natalie squeezed her eyes shut and tried to focus. Had people listened? It was getting harder and harder to sneak away from the ones who chased her. But it was a risk she had to take. So everyone would know.

The bad men had met again since she'd ventured out. Perhaps more than once, but she was only aware of the one time. She'd forced herself to listen closely. Remember. This time she wrote a few scribbles down on her notepad. She went over them again and again. That should help. If she could only find someone who would listen. Someone with power to do something to stop the bad men.

Oh, Lord, show me who to talk to. Who to trust. I can't do this alone.

Natalie recognized several of the voices now. Especially the one in charge. The one the others called Griz. He wasn't a nice man. And he had more than one plan. Too many things to sort through and keep straight. It hurt her head.

But she was called to let people know. She couldn't let those bad men hurt innocent people. She wouldn't. If Tito were still alive, he would protect them.

Now the burden fell to her. If it was the last thing she did on this earth, she would give it her best.

Sleep overtook her mind. and she relaxed under the blanket.

Thump, scrape.

The sounds brought her awake. Where was she? Blinking away the remnants of rest, she listened.

Footsteps sounded above her head. She shivered under her blanket. She opened her mouth to call out for Tito . . . the voices above made her stop.

She couldn't call for Tito. He was gone. She was alone. And the bad men were back.

Moving as quietly as she could, she perched herself under the floorboards where she had a tiny view through a slit between the wood. *Focus, Natalie.* This was important.

There were only two men this time. Odd. Hadn't there been more?

Their voices were muffled. What were they saying? Something about the pipeline. If only she could hear them better . . .

"Not a word to anyone. Got it?" That was a new voice, wasn't it?

She strained to catch the response. But the whispers of her husband called to her. In her mind's eye, she could see him sitting across from her. At the dinner table. She'd made him a stew and his favorite sourdough bread.

Tito's broad grin made her stomach do a little flip. Oh, how she loved him.

A noise above her head made her frown, and the vision of her husband vanished. What had that man said? Shouldn't she be listening? The urge to pay attention was strong.

But then the cool cellar around her morphed into a familiar space and the warmth of the fireplace made the room cozy and romantic.

She shook her head—she'd much rather be with Tito anyway. The soft glow from his eyes begged her to stay with him.

So she did.

CHAPTER EIGHT

16 Above Zero
October 24—9:43 a.m.
Emergency Operations Center

THE WEATHER DATA SPREAD OUT across Darcie's desk was fascinating. Fairbanks definitely dealt with extremes. While they'd had a record-hitting summer this year, it was long gone now. The leaves had turned and fallen before she'd arrived. Fall colors in Alaska had a reputation of being short lived. Darcie had never seen them last longer than four weeks. And that had been a record. But most of mainland Alaska boasted about a week or two of fall.

Typically the leaves changed colors and the winter winds tore them from their trees within that short time frame.

The scent of woodstoves and fireplaces filled the air now as temperatures steadily dropped for all-out winter. A season she loved. Snowshoeing, snowmachining, skiing, and running with sled dogs were some of her favorite activities. And up in Fairbanks, they would get a lot more snow than she was used to. The first heavy snow had yet to fall, but she couldn't wait. It was what made winter in Alaska so amazing.

As her eyes scanned the data, she was impressed with how hardy the people must be to go through such incredible temperature ranges.

"Hey, Darc." Misty popped her head in. Over the last couple weeks, they'd gotten into a good working groove. Her assistant was easy to work with and was great at anticipating Darcie's next move. Something she appreciated more and more each day. "There's a trooper on line two waiting for you."

"Thanks." Her stomach dropped. This wasn't about Jason, was it?

Darcie picked up her desk phone. "This is Ms. Phillips."

"Ms. Phillips. This is Trooper Thompson. I'm calling you to follow up on your request." The deep rumble of his voice was scratchy. As if he'd had one too many cigarettes in his day.

"My request?"

"Yes, about the woman who was touting the end of the world?"

Oh. That request. "Did you find out who she was?"

"As of right now, we have no ID on the woman. But we will keep our eyes and ears open. FPD is also aware and working on it."

That wasn't encouraging. "Trooper Thompson, I know your job is to ensure the safety of the citizens here, and that is my job as well. Should I be worried about this woman and the predictions she's making?" Even as she said it, she cringed. She couldn't tell him how much she wanted the woman to be found simply so Darcie could see her in person. Look into those desperate, pleading eyes.

"Ms. Phillips, there is nothing to substantiate the woman's claims. At this point, we believe she's just another superstitious, perhaps mentally challenged individual."

That should make her feel better. But it didn't. "You'll keep me informed if you discover anything else? You know how the press likes to get ahold of these things. If I don't have my bases covered, I would hate for this to come back and bite me." Man, she'd gotten really good at faking it, hadn't she?

He laughed. "Yes, ma'am. Like I said, we're keeping our eyes and ears open."

"Thank you. I hope we won't have any more trouble from her. Not that she has caused trouble, per se, but she comes up in conversations quite often." Why did she say that?

"Yes, ma'am. Have a good day."

"Thank you." She hung up the phone. "Misty?" she called out her door.

Her assistant appeared with a folder in her hand. "Whatcha need?"

"The state troopers and FPD haven't come up with anything on our mystery woman."

"You mean the Prophetess?"

The name the media had given her sounded so . . . weird. "Yeah. But I'd rather refer to her as the mystery woman."

"Mystery woman it is."

"Have you seen anything else?"

"No. My contact at the newspaper said things had been pretty quiet for a while."

"Do you think she's okay? She hasn't shown up in the hospital or anything, has she?" For some reason, the thought of that poor woman being sick hurt Darcie's heart.

"I've given my contact info to everyone at the hospital. They assured me if she came in, they would let me know." Misty tipped her head to the right. "What is it about this woman that has you so concerned?"

With a shrug, she leaned back in her chair. "I don't know. She just seems so . . . passionate about what she's saying. Not like she's trying to scare people, but that she's worried about us, ya know?"

"How many times have you watched that video?"

"A few dozen." As she admitted it, she allowed a sheepish expression onto her face. "Is that weird?"

"Not at all." Misty plopped into one of the chairs in front of Darcie's desk. "I have to admit that I find myself watching it over and over again. I can't figure out anything about her though." She lifted the folder in her hand. "But *this* group? It's full of colorful characters."

Ugh. The group from her first day. "Don't remind me."

"I thought you were exaggerating at first, but the more I dug? Man oh man, these guys would give any psych study a run for their money." She gave a few pieces of paper to Darcie. "This is what I've handled so far. They seem to be compliant for the time being."

That made her eyebrows raise. "Seriously?" She let out her breath in a whoosh. "That's a relief."

"I'm not saying we're done with them, but they are appeased for now." Misty sent her a conspiratorial grin. "I have to admit, I had permission to give them a number for a new guy at the governor's office."

"Throwing another new guy out to the wolves?"

"Yep. This is right up his alley, so to speak."

"Perfect. As long as I don't have to deal with them again." She handed the sheets back to Misty. "Keep it all on file, and we'll keep our fingers crossed that we don't have to pull it anytime soon."

"You got it." Misty stood. "Do you need anything else?"

"An iced vanilla latte would be great. Any chance you could run down to the Mocha Moose for me? And get yourself whatever you want, my treat."

The gleam in her assistant's eyes made her smile. "I'll be right back."

Darcie turned back to her laptop where she had the local radio news streaming. She turned up the volume so she could hear snippets and went back to all the data in front of her. Dealing with extreme temperatures was nothing new to Alaska. The Fairbanks Police, state troopers, hospitals, and utilities all had their own emergency preparedness. All she was doing was adding another layer to that preparedness.

"In breaking news, we've just heard that the Prophetess was back in the streets of Fairbanks just a few minutes ago—"

Misty ran back in. "Are you listening to it?"

"Uh-huh." She'd cranked the volume.

"You must listen . . . please." The woman sounded like she was crying, the plea was so intense. "When it reaches twenty-six below, people will die . . ." She broke into great sobs.

"There you have it, folks." The host was back on. "The world will apparently end soon." Another voice joined in, and they bantered back and forth about the woman and her dire warning.

Darcie turned it down. "See if you can find out anything?"

"On it!" Misty rushed out of the room.

In less than a minute, she was back with her cell pressed up to her ear. She held up a finger while she listened. "Thanks. I appreciate it." She shoved her phone into her back pocket. "Apparently, our mystery woman started shouting her predictions at city hall. Quite a crowd was already present because of a protest. The press was also there and got her on video. But as they went after her, the protesters rallied around her, and once again she vanished."

"She's going to end up getting hurt." The thought made Darcie wince. She hated to think of anything happening to the older woman. Why? "Did any of the video footage show anything?"

"Other than the woman clutching a small notebook, no."

The phones started ringing. "Great."

"I'll get those at my desk." Misty ran out.

What did the woman have to gain by causing a commotion like that? Unless she actually knew something. But how? Maybe she *was* mentally ill . . . It really didn't make sense. Shaking her head, Darcie opened her email and clicked on the first one.

"Darc." Her assistant was back at her door, out of breath. "Line one is the governor."

"What? Like the *governor* governor?" She sat up straighter. While she'd dealt with the office, the actual person was another story.

"Yep." Misty bit her lip. "Line two is the mayor."

"Please ask the mayor if I can call her back while I speak with the governor."

"Of course." Misty dashed back to her desk.

Darcie picked up the receiver and went to press the button for line one. But the open message on her computer screen made her do a double take:

We're tired of being nice. Resign. Or face the consequences.

*   *   *

14 Above Zero
October 28—8:52 a.m.

With his hands shoved into the pockets of his coat, Jason took the stairs up to Darcie's office to burn some calories. And get his head on straight.

He was done with the reprogramming at the pipeline a few days ahead of schedule. Maybe his early appearance would help to smooth things over with her. Twice now he'd royally made a mess of things. That wasn't his style.

But the only thing he could do now was move forward. Prove to her he wasn't that man.

The one that stuck his foot in his mouth and threw her under the bus.

Or the one that was arrested for standing over a dead man.

Most definitely not the one who couldn't get the job done and follow through.

No. He needed her to see what kind of man he really was. Because somewhere deep inside her, he knew she was wounded. By what or whom he wasn't sure, but he hoped to find out.

As he reached the fourth floor, he shook his head. This was neither the time nor the place. He was sent here to do a job. And his motivation was always to do things to the best of his God-given ability. He should stop caring about what people thought of him. Plain and simple.

Even the very interesting Miss Darcie Phillips.

Misty opened the door for him before he even reached it.

He raised his eyebrows. "How'd you know I was coming?"

"Security cameras in the stairwell." She held out her hand. "Glad to have you here, Mr. Myers."

"Good to finally be here." With a nod, he followed her through the office.

"We've set you up right over here." She pointed to a desk with four monitors. "Ms. Phillips would like to see you in her office in five minutes. That will give you a chance to get settled and grab a cup of coffee."

"Perfect." He set his laptop bag down beside the desk and studied the computer setup. Not bad. Looked like maybe Darcie had done some of that dense reading. He'd have to ask her about it.

He pulled out his laptop and grabbed that cup of coffee.

Five minutes on the dot and he tapped on her doorframe, laptop in hand.

She stood from behind her desk and smiled. "Thanks for letting us know you were done with the pipeline project early." With her hands to the back of her straight skirt, she smoothed it and settled back into her chair.

He took his seat, appreciating her femininity, then forced himself to focus. "Glad it's over." Whether or not it was definitively would still have to be determined. But in his mind, the happenings at the pipeline and trooper station were sketchy at best.

"We've been granted permission to hire two more full-time employees for this office, with the budget to do so. I was hoping to have them in place before you got here so they could be in on this from the ground up and understand every facet, but we haven't found anyone qualified yet."

He leaned forward. This was perfect. "I've got two young guys who interned under me in Anchorage last summer. I know they've graduated and have been looking for permanent work. One of them called me last weekend."

Her eyes lit up. "Do they have any training in emergency management?"

With a wince, he squinted at her. "No. They are both cyber specialists, but they worked with me on a project a buddy of mine from the ACI did. Which was all about cities' preparedness and emergency management."

One eyebrow lifted. "What's the ACI?"

"The Army Cyber Institute. It's at West Point."

"Oh. I see. And the project?"

Jason opened his laptop on the corner of her desk and typed in the search bar to bring up the screen for the ACI and their Cyber Research Project. He turned his computer screen toward her. "As you can see, testing a city's cyber response capabilities is exactly what we need to implement here. In my opinion the biggest terrorist threat is now cyber. That's where we're vulnerable. Everything relies on computers. Everything."

Darcie stopped and read the screen and scrolled. Several minutes later, she pursed her lips. "These guys worked with you on this?"

"We went through the project and scenarios, yes."

Her brow dipped and she studied him.

"Like a war game done online. A distributed exercise where we go through all the different scenarios and make a continuity-of-operations plan. Not all attacks can be prevented. So the exercise was to help us discover what our plan would be for dealing with any cyberattack. How we would keep the infrastructure functioning and communicating."

Darcie bit her lip and gave him a slow nod. "Now I understand even more why they sent you here. I might be an expert at emergency management, but I am not prepared for something of this magnitude." She pulled a notebook toward her and opened it up. Flipping through several pages of handwritten notes, she landed on a page and pointed. "Here's all the questions I have about the reading you sent me. Everything that I need you to teach me and make me an expert. It's the only way I can do this job well." She shifted the notebook so he could read her list of questions.

"I'm impressed you made it through all the material."

She shrugged. "Information nerd."

Jason struggled to keep from grinning too wide. "Well, I can address all of this today if we hunker down and sequester ourselves."

Darcie scrunched up her nose as she shook her head. "Actually, our first plan of action is a press conference. Sorry—not sorry—about the last-minute notification, but I had already scheduled the conference for today before I knew you would be here. I'm hoping that you can be my backup and answer any questions that might be your forte." She pushed her chair back and stood. Her black skirt over a pair of black boots was professional looking. When she slipped a jacket over her white shirt, she looked even more the part.

His casual dress of polo shirt over khakis wasn't what he would have chosen had he known she'd wanted him to be a part of an official press conference.

"I apologize for not giving you a warning about this, but when the governor calls and gives you an earful, then the mayor, you kinda have to do what you're told." A light laugh escaped her lips. "Including wearing a skirt and jacket."

"You look great. Very official." He stood and followed her to Misty's desk. "Do you have any talking points you need me to address? Or just answer questions?"

Misty handed both of them a printout—basic bullet points of what needed to be covered.

Darcie scanned the page and nodded to her assistant and then looked back at him. "How about you give some really good high-tech cybersecurity stuff that shows we are prepared for anything and everything?"

He didn't like where this was headed. "But we're *not* prepared for it. Not yet."

"I know that. And you know that. But we are going to work our tails off to be prepared. As soon as we can. The governor was adamant that we keep people calm. Apparently, our mystery woman who shouts in the streets about the end coming has gotten under the skin of a lot of the citizens. As the temperatures drop, the governor's office receives more and more phone calls. Couple that with the rise in violent crimes, and people are on edge."

"How many times has she appeared?"

Misty piped up to answer that one with a raised hand. "Five to eight times so far. Only two are confirmed. But hundreds of people have called in about it."

Jason sat on the corner of her desk and tapped the press sheet on his thigh. "What exactly does she say?"

"I'll let Misty field that one. She's been keeping a log." Darcie buttoned her jacket.

Her assistant swiped up on her iPad. "The main talking points have been that the end is near, we must prepare, when it reaches twenty-six below people will die."

"Any substance to the woman's claims?" Jason frowned. This was odd. And very specific.

"Not that anyone can find. And no one knows who the woman is or how to locate her." Darcie licked her lips and tucked her hair behind her ear. "When the temperature gets that low—which isn't abnormal here—it's dangerous for anyone to be out in the elements. Dangerous for people to get stranded in their vehicles. Dangerous if utilities fail."

Jason's mind reeled. The threat here was very real. But how much should he say?

"I can see your wheels are turning. What are you thinking?"

The woman in charge might not want to be in charge if he told her what he really thought. "The cybersecurity risks are huge." He'd leave it at that.

She straightened. "Alright then. Let's not mess around. We will get the press conference over with and assure the public that we are here to prepare, prevent, and respond to any and all crises. After that I'd like to talk to the people you think would be a good fit for our office here and get to work. I hope you don't mind long hours, Jason, because we are going to do whatever is necessary to keep our people safe."

"You got it." He stood again and sent a smile to Misty. "Thanks for printing me a copy." He held up the paper.

Darcie headed toward another part of their offices. Keying in a code to the door, she opened it, and they entered a pressroom with a podium and seal of the state of Alaska. Shutters clicked as he followed her to the front of the room. At least thirty people were packed in there.

Taking a deep breath, he took an at-ease stance with his hands folded in front of him, the paper in his grip. Now all he had to do was help convince everyone present—including himself—that they were prepared for whatever came their way.

CHAPTER NINE

11 Above Zero
October 28—10:15 a.m.
Pressroom

SO FAR SO GOOD. SHE'D given her speech about her position and given a short résumé like the governor suggested so that people would know and trust the person in charge. She hadn't stuttered one bit. Thank you very much.

After addressing the list she'd prepared, which encompassed her office's responsibilities and duties for the citizens of the area, she introduced Jason as the specialist and expert he was. Now she could catch her breath and psych herself up for the litany of questions that was sure to come.

Jason appeared calm and in control. His words captivated the crowd. ". . . all of this is Homeland's critical infrastructure defense. I'm proud to be a part of the team here and to help Alaska stay strong." His gaze turned toward her before he walked away from the podium.

As she took center stage again, she breathed in through her nose and prepared for her least favorite part. "We have time for a few questions."

Then it began. The barrage. For thirty minutes. Sometimes she answered. Sometimes she asked Jason to chime in. Most of it was simplistic. Not weight-bearing. Which was fine by her, but tedious nonetheless.

The only reason she kept allowing more questions was the hope that the press would relay to their listeners, readers, viewers, that all was in hand and there was no reason to panic.

Her thoughts flew back to the woman in the streets. She could still see the older woman's eyes. Passionate, pleading. If only she could help the woman in some way.

"Ms. Phillips?"

"Forgive me. Would you repeat the question?" The room fell silent. What had she missed?

"With another cold snap on its way—the temperature has already dropped three degrees since we arrived—what are your plans to address the twenty-six-below prophecy?"

Several in the room laughed as she gave what she hoped was a very teacherly glare to the man.

He laughed along and then help up a hand to the crowd. "Alright. How about a more serious question?" The man in the front of the pack of ravenous reporters drilled her with his gaze. "Rumor has it that after your wedding was called off, you had a mental breakdown. Could you please explain to us how a woman who couldn't even handle a bit of personal adversity is supposed to handle the life-and-death emergency preparedness for a region with almost one hundred thousand people?"

Everything in her stiffened. Even the air she breathed. Of course someone would bring up Greg. She'd prepared for this question many times over the past couple years but never had the chance to give a response. Until now.

Darcie cleared her throat and hoped her features were neutral. "It isn't a secret that I called off my wedding two years ago after I discovered that my fiancé was embezzling money from his father's own company. There was no mental breakdown. I do admit to taking *two* days off to examine things in my life. How this man had pulled the wool over so many friends' and his family's eyes. There were a lot of people hurt by his actions. I was one of them. But rather than it making me the incompetent, mentally fragile female you are trying to insinuate I am with your question, it made me stronger. More capable of handling disastrous situations." The last words held a bite to them, but at the moment that was tame. She struggled to control her anger but held it in check. How dare he?

The room exploded in questions. Misty nudged her to go, but Darcie shook her head. If she left now, it would only lead them to speculate. And she wasn't about to give them that opportunity.

Everyone vied for attention, and Misty pointed to a slight girl in jeans and a sweater in the corner of the room.

Her question was drowned out by the crowd.

"Quiet, please!" Jason's booming voice brought the room to a hush.

The young woman in the back lifted her pencil and started again. "Mr. Myers, you were helping out at the pipeline before you came to assist Ms. Phillips."

"That is correct." He didn't even step to the microphone—just took command from where he stood.

It thrilled Darcie more than she could put into words that the subject had been changed. But she stood there hoping to give off a confident air.

"Do you have any comment on the body they found on the fourteenth of October?"

The man in the front made a mocking face. "That's old news, rookie. Why don't you—"

"Excuse me." The tiny woman had some fire in her and shot the man a glare. "But I just confirmed that the bullets that killed the man at the pipeline were a match to bullets at another murder scene on October twentieth." She looked down at her notepad. "The victim was found behind the auto salvage yard on Van Horn."

Darcie and Jason whipped their gazes to each other at the same moment.

Every person there started talking at once. Darcie blinked several times, and Jason's eyes widened at her. That's right. The crowd was expecting a response. "Mr. Myers and I do not have any comments about the victims or the crimes committed. You'll need to speak to the state troopers about that." At Misty's nudge this time, she didn't ignore it. "If you don't have any other questions pertaining to emergency preparedness, we'll return to work." Darcie raced out of the room with Jason on her heels.

Once they were through the secure door, she put a hand to her forehead. "At least Misty knows how to handle a crowd. Hopefully, she can defuse things a bit and get them back on track before they go home."

Jason had his hands on his hips and paced back and forth in front of her. His lips in a thin line. His jaw clenching and unclenching.

No longer was she worried about what the press would say about her would-be marriage to the embezzler. Watching Jason pace tugged at her heart. Sympathy broke through her carefully constructed shield. The weight on him was unmistakable. "You're worried Kirk had something to do with the murders, aren't you?"

His dark eyes snapped to hers, the pain and anger so evident she could feel it like heat on her skin.

It'd been a long time since she'd empathized with another human being. The door that it opened wasn't as painful as she'd expected.

He opened his mouth, but Misty burst through the door, staring at her phone screen. "Apparently we all just missed our mystery woman."

Pulling her gaze from Jason, she went back into work mode. "Where?" Darcie doubted there would be any footage since most of the press were here in her building.

"In front of the university."

*　*　*

10 Above Zero
October 28—10:03 a.m.
Emergency Operations Center

Jason looked between Misty and Darcie. "Are there any reports about what she said?" Whether the woman was crazy or not was beyond his knowledge, but if she continued to get people worked up, then that could be a problem. What they really needed to do was find her, question her, and determine if there was any validity at all to what she was saying.

"Same as usual"—Misty tapped her phone—"except this time she said something about power being lost."

He closed his eyes for a moment and grimaced. "Which is not what people want to hear when the temperatures drop." The highs during the day were predicted to be single digits the next few days—the lows dipping close to ten below. The closer they crept to the dreaded number, the more fear and panic would take over. Which meant they needed to figure this out and fast.

Darcie unbuttoned her jacket and made a beeline for her desk. "Jason, bring your computer. Misty, you too."

Packed into Darcie's office, they opened their devices. Jason went straight to trusted sources. He shook his head. "I don't see anything from the FBI or CISA about a generalized warning."

"CISA?" Misty lifted her pen. "Spell that?"

"C-I-S-A. It stands for Cybersecurity and Infrastructure Security Agency."

"Gotcha." Shoving the pen between her teeth, the woman went back to her laptop, and her fingers flew over the keys.

"Those would be the first two that would send out warnings if there was any chatter or evidence of hacking. But that doesn't mean it isn't out there. We may not be looking at a cyberattack though—even though the Ukraine power grid hack from 2015 still haunts people. Since I'm new to this area, I better get an understanding of the protocols in place." He looked to Darcie. "Can you give me a brief rundown so I know what we're dealing with?"

She turned those brilliant blue eyes toward him. "GVEA—Golden Valley Electric Association—has a diverse supply for its power. There's power plants—Zehnder, Delta, North Pole Plant and its expansion, and Healy. There's also the Eva Creek Wind Farm, a solar farm, and Bradley Lake Hydroelectric. When more power is needed,

GVEA purchases it, and it comes through the interties with southern utilities."

He typed as quick as he could in a form of shorthand he hoped he could decipher back at his desk. He'd have to do a lot of research on all this. Looking back up at her, he nodded. "Alright, what else?"

"Then there's the BESS. Battery Energy Storage System. I'm sure you are aware of it. It was completed in 2003 and can supply twenty-five megawatts of power for fifteen minutes. It has since been upgraded, and so we call her BESS 2.0. Unless there's physical damage to a line—such as a tree falling on one or a transformer blowing—the BESS can prevent a lot of outages. And she has done just that."

"Wasn't it awarded a Guinness World Record certificate?" Misty piped up. "I remember my dad talking about it once."

Darcie scanned her computer. Then nodded. "Yep. Right here it says that on December 10, 2003, it was shown to be the world's most powerful battery."

Jason breathed deep and leaned back. "So if someone wanted to turn out all the power, what would they have to do?"

Eyes wide, Darcie frowned. "I don't even want to answer that out loud. But I know that's our job. To prevent it from happening, we have to figure out how it could be done."

"Yep. And thinking like the bad guys isn't fun. Just sayin'."

Darcie chewed on her lip.

A habit of hers that he couldn't deny drew him like a magnet.

"Before we do anything else, give Misty the contact info for the two men you recommend." She looked to her assistant. "Get us some video interviews with the candidates set up ASAP. And I mean today if at all possible."

"You got it." Misty hopped to her feet and headed for her desk.

"I'm emailing it right now." Jason shot a smile at her and then turned his attention back to Darcie.

"Jason, you stay here. I want to hear more about the exercise you went through with the ACI, and I'm going to contact a friend of mine who's an emergency manager for her town. It would be good for all of us to be on a call together."

"Sure." Even though the idea of an old woman in the streets being correct about the power going out at twenty-six below was ludicrous, they had to do their due diligence.

"I also want us to work on a system for this ops center. Everything needs to be connected and streamlined so that in case of emergency, there's no way for our communications to be down. Can you do that?"

It would be a huge project, but he loved a challenge. "Of course. But first, may I suggest that we up the security on all the emergency systems' computers? I have a program I've created that I could get up and running pretty quick."

Her eyes narrowed, and she studied him for several moments.

Was she assessing him? Wondering if she could trust him? He wouldn't judge her for either.

"Have you implemented this before?"

"My company in Anchorage has had it going through testing for the last few months. This would be the first place to use it. But it was my boss's suggestion, so I know we have his green light of approval."

She sighed. "Since we have so much to do, and I'm even more concerned than ever about getting our operations up and running at full speed, I will trust you to do what needs to be done. Cyber is your area of expertise. I need you in my corner to get all this set up." She handed him a sheet of paper. "This is what I need to streamline immediately."

He scanned the list. Letting out a whistle, he raised his eyebrows. "You don't mess around, do you?"

"No." Her attention fixed back on her computer, she pointed a finger at him. "Amanda can be on Zoom with us in ten minutes. She's emergency manager in Mount Pleasant, South Carolina."

"What do you want to talk about?"

"I need her advice. We were in the Air Force together, and she's mentored me for years. Probably the smartest person I know. I'm going to ask her if I'm on the right track with my plan. I don't have time for mistakes or blunders. We need to do it right the first time."

Once again, he was impressed. "I'll get Zoom set up on my desktop out there and get my headphones ready."

"Darc!" Misty was at the door, breathless. She clicked on the TV in the corner. "You won't believe this guy. He was bashing you before the commercial break."

The talk show banner showed up on-screen, and then the camera focused in on two men sitting in comfortable chairs with a small table between them. They were laughing about something.

"Great." If the look on Darcie's face was any indication, she didn't like one or both of the men.

"Do you know them?" He kept his voice low.

"The guy on the right is Darrell Collins. He tried to get this job. I have no idea why he's still in Fairbanks."

"You've just started your own company in Alaska, as an expert in your field of emergency management." The man in the left chair furrowed his brow.

"He's not an expert!" Darcie jumped to her feet and headed over to the TV. "Just what we need."

The interviewer continued, "In all seriousness, what did you think of the press conference today?"

"No offense to Ms. Phillips—she is a perfectly lovely person—but she and her team are unprepared. I don't know what the governor's office was thinking." Darrell took a sip of his coffee. "Every threat that comes through has to be taken seriously."

"You don't think she's taking it seriously?"

Darrell harrumphed. "Did you see the glare she shot the reporter who questioned her? She obviously thinks this is all a prank."

The interviewer gave a dramatic nod. "So you're saying that the public should be concerned?"

"*Very* concerned. There is an incredibly real threat out there."

CHAPTER TEN

8 Above Zero
November 1—1:37 p.m.
Undisclosed Location

"HOW MUCH HAVE YOU EXTRACTED so far?" Griz narrowed his eyes at the scrawny hacker in front of him.

"Everything we need to know about how they are setting up their systems. Once the temp hits the magic number, we will send the ransomware. Until then, we get to watch every move they make and learn." Julian pushed his glasses up his nose and smiled.

The kid was always smiling, as if everything were a game. "Gotta love government funding."

The new guy—a taller, chubbier version of Julian—stepped forward. "We may have a bit of a problem. The new hires at the Emergency Operations Center's office all have cyber backgrounds."

Griz hated it when people didn't just get to the point. "Which means?"

"They might get tipped off before we play our winning hand." The guy shrugged. "If they're smart."

"So you're saying anyone smart can foil your plan?" The gravelly voice of Griz's boss echoed as he stepped out of the shadows.

The new guy paled and shifted his weight. "Um no . . . that is . . . well, if they're trained—"

"What is your name?"

Chubby guy cleared his throat. "Nick."

"Alright, Nick. You're trained. Correct?"

Nick's face paled.

"It's your job to make sure that doesn't happen, now isn't it? Or do I need to find someone else to replace you?"

"I can do it." Chubby guy lifted his chin.

"Good." The boss walked over to the row of computers. "If you want your payday, then this better go off without a hitch."

His boss walked over to Griz. "Follow me."

They went into a back room.

"You've met with the others?"

"Yes." Multiple times. Going over every detail of his plan.

"No issues?"

"Not one."

The boss grinned. "I love it when it all comes together."

So did he.

"This time next month, the governor and I will be having a heart to heart. Then the fun will really begin."

The man was a fool. Didn't he understand that the government was the problem? He pinched his lips together. No matter. Two could play this game. And Griz would win. His idea was more than brilliant.

"I trust you'll keep everything running?"

"Like a well-oiled machine, sir." He dipped his head.

The boss left, and Griz strode back into the main room. The hum of the computers around him was invigorating. All eyes were on him.

He sent a grin to their number one computer geek. "You know what to do."

Julian rubbed his hands together and sat at his keyboard. Smiling. Always smiling.

*   *   *

4 Above Zero
November 2—6:14 a.m.
Emergency Operations Center

The dartboard on the back of Darcie's door gave her the sudden urge to picture Darrell's face there and sling a few darts in his direction. After all, that's what he'd done to her.

No. She wouldn't stoop to his level.

Whatever he was up to, though, made her nervous. She'd asked Misty to keep her eyes and ears open.

Darcie took a long swig of her coffee and sat in her office in the quiet of the early morning hours. Their first big snow had rushed in overnight, and now at the end of the squall, huge, soft snowflakes fell. As they floated down, she thought about her counseling session last week. While the woman had helped by giving her some exercises to tame her anger, the numbness was still her normal. Was she destined to always be like this? Incapable of feeling?

And yet there were a few times recently when the numbness wasn't prevalent. When Jason was around.

She closed her eyes and took another sip. These thoughts were not how she should start her day. Look what happened last time she allowed herself to open up to a man.

Setting her coffee down, she smirked. Maybe a little stooping would do her some good. With a hop to her feet, she grabbed a dart. Then laughed as she pictured Darrell. Her wrist, arm, and muscle memory took it from there. As it sank into the red center, she grinned. There. The satisfaction that filled her couldn't be squashed. No matter what Darrell Collins thought he could do with all his TV interviews.

Darcie removed the dart and straightened her sweater. Back to work. But it was so much sweeter now.

She opened her door, stepped back to her desk, picked up her coffee, and stared out at the snow-filled sky.

Six on a winter morning in the lower forty-eight was probably still dark too. But as they barreled toward the shortest days of the year up here at the top of the world in Fairbanks, the sunrise was half past nine now, with the sunset a little after 5:00 p.m. By the time December 21 rolled around, sunrise would be around 11:00 a.m. and sunset around 2:45 p.m. People unfamiliar with Alaska always asked her what it was like to deal with six months of daylight and six months of darkness.

She chuckled to herself as she wrapped her hands around the warm cup, sat in her chair, and gazed out the window at the dark sky.

Funny how people created stereotypes in their minds. She didn't endure six months of darkness. In fact, even up in Barrow, which was the most northern point of Alaska, it was only three months without an actual sunrise. Here, they lost seven minutes a day during the fall and winter and then gained seven minutes a day in the spring and summer. Something she'd always loved. Of course, she was an Alaskan through and through, so the pattern was normal to her.

Noise at the office's main entrance pulled her from her thoughts. She swiveled in her chair. Her team had arrived. They'd spent twelve to fourteen hours at the office for five days straight. Jason's guys—Chaz and Simon—had arrived in record time from Anchorage with their cars stuffed with duffel bags and backpacks. The rest of their belongings had been shipped. They'd crashed at Jason's apartment while they looked for places to live. Raring to go with the new jobs, the two were brilliant.

Darcie was amazed at their brainpower but exhausted by their energy. When had she gotten so old? Their youth seemed accentuated in everything. In their early twenties, their regular attire was gaming T-shirts, jeans, tennis shoes, and hoodies. Not that she was about to enforce a dress code. Whatever worked for them, worked for her.

Their vocabulary also took some getting used to. Active attack, passive attack, GOAT, camping, deepfake, RNG, white hat, black hat, gank, peel—she continued to make a list and asked Jason what the words meant and if they were for gaming or cybersecurity.

But the two guys were impressive—she'd give them that. They had done more in the two days since they'd arrived than she and Misty could have accomplished in a month. They knew their stuff. And most importantly? They passed security and background checks with flying colors.

Jason trusted them. And she trusted him.

"Hey, Darc." Misty was the first to pop her head around the doorframe. "Need anything?"

Her assistant was a godsend. "I've got coffee, so I'm good for right now."

"Conference room in ten?" Misty's normally smooth hair was pulled up into a messy bun today. Maybe a bit of the influence of the guys. Darcie supposed it couldn't hurt.

"Perfect."

"I'll let everyone know." She bounced away.

Darcie relaxed in her chair. A few more minutes to gather her thoughts before the day rolled out at full speed. Each morning they met in the conference room, divvied up assignments, came back at lunch, ate, downloaded info, and did it again. By the time dinner rolled around, they returned for round three.

Ever since the press conference, Jason had become invaluable to her. They worked together well. He had strengths in all her weak areas. And frankly, the thought of him leaving in a few months made her heart sink. Good grief, that was the second time in five minutes that her thoughts had drifted to the guy. Her cheeks warmed. What was wrong with her? She couldn't allow herself to feel anything for him. No matter how great he seemed to be.

Feel. Ha. The only feelings she was capable of right now were stress and anger. Especially when certain people insinuated she couldn't handle her job.

A subject change was necessary. She shook away the thoughts. This wasn't helping. The best thing she could do was learn everything humanly possible from Jason while he was here.

Her mind shifted to the mystery woman. No one had been able to locate her. And Misty was a bulldog when it came to finding people.

Things had been quiet for a few days. No badgering from the press. No dire predictions in the streets. No murders. But as the temperatures dropped, the woman's warning was at the back of Darcie's mind on a regular basis.

Why the exact number?

The only logical explanation was that someone had something terrible planned and would enact it at twenty-six below zero. But the woman didn't look like a criminal or a terrorist. She seemed deeply concerned. Wanted to warn people to save them. But from what?

That was the prize-winning question.

The only way Darcie could get to the bottom of it was if she found the woman. Before it was too late. But there hadn't been time or manpower to dedicate to locating her.

Shaking her head again, she set her cup down. They'd all heard it so much and talked about it so much that now her brain was taking warning as fact. Not a good idea.

Even if her gut was telling her that she should.

Picking up her iPad and notebook, she marched to the conference room. She had a lot to do—it was best to rein in her thoughts as much as possible.

Later that night, Darcie slipped into her bed a hair before midnight. She'd probably only get five hours of sleep, but that was her life.

The day had brought about a lot of accomplishments. She'd had meetings or phone calls with every head of every program, hospital, utility, and anyone else who worked with the Emergency Operations Center. They were all on the same page. Each department was putting emergency procedures in place. The new communications system was being tested. They would be ready to execute their first test runs in a week. Granted there would be a lot of tweaks the team would need to make. Other things to be implemented as they learned, but this was a great start.

Now if she could just get her brain to stop spinning so she could sleep, that would be wonderful.

She closed her eyes and took long, deep breaths. Exhaled slowly.

The snow was so deep. Darcie trudged through it, every fiber in her being feeling the cold.

But every door she tried was locked. No lights glowed through windows.

No streetlamps were lit.

Only the stars and moon lit the town of Fairbanks.

Wails echoed in the streets. They turned to screams.

Looking over her shoulder, she saw a crowd. Getting closer and closer.

She picked up her pace, but the snow kept her from running. It seemed to grow deeper with every step.

The crowd followed her, begging for help. They pulled at her coat, grabbed at her arms and legs.

She spotted the old Lamar diner ahead—their large non-digital thermometer spinning out of control. Everything in her told her she had to reach it.

With painstaking steps, she worked. Grunted and groaned her way.

Until she was in front of the thermometer.

The moans of the crowd grew to a roar. Pleas for help rang out.

Her eyes were drawn upward. The thermometer stopped spinning.

Twenty-six below.

CHAPTER ELEVEN

Zero Degrees
November 4—6:15 p.m.

ANOTHER LONG DAY AND JASON let out a sigh. It was his turn to be in charge of dinner, so he thought it would be great to surprise everyone with food from his favorite place. They'd had plenty of pizza, fast food, easy food, and snacks. It was time for a real meal.

Checking his watch, he got up from his desk. The delivery guy with Grub Hub should be there any minute. Taking long strides to the stairs, he worked out the kinks in his back. The least he could do for the poor delivery guy was meet him at the door.

He jogged down the stairs and reviewed their progress in his mind. Everything had been going well. They were getting a handle on the lists and systems that needed to coordinate seamlessly with each other, but there was a long way to go. Even though they'd checked off three pages of the tasks Darcie had lined out for the ops center, there were still umpteen more to get through.

At least they now had a decent team to tackle it. Darcie was extraordinary. Organized. Intelligent. A multitasker. Great admin and delegator. Misty was the perfect right-hand person. That girl could tackle it all and just about read her boss's mind. Simon and Chaz had both proven they were worth their weight in nachos—as Simon put it. Easygoing and yet workaholics, they almost had Jason wishing he had them working for him full-time.

Those thoughts made him grin. Jason's boss back in Anchorage had already started asking questions about opening an office for Cybersecurity Solutions in Fairbanks. Where he'd put Jason in charge and in the lead. Wouldn't that be a dream come true?

The biggest question? Was Fairbanks the right place for the next expansion? It was the second largest city in Alaska, true, but it wasn't that big in the sense of population. Of course if they included the whole borough, it was massive. At least size-wise. The need was obviously here, with the pipeline, Eielson Air Force Base, Fort Greely, and Fort Wainwright. The more technology grew, the more the need grew. With each passing day, cyberattacks around the world increased.

Most people were completely content to surf the internet, stream their favorite shows, and blast out every second of their days on social media. And the majority of them had no idea what threats lurked.

Or if they did know, they chose to ignore it. Ignorance was supposed bliss, right?

A little red Subaru pulled up in front of the building. Jason waited for the guy to get out with the bags of food and then opened the door for him. Jason gave the delivery guy a hefty tip and told him to stay warm as an arctic blast threatened to pull the door out of his grasp.

He blinked several times and relocked the door. Wow. Winter was definitely here.

Taking the stairs two at a time, he kept his pace slow and balanced the bags between his arms. Since they'd started working such long hours, his exercise routine had been reduced to taking the stairs multiple times a day.

If he had his own office, he'd install one of those fancy desk bikes. Maybe a standing desk and treadmill too. As tempting as it was to think about running his own office, he needed to push the selfish thoughts aside. He had a job to do here first. And he intended to do it well. He could hash it out with his boss once security protocols here were up, tested, running, and perfected.

Reaching the secure door to the ops center offices, he switched the food bags to one hand so he could enter the key code.

As soon as he entered, Chaz ran toward him. "Dude, I thought you'd never get back. I'm starved."

Jason shook his head as he laughed at the young guy. "Yep, you look like you're wasting away before my very eyes."

He carried the food into the conference room as everyone congregated. Smiles and eager faces greeted him.

"What smells so incredible?" Darcie licked her lips and put a hand to her stomach.

Jason couldn't contain his grin. "I thought I'd treat you guys to something special tonight." He pulled containers out of the four large grocery-bag-wrapped brown bags. "We are going to feast this evening, my friends. Seafood risotto, grilled halibut, grilled Alaskan salmon, pan-seared crab cakes, crab mac and cheese, fresh steamed clams with reindeer sausage, coconut shrimp, and parmesan-crusted zucchini sticks."

They all stared and then reached for the food.

"Wait." He held up a hand. "I have a request."

Eight hands pulled back in slow-motion.

"I'd like to pray before we eat if that doesn't offend anyone." He held his breath, waiting and watching for their responses. It had been a last-second idea.

Chaz shrugged.

Simon did as well. "Cool, dude. My mom's religious."

Misty's eyebrows raised. "I'd appreciate that."

Darcie's expression wasn't decipherable. It didn't appear to be anger or happiness. Did she not care one way or the other? And she shrugged as well. "That's fine."

"Awesome." He bowed his head. "Thank You, Lord, for this food. For this team. And for all the work we've accomplished so far. Help us to do our very best to keep our community safe. In Jesus's name, Amen." He looked up and grinned. "Feel free to dig in. I figured we could all share—family style. There's plenty." Hopefully, he hadn't stepped over any lines. All he needed was a phone call from the governor's office telling him how inappropriate his request had been.

The scents filled the room as each container was pulled out of the bags. In addition to everything he'd listed, there were salads, parmesan roasted potatoes, the chef's vegetables, and enough seafood chowder for all of them.

Misty came to his side while the others opened up everything and oohed and aahed over it. "Thanks for that." Her words were barely a whisper. "It's been a long time since I've had anyone of faith in my workplace. Didn't realize how much I missed it." She grabbed a paper plate and joined the ruckus and dishing up of food.

It took him aback for a moment. Granted, it had been a week or so since he joined the team, but it was sad that she just now knew he was a man of faith. Had he hidden it?

In this day and age, Christians had to keep their mouths shut at their workplaces if they wanted to be treated fairly. But it shouldn't be hidden. Someone—anyone—should be able to tell by how he lived his life that he was a man of faith, right? And since Misty—quite possibly a believer—hadn't noticed it in him and he hadn't noticed it in her, that meant he was failing. Big time.

The job wasn't more important than his faith. Security wasn't more important than his faith. Whether people liked him or not wasn't more important than his faith.

And yet he hadn't found a church. His accountability brothers had prodded him about it, but he'd put them off.

Jason let those thoughts sink in. Something needed to change.

Darcie elbowed him. "This is incredible. I'm sure it put you back a pretty penny." Her smile was hesitant, but at least it reached her eyes. Was she hesitant about him? The cost of the food? Or the prayer he'd just offered up?

"I found this restaurant—The Pump House—and it became my favorite place to eat after the first bite. Just wanted to show my gratitude to all of you. Hope you like it." He took a paper plate from her and went to the other side of the table and filled it. The guys were chowing down and would probably want seconds soon, so he better get what he wanted now.

They reminded him of himself as a teen. Constantly growing and working out for cross country and swimming. He ate his parents out of house and home. At least, that's what Mom always said.

Chaz finished off his first plate and stood. "Mind if I get seconds?"

Jason exchanged a look with Darcie. "Dude . . ." He laughed. "I just sat down with my first."

She laughed along as she placed a napkin in her lap. "As long as you leave some for the rest of us." The intimate expression she sent him across the table made him feel like they were the old couple among a group of kids. With a shake of her curls, she pointed her fork. "That totally sounded like my grandma."

Laughter filled the room.

After she took a bite, she lifted that fork again. "Don't go getting ideas. I will *not* be known as the group grandma." She took a sip of water. "Dibs on the rest of whatever this is." She pointed to the crab mac.

"I didn't know dibs was allowed. No fair." Simon's dramatic whine caused Jason to choke on his Dr Pepper. "I'll arm wrestle you for it?"

Darcie narrowed her eyes and leaned over the table. "How about a game of darts?"

"Nuh-uh. No way." Simon lifted his hands like he was surrendering. "I've seen your dartboard."

A satisfied smirk lifted Darcie's lips as she reached for the container of rich crab ensconced in layers of cheese and pasta. "Wise choice, young one."

Conversation was easy around the table as they enjoyed their food. Darcie asked everyone about their college experiences, places they'd traveled to, their bucket lists.

But it was interesting that she didn't ask about friends and families, and she certainly didn't offer up anything personal about herself. From all the laughter, he was pretty sure no one else noticed.

Misty slipped out and returned with a pie plate. "It seems like the perfect time to bring this out. It's a Tollhouse Pie. I made it last night."

"When did you have time for that?" Darcie's voice squeaked on the end. "Do you not sleep?"

Misty shrugged. "I bake when I'm mulling over things."

Jason glanced at each person around the table. "This could be our reward for finishing up whatever the boss has on docket for tonight." He sent Darcie a conspiratorial grin.

"Sounds like a plan." Misty cleared away all the empty food containers and then placed the pie in the middle of the table with small dessert plates and forks.

Two hours later, they were exhausted but content after celebrating their accomplishments with the gooey pie. Simon and Chaz were the first to head out the door, backpacks on their shoulders. No coats. Of course. Talking about what game they were going to play that night. Probably until the wee hours of the morning.

"Oh to be young again." Jason chuckled.

"You make it sound like you're ancient." Misty made a fist and bumped his shoulder. Then waved and grabbed her bag. Around a yawn, she said her good nights.

"I hear you though." Darcie didn't look up from the paperwork spread out in front of her. "I didn't realize that a simple decade between us and the young guys would make me feel like I should be using a cane."

He laughed with her and then studied her for several moments. With everyone else gone, Jason took the opportunity to go deeper than the surface. "You're doing an awesome job leading this team."

"Thanks." She scribbled something else in her notebook.

"You about done? It's late, and I don't want you to have to walk out by yourself."

Her eyes snagged his, and then she glanced around. "Guess I didn't realize everyone else had gone." She looked at her watch. "Crud. It's later than I thought." She straightened up the papers in front of her and then shoved everything into her enormous leather briefcase. "Didn't mean to keep you so late."

Jason stood and shoved a hand into one of his pockets. "Not a problem." He reached for his coat and followed her out of the conference room.

She wrapped a scarf around her neck and pulled on a pair of gloves. Clicking her truck's auto-start, she shivered. "I should have started that a few minutes ago. But oh well. Wanna take the stairs? It will waste a bit more time."

"Sure." He hit the button for his own truck and lifted his computer bag to his shoulder. In the quiet of the evening, he risked a personal question. "Hey, so I know you're from Juneau. Is your family back there?"

"Nope."

A one-word answer. Was that a touchy subject? "Are your parents still living?"

"Yep."

Great. Definitely not a friendly topic for her. "Do you have siblings?"

"Nope."

Why did it feel like the space had filled with icicles? Hopefully, if he kept on gently probing, she would open up. Not clam up more. It was her idea to take the stairs after all. "Friends still back in Juneau?"

"A few. But I won't be going back."

"Because of your fiancé?"

She stopped on a step and turned toward him. The steely look in her eyes was hard. Angry. "Look, I appreciate that you're just trying to be a friend. But it's none of your business. My personal life as a topic is closed. Got it?"

He met her stare. "Yeah. Got it." What had built that great big wall in her eyes? For all the glances they'd shared the past few days, all the long hours they'd put in together problem solving and sharing ideas, he'd thought they were both feeling the comfort of being together. The attraction. Had he misread her? That was a tough pill to swallow. Because the more time he spent with Darcie, the more time he *wanted* to spend with her.

They walked the rest of the way down the stairs in silence. Every time he thought to open his mouth, he clamped it shut. Obviously he had touched a nerve. She wasn't happy with him, and nothing he could say or do in that moment would fix it. He'd learned that much about her.

Once they were at the doors, she lifted her scarf to cover her mouth and nose and paused as she looked straight into his eyes. "I'll see you tomorrow, Jason. Thanks for dinner." But her tone was more cold and dead than he'd ever heard it.

And it was all his fault.

CHAPTER TWELVE

2 Degrees Below Zero
November 5—12:07 p.m.

AROUND THE CONFERENCE TABLE AT lunch, no one said a word. Probably because Darcie had snapped at every one of them at least twice today. Jason guessed some of it stemmed from their stilted conversation last night. He probably should apologize for getting too personal with her. But her frustration with him didn't mean she had to take it out on the rest of the team.

Of course, the day hadn't gone as planned. Every emergency service and program they'd single tested had at least one snafu. First, the fire department had issues with the backup dispatch system. Then the emergency communication server only allowed outgoing calls. The list went on and on. They were only able to fix two to work in every facet. The pipeline and the troopers. What would happen if they truly had an emergency and needed everything to work together?

He dug into his sub sandwich and studied his notes. He'd gone back and double-checked so many different systems that they were all beginning to blur.

A knot started in his gut, and he stopped chewing.

Wait.

The pipeline computers.

The state troopers' computers.

Different problems. Different systems.

Both were connected to the Emergency Operations Center now.

What if . . . Jason bolted to his feet and ran back to his desk. He didn't even want to finish the thought. But it made sense. No wonder his instincts wouldn't leave him be about the earlier problems.

Simon and Chaz were at his side in seconds, scarfing their own sandwiches.

"Whatcha thinkin', Jas?" Simon pulled up a chair.

"I'm thinking that it was *no* coincidence the pipeline software went offline and then had issues." He scrolled through pages and pages of code. Then picked up his phone and dialed the troopers' office. "Trooper Lindsay? This is Jason Myers. Can you transfer me to your IT guy?"

"Sure, but I should warn you that he's new. We're underfunded for cyber. The state sent him since we've had so many issues."

After several minutes talking to the cyber officer at the trooper station, he was convinced. He looked at the two young guys. "Here— I've got a job for you. The IT man from the trooper station is sending over a couple things for you to look over. Go through it with a fine-tooth comb."

"Sure thing." Chaz stuck a sucker in his mouth, the sandwich long gone. "Anything in particular to look for?"

"Anything intentional. The troopers said that their systems went down several times. I don't think that was an accident." The more Jason mulled it over, the more it made sense. He couldn't say his theory out loud yet—they might all think he was crazy. "Simon, I want you to double-check my work and then Chaz's. We've got to figure this out." Because something in the pit of his stomach told him that things would get a lot worse.

"Hey, guys, let's make a plan for this afternoon." Misty waved them to the conference room.

They all nodded and headed back. Should he tell Darcie his suspicions?

At this point, would she even listen to him?

The woman of his thoughts stood behind her chair, her brow furrowed. "Before we get started, I need to apologize to all of you. It's been a rough day, and I shouldn't take my foul mood out on you. As the head of this team, that's unacceptable. Please forgive me."

Murmurs of acknowledgment rounded the table.

She ran a hand through her curls and lifted her chin. "I've come to realize that what we're trying to accomplish is much larger than I had hoped. It's incredible what we've pulled off in a short amount of time, but we need a great deal of man-hours to get this done before my hoped-for deadline."

"Is there anything we can do to help you, Darc? Just like you said—we're a team." Misty's voice was soft, encouraging.

With a stiff posture and arms crossed over her waist, Darcie shook her head. "You guys are doing a lot already." For several seconds she stared out the window and then took her seat again. "I've been expecting too much. Please know how much I appreciate each of you and everything you've put in so far."

Her discomfort was clear. Had he contributed to that by pushing too far? This was deeper than anger over his personal questions. She was hurting.

She passed a sheet to each of them. "This is the agenda for this afternoon. We need some brainstorming sessions, conference calls with the mayor's and governor's offices, and then back to getting everything in working order. So far the only two successes we can claim are with the state troopers and TAPS."

Jason narrowed his eyes. Strange. Only time would tell if it turned out to be what he suspected. But Darcie had continued, so he paid attention.

". . . hospital, EMTs, ambulance services, fire, police, GVEA, the BESS, the interties, the Emergency Alert System, news and radio . . . Am I missing anything?"

Misty shook her head. "Looks like that's the complete list."

Their boss sent him a look. And for a moment, the guard around those blue eyes was down. Then just as quickly it went back up. "Jason, do you have any ideas of how to streamline this process? How to get everyone on board with the same system efficiently? And then just as important, the backup system? Since you went through the event with the ACI, you're the one with the most knowledge for our scenarios."

His respect for her shot up a notch. Even though she was the leader, she was humble and willing to rely on others who might have more experience. "Let me put some thought into it and check all my notes from the event. You've done a great job so far." In that moment he had to admit that he wanted more than their professional working friendship. He had no idea what that looked like. Or if it was even possible. He wouldn't treat her any different. Maybe one day she'd let him in.

"Well then, let's get ready for our call with—"

Every cell in the room wailed with an alert. They all looked at their screens.

Active shooter! At an elementary school . . .

God, help us!

* * *

2 Below Zero
November 5—12:54 p.m.

Every person in the room scrambled to their computers. Darcie waited for the call that should come from the FPD or the troopers. The public safety system was set up through Wireless Emergency Alerts to send out warnings through cell phones about missing children, dangerous weather, or other critical situations.

This was one scenario she'd never wanted to deal with. But what person would? Even with all her training, she couldn't stop her heart from racing with this one. Weather, she could handle. She'd been a weather specialist after all. Terrorist attacks, well, those scared her, but she had years of military training to help her deal with it. Children in danger, on the other hand? That was like being tossed into a bottomless pit.

Every evaluation she'd had in emergency scenarios had shown her biggest weakness was in this area.

But she couldn't let that get in her way today. This was where the rubber met the road, so to speak. This was what she was hired to do.

But her phone didn't ring. And that concerned her the most. According to their new protocol, she should have had a phone call *immediately*. Before the alert even went out. The seconds ticked by in agonizing snail pace.

Narrowing her eyes, she couldn't take it anymore and clicked on the TV to let the news scroll. The anchors were scrambling to get information. The only thing they knew for certain from their tip line was that every parent with a child in school in the Fairbanks area had gotten that screeching alert.

Schools were in chaos as they evacuated.

What was going on? Why were *all* of the schools evacuating? Was there another threat? Multiple shooters?

Why wasn't she getting any information on the secure portal?

None of this was working according to protocol.

All of a sudden, the phones rang in her office.

She grabbed for the speakerphone on the conference table. "This is the Emergency Operations Center."

"Ms. Phillips?"

"Yes, this is Darcie Phillips."

"Please hold for the mayor."

A brief click and then some muffling. "Ms. Phillips, what do you know of the situation?"

"Nothing, ma'am. This is the first call I've received to the office. The alerts came through to our cell phones almost ninety seconds ago. But the portal is blank." Glancing at her watch, she shook her head. That was an eternity of time.

"I haven't received anything either. But what I'm seeing on the news is not encouraging."

"Yes, ma'am. I was watching myself. Apparently our protocols have fallen to the wayside." Darcie wanted to throttle someone . . . something. How had this happened?

"None of my people can get through to anyone." The woman sounded exasperated. "Not to the police, the state troopers, the schools. Nothing."

Darcie looked out to each of her people—they all shook their heads. "My team is having the same problem." Add the phone systems to their investigation and new systems' checks. This was unacceptable.

"Hold please." More muffling. Mayor must have put her hand over the phone. "Ms. Phillips, I need your team to find out anything and everything they can. I'm headed out to Blakeslee Elementary. Use my emergency cell number if you find out *anything*."

Wait? Blakeslee Elementary? "But, Madam Mayor, my alert said the active shooter was at Alexander Elementary."

More muffling. "We have a serious situation on our hands. Apparently, seven active shooters have been reported. I'll be in touch." And with that, she disconnected.

Seven active shooters? That couldn't be.

Darcie fell back in her chair, the horror of the situation hitting her chest like an anvil. She allowed herself five seconds of shock and then bolted from her chair and headed to her team. "Alright, guys, we have to figure out what is happening. The mayor just called, and there are seven active shooters. No one can get ahold of the police or the state troopers or the schools. All schools are being evacuated."

She took a breath. "Misty, be the liaison. Call anyone and everyone. So far the news station tip line seems to be the only one working. Chaz and Simon, figure out why our new emergency portal isn't working. Jason, grab your laptop and join me in the conference room, please? That's going to be our HQ for now."

She marched back to the conference room and stared at the TV screen with hands on her hips. No reports about how many were injured or worse. No reports on shooters. Just chaos. Evacuation. Parents panicking and flying to their children's schools.

Police in heavy armor with shields crouched and moved quickly into the elementary school on the screen while crowds in the distance waited. Even the reporter at the scene seemed to hold his breath.

No shots were heard in the distance.

Since nothing was happening, the news changed locations to another school where the same scene played out.

"Darcie?" Jason was at the table, staring at his computer screen. "None of this makes sense. I can't log in to the Emergency Alert System."

"What?" She walked over to stand behind him and leaned over the table. "Let me try." But the same thing happened. Log-in failed.

"Hm." Jason closed out of that screen and went to their secure portal. He logged out and tried to get back in. "Can't get in here either."

Darcie raced to her laptop. Logged out of the portal and tried to log in again. Same thing. No access. She put a hand to her forehead. "Is there a chance that someone has hacked the portal and the Emergency Alert System to keep us from gaining access?"

"Not just a chance. They've done it."

Her heart sank, and it felt like every drop of her blood drained out of her body. This couldn't be happening.

CHAPTER THIRTEEN

2 Below Zero
November 5—12:59 p.m.

"Look, we'll figure this out. I've got friends at the FBI and CISA that will be all over this." Jason stared at Darcie, willing her to believe that they would make it through. But the look on her face was one of devastation. Failure.

Her gaze snapped to the TV. "Wait." Her voice was hushed. "There hasn't been *one* report of injuries." Darcie turned to him. "Only evacuations, chaos, and the police going to each campus." She pointed to the screen.

With a nod, he was pretty sure he understood where she was going with this. "You think it's fake? Not an attempt to tie our hands during a real emergency?"

"Could that be done?"

"It's a possibility. *Anything* is possible." He dove back into his laptop. "I still can't access anything here. Let me make a few calls."

He jogged out of the room and went to his desk. Using every trick he knew, he tried gaining access through the more powerful system, but to no avail. He called his buddy at the FBI and was put on hold. He paced around his desk. Watched Darcie make call after call. Misty, Chaz, and Simon scurried from one desk to another as they shouted things to each other across the space. What was going on?

The longer he spent on hold, the more he prayed that it was indeed fake. Surely they would have heard of injuries or casualties by now if it wasn't. And the thought of children being the victims made him want to pound the perpetrator like he pounded his boxing bag.

Ten long minutes later, he heard the connection go through.

"Jason—glad you called. We're tracking the active shooter alert up there." Trent's voice sounded ragged. "You got anything?"

"Something's fishy. First, the alerts apparently went out to all parents of any child in the school system. We all got them here too. Our communications seem to be partially down. Phones, log-ins to the Emergency Alert System, and our emergency portal. Then there's the fact that there's been no report of injuries. The mayor can't get through either, and the only phones that seem to be working are at the news station, of all places."

"Any demands?"

"Nope. Not that we know of."

His friend huffed. "Hold on a sec, Jas."

He counted to twenty while he watched his computer scan code.

Trent groaned. "Just got word. It's a hack. It's not public knowledge. My boss is trying to get ahold of the governor and mayor right now."

"Can you guys trace it?"

"Look, this is bigger than we imagined. I'll be in touch and send you whatever I can, but I've gotta go."

"Thanks." Jason barely got it out before his friend hung up. He jumped up from his chair and jogged back to Darcie in the conference room. "Darcie, it appears it's a hack. My friend at the FBI will send me what he can when he can, but that's all I've got for now."

"I need to alert the press." She picked up her phone.

He put his hand over hers. Wishing he could do more to help. Give her the answers she needed. "His boss was on with the mayor and governor. I have a feeling they will be saying something soon."

She deflated in front of him and practically collapsed in her chair. "Chalk up another fail for this office. Parents will be in an uproar because the system that's supposed to warn them of danger has been hijacked. The governor's and mayor's offices will most likely do a smash-bang-up job with the press and then the hammer will fall on this office. On me." Shaking her head, she frowned. "Here we are supposed to be helping people, and our hands were completely tied . . ."

"It's not a fail. We're not even up and fully functional yet. Estimations were that it would take one full year to get everything in place, right?"

Her curls fell around her face. "But thanks to the press, everyone already knows about our office. They're expecting results. We live in an instantaneous world, remember? My goal was for the first of the year."

He let out a loud laugh. "I can't even get all the software and programming done by then."

"This is no laughing matter, Jason Myers." Her eyes snapped at him, and she slapped a hand on the table. "People's lives are at stake."

Okay, so maybe he shouldn't have laughed. "I'm sorry. But giving yourself unattainable goals isn't going to help either." He pointed to the offices beyond the conference room. "You've got a great team. We're all working our tails off and will do whatever we can. But you have to be realistic. It's better to do something right the first time than to rush it and get it wrong."

Fire lit her eyes. Then her gaze tore to the TV. She lifted the remote and turned up the volume.

". . . if you are just now joining us, the all clear has been given by the police. All of the students are safe. No injuries. No active shooters found. I repeat: no active shooters found. At the top of the hour, the mayor will hold a press conf—"

The phone rang, and Darcie muted the TV and punched the Speakerphone button. "This is Emergency Operations."

"Ms. Phillips, please hold for the mayor."

Everything was quiet for a second.

"Darcie, Mayor Crandall. Please come down to city hall for a press conference. I'm shooting completely blind here, but I was told by a message from the FBI that you might have some more information?"

"Yes, ma'am. I'll have Mr. Myers fill you in on what little we have ascertained." She nodded at him.

Jason cleared his throat. "This was a hack, Madam Mayor. Quite elaborate, too, since it was the Emergency Alert System, plus some communications. My friends at the FBI will keep us informed and help us to navigate from here."

"Both of you come to the press conference. We don't want to give the hacker or hackers more time than they are due. So we will keep it short and sweet. We'll tell the public that we have been working on a complete overhaul of our systems so in the future, this won't happen, again. Clear?"

"Understood." Darcie's voice was succinct and strong.

"Good. I'm not even sure how we will clean this up, but our main objective is to keep the public calm and to keep panic from taking over. I'm counting on you, Ms. Phillips, as the head of our Emergency Operations Center, to be the face and voice of calm and reason. I know that's a hefty task, but that's your job. No better time than now to start showing the people they can rely on us. You're not a politician, so they'll trust you more. I'll see you both in a few minutes."

The call ended, and Jason let out his breath. He wasn't exactly dressed for a press conference, but his polo and jeans would have to do. "You want me to drive?"

"Actually, let's ask Misty to drive. You and I have to come up with some sort of plan to share the smallest amount of information that will pack the biggest punch and keep the people feeling protected."

"Mind if I go along?" Chaz shouldered his messenger bag and dropped his laptop into it. "I want to be there . . . just in case."

"You got it." Jason jogged back to his desk and grabbed his laptop to make notes.

He looked at his watch—1:17 p.m.

The longest twenty-three minutes of his life.

Now he just had to help convince a hundred thousand people that they were prepared to face disaster together.

When they weren't even close.

*   *   *

5 Below Zero
November 5—1:19 p.m.
North Pole, Alaska, Beside the Tanana River

The shiny black Escalade's exhaust puffed in the frozen air. "Your little stunt was a bit extreme, don't you think?" Boss eyed him with a look that said Griz had overstepped.

Standing next to the vehicle, Griz shoved his hands deep into his pockets. "You wanted people to know we weren't to be trifled with." He didn't need to defend his actions, but he'd play along.

The older man let out a ragged breath, the condensation clouding around his face. "I know you have been restless the past few months. Wanting to accomplish more. But I've hired you to do what you're told and to carry out my plans. There will be plenty of time—believe me—to take this to the next level. So don't let me hear of you pulling something like this on your own again, got it?" The stare was cold. Calculating.

Was the guy seriously that naive? Griz cut his gaze to the vehicle. The boss's driver was still in the Escalade, probably enjoying the seat warmers.

So he pulled out his Glock and drilled three rounds into his boss's chest. Thanks to the silencer, the sound wasn't even enough to scare the birds.

The look in the man's eyes as he dropped to the ground made Griz grin. He walked over to the SUV and opened the driver's door. "So . . ." He pointed the gun at the wide eyes of the slimy chump. "Are you going to be a problem?"

The other guy stared him down for a few seconds and then attempted to reach for his gun.

Two more shots and the driver fell out of the SUV. A shame to dirty up such a pretty vehicle, but he really didn't care.

Holstering his gun, he walked toward Diversion Dike and his

waiting vehicle. Let the wild animals do their thing with the bodies. It would take a while before anyone found the corpses. *If* they found them.

His plans were going to keep everyone very busy.

This wasn't about what his previous boss had planned. It wasn't about what that stupid environmental group thought was planned. It wasn't even about the tyrannical government that spouted lies at every turn.

No.

This was about power.

And he was ready to unleash it.

CHAPTER FOURTEEN

5 Below Zero
November 5—3:12 p.m.
Driving Through Fairbanks

MISTY'S SUV HUMMED ALONG THE streets as they headed back to the ops center. Chaz sat in the front passenger seat jabbering away about politicians and how he was glad he wasn't one.

Jason let out a long breath. They'd survived the press conference. In fact, it had gone quite well. He glanced at Darcie, who stared out the window. Better than either of them had expected actually. The mayor had commended them.

Crisis averted.

Now they just had to figure out who did it and how to never let it happen again. Easy, right?

But one hurdle at a time.

Misty cleared her throat and looked at him in the rearview mirror. "I think this calls for a little pat on the back, don't you? I mean, nobody was hurt. The public seems to be appeased. The mayor and governor are content with how quickly our office responded and handled things . . . and all those kids are safe." Her relief that all the kids were accounted for and unharmed practically oozed through the car.

"You're right, Misty. Rather than looking at this negatively, we should be grateful." He'd caught a bit of the optimism and reached over to give Darcie's hand a squeeze. Just to reassure her that they would figure this out.

She yanked her hand out of his grasp so quickly it shocked him.

All right. Big mistake.

No words. Nothing. But a glare that told him he'd overstepped and he better keep his distance.

So he did.

Which was difficult under the circumstances. They worked together.

Misty must have seen the whole thing, because she shot him a compassionate glance and changed the subject. When Darcie didn't respond, Chaz picked up the slack.

The more Jason thought about it, the more he wanted to kick himself. Gestures like that weren't his norm, and he hadn't meant it to be intimate. But he had to admit there was part of him that was drawn to Darcie. She was strong and smart, and he longed to help ease the pain of whatever was locked behind that wall of hers.

For years he'd longed for a companion and a family. Most red-blooded males filled their time with chasing down their next conquest. But he'd spent his adult life chasing down his brother. Which had probably kept him out of a lot of trouble himself. There hadn't been time to focus too much on his own personal life. He'd made a promise to his parents, and he intended to keep it: find Kirk and bring him home.

He shook the thoughts away. It wasn't like the gesture meant he was seeking a relationship with her. She was his boss, after all. And he didn't even know her. Didn't know where she stood spiritually.

And most glaring? Darcie was wounded, and he liked her enough that he didn't want to be the cause of wounding her further.

Time. That was what they both needed.

Time to do their jobs.

Time to let things settle down and rest.

Time for peace and calm to cover them like the deep snow that sheltered Fairbanks every winter.

If only time truly healed all wounds.

* * *

7 Below Zero
November 7—11:31 a.m.
Emergency Operations Center

Jason paced in the stairwell. It was his only place to get away and think.

The weather had been weird. Calm. Clear. And cold. Very cold. The highs during the day weren't even reaching Zero, and the lows were hovering awfully close to the number no one wanted to say out loud.

Things had been torturous at the office since the active shooter alert. Darcie had built a firewall so thick and impenetrable that he was afraid he'd forever be locked on the outside in the cold. Whatever had triggered it, he wasn't certain.

He didn't want to go there but had to accept this was where things stood.

Two days had passed, and they'd spent every hour together working except the time when they slept on couches and chairs. Darcie hadn't gone home, so no one else had either.

Chaz and Simon both looked supercharged and like they could bounce off the walls, but that was probably all the high-energy drinks they'd been inhaling.

Misty had dark circles under her eyes, her hair pulled up in a ponytail.

Darcie's eyes were bloodshot, but other than that, she looked the best out of all of them.

Pretty good for the person in charge of the emergency center.

Him, on the other hand? He needed a shower. Real food. Sleep in a real bed. And an hour or so with his punching bag to work off all this stress.

No one wanted to say it, but none of them understood why Darcie was so all-fired insistent that they fix everything. Right now. When the fix and answers weren't easy.

They all knew that. But worked themselves crazy anyway.

Footsteps sounded on the stairs above him, and he stopped his pacing on the landing long enough to wait for whoever it was.

Because if it was Darcie, he'd give her a wide berth. Anyone else, he could use a chat. A sounding board.

Misty's slight frame appeared as she came around the stairwell. "Hey, Jas. Pacing again?" She quirked that one eyebrow up at him.

His team knew him. Hadn't taken them long to figure him out. "How'd you guess?"

"I'm off to get lunch. Need anything?"

"Oh, only a way to find and stop the hackers?"

"Nice try. I'm not *that* much of a miracle worker. But I will bring back some food. How does that sound?" She let out a loud sigh. "To be honest, I'm looking forward to the fresh air. Even if it is frozen." The grin she sent him was halfhearted, but they all could use some sleep.

"Food and fresh air." He stepped toward the stairs to go back to the office. "I guess that will have to do. For now." Giving her a wide grin, he took the stairs two at a time.

Now if he could only get through to Darcie and convince her that he was safe and on her side. And to let them all go home and sleep. Shower. Recharge.

For that, he needed a miracle.

* * *

10 Below Zero
November 9—1:59 p.m.

Natalie roamed the streets, searching for the right place. Rubbing her gloved hands together, she kept her pace quick. She needed every bit of warmth she could muster. This might take a while.

Breathing through her mouth, she tried to keep her breaths steady. She had layered two scarves around her neck and up and over her nose and mouth. An old pair of ski goggles kept her eyes covered for now. But it was her coat that really did the job. Tito had bought it for her years ago. The fur lining and thick hood had helped her stay warm through many winters.

The urgency in her grew. She had to tell them all before she forgot what she'd heard. But who should she tell? Would they listen? She had to make sure they did. No matter what. It was truly awful. But someone needed to stop those bad men.

Crossing the street, the blue-gray building in front of her had a new sign. In fact, there was a man finishing the installation right now.

The lights in the sign flickered as the man did something at the back of it. Then he closed the clear shield over the front and closed a box at the base. He walked to a van and drove away.

Natalie got closer. Her eyes stung. She was tired. Everything was blurry.

But then the words jumped out at her.

Emergency Operations Center.

This was it. These were the people she needed to tell.

Lifting her goggles, she closed her eyes and asked for Tito to help her. She needed his strength to do what was right. He would remind her to trust in God. He was right.

Tito was always right.

God . . . I'm not as strong as my husband. Tito had better faith than I do. But I need help. Please . . . I need someone to listen.

In that moment, strength rushed through her limbs. "It's getting colder every day. When it hits twenty-six below, it's going to be horrible." What was it she was supposed to remember?

"A disaster!" She yelled for all she was worth. "People are going to die! Please listen! Help! You've got to help!"

She repeated what she could remember. "You can't let people die!" Her voice cracked, the bitter cold air chilling her lungs all the way down.

But then people exited the building. They ran toward her.

Natalie backed up. She couldn't let them get too close.

A lady with curly hair and brilliant-blue eyes waved the others back. She stepped slowly. One step at a time. "Please. I won't hurt you."

"You have to save people." Natalie cried the words but couldn't trust the woman. She slid back. Ready to bolt.

"That's my job. To save people. I just need to know what to do. How can I save them?"

Natalie shook her head. She didn't know the answer. "When it hits twenty-six below, bad things are going to happen. You have to prepare. You have to save them!"

"Save who?" The woman's voice was calm. Soothing. But she shivered. The younger woman only had on a coat.

"You've got to believe me!" Natalie took several steps back. Looked over her shoulder to make sure no one was there.

"I do. I do. Just tell me what I need to do."

She shook her head. It was blurry again. Fuzzy. Why couldn't she remember? Her notepad! She struggled to pull it out of her pocket with her thick gloves on. Tried to read her writing. The words she read made her want to vomit. "Bad men. Very bad men . . ." Placing both hands on the sides of her head, she squeezed.

"The lady's crazy." A man from the building next door traipsed across the parking lot. "I'm not going to put up with this. I've called the police."

The woman with the blue eyes headed the man off. Protecting Natalie. "Please. Go back inside, sir."

"Haven't you heard what this lunatic is saying? It's been all over the news. It's ridiculous. She's not a prophetess. She's obviously out of her mind." The man waved a hand at her.

Natalie's temper raged. How dare that man? "I'm *not* out of my mind." She spat the words toward the man. Pointed the notepad at him. "People are in danger. If you don't believe me—there's more bodies. Out by Diversion Dike."

"Oh, this is ridiculous!" The man charged her, but the others stepped in front of him. They argued, and she turned and ran for all she was worth.

Maybe the lady with the piercing eyes could do something. She was their only hope.

*　*　*

12 Below Zero
November 9—2:26 p.m.

Darcie did laps around the conference room table while she waited for a call from the police or the state troopers. Anyone really. Anyone with information on the woman . . . or who could substantiate what she said. None of the others seemed to think much of the woman's "prophecy"—but that didn't mean they shouldn't pay attention. If that outspoken man from the office building next door hadn't interrupted, they would have been able to follow her when she ran. But no. In protecting the woman from the angry bystander, they'd lost her.

It infuriated Darcie.

She was supposed to be in charge. In control.

And yet she didn't have control of anything.

Misty had been brilliant. Without bringing attention to herself, she'd pulled out her cell and filmed the mysterious woman. She'd sent the video to the FBI so it could be analyzed. Perhaps the FBI would have luck with facial recognition. But unlike the quick responses that happened on her favorite show, *NCIS*, in real life that could take days or even weeks.

What haunted her was the look in the woman's eyes. She hadn't appeared like a crazed lunatic. The only way Darcie could describe it was desperation. For someone to listen to her.

The woman believed what she was saying.

Deep down Darcie believed it too. She had no idea why. Her gut? Like the famous Gibbs's gut on *NCIS*? She shook her head. If she started saying things like that out loud, everyone would think she was the crazy one who watched too much TV and wasn't grounded in reality.

At least she'd come to her senses and sent everyone home a couple days ago and realized she couldn't push everyone to the very limits. Maybe Jason had been correct.

Who was she kidding. Of course he was right. But she'd been too stubborn to admit it.

Steps sounded behind her.

Darcie turned.

Jason.

She let out a breath. She hadn't been very nice to him lately. Her emotional survival instincts had kicked up a notch ever since he'd grabbed her hand. Oh, she knew his motivation was encouragement. It had been spontaneous. But she'd still freaked.

"Sorry to bug you." He shoved his hands into his jeans pockets. "I just couldn't get that woman's eyes out of my mind and was wondering what you were thinking."

Darcie studied him. He was a decent enough guy. More than decent. She liked him. It wasn't his fault that the last time a guy grabbed her hand like that . . . "You probably will think this is crazy, but I want to believe her."

"I don't think that's crazy at all. But which part? The dire prediction or the bodies?"

Letting her shoulders relax, she took a seat. How much should she say? His deep-brown eyes bored into hers. Drew her in. The intensity in them frightened her more than she wanted to admit. The fact that he was willing to ignore her harshness, forgive, and move on sent a rush of humiliation through her. Her heart sank. She was better than this. Wasn't she?

"Sorry. You've obviously got a lot on your mind. I'll get back to work."

"Jason. Wait." Deep breath. Time to put on her big-girl pants and deal with her issues head-on. "It's time to clear the air."

"Alright." He crossed his arms over his chest.

"Look, Jason. I'm horrible at apologies. But I'm sorry for how rotten I've been to you lately. It's not you. Just a reminder of something that happened to me a long time ago." She shouldn't have said that out loud, but oh well, it was out there now. "When I'm stressed, I close off. I shouldn't do that with all of you—this team. It's imperative that we trust one another. We spend pretty much all our time together, and as we have so much to do—"

"Sorry to interrupt." He held up a hand, and his jaw clenched. "But *I* need to apologize. You don't need to do any more explaining. I'm the one who made you uncomfortable or did something inappropriate. I'm sorry."

She shook her head. Couldn't allow him to take the blame when she was the messed-up one. Good leaders didn't do that. "That's the thing. You didn't do anything wrong." How much should she say? "But you are forgiven. I hope you will forgive me too."

"All's forgiven." He pulled a chair next to her and sat as well. "Look, I know we haven't known each other a long time, but we have worked side by side a good deal of that short time. I've seen what an incredible work ethic you have. You are strong, capable, have great leader skills. Then you have also been humble. Willing to sacrifice whatever you have to for the sake of our team. You've apologized—when you didn't have to. You've asked for everyone's opinions. You've made everyone feel like a valued member of the team."

The words weren't fluffy. His compliments brought on a swell of emotion. And that confused her. She blinked.

"Thank you." Their eyes connected for several seconds. Heat traveled up her neck, and she tried to swipe it away with her hand. "I trust you, Jason. I trust your knowledge, your wisdom, and your instincts. Needless to say, I need you here. You're a valuable asset to this team."

He studied her for several seconds and then glanced away. "I appreciate that. My instincts are saying we need to find out more about our mystery woman." It looked like he wanted to say more, but he hesitated.

The phone in the middle of the conference table rang, startling her out of the moment. Darcie tapped the Speakerphone button. "This is the Emergency Operations Center."

"Ms. Phillips?"

"Yes, I'm here."

"This is Trooper Lindsay. We've spoken before. About Mr. Myers."

For some reason, that made her smile. She sent a look to Jason. "Yes, he's here as well."

"The reason for my call is to inform you that the tip you gave us was true. We just returned from the scene. Two men were found. Both shot in the chest."

That meant the old woman was right. Shifting her gaze to Jason, Darcie raised her eyebrows.

He frowned and blew out a breath.

What else was their mystery woman right about?

CHAPTER FIFTEEN

13 Below Zero
November 10—11:56 a.m.

JASON DOUBTED ANY OF THEM had slept much the night before. Not since the bodies were found out by Diversion Dike.

The minute the news caught wind of the bodies and the source of the tip, the team was flooded with calls from news stations. And not just local or statewide. They were fielding inquiries from around the country.

Guess it had been impossible to hope that they'd be able to keep it out of the news. Now everyone was looking for their mysterious woman. Of course, to law enforcement she was a person of interest in the murders.

They wanted to find her to ascertain how she knew about the bodies.

The media wanted to find her so they could record interviews and splash sensational stories across the internet and TVs.

Jason needed to find her because he had a feeling she knew something.

Something that could help them prevent a disaster.

He spread out all the information he had put together so far on his desk. Refusing to answer any more calls, he knew the best use of his time was to figure out this crazy puzzle.

Jogging to the break room, he grabbed another cup of coffee and went back to his desk.

With a swig of the hot brew, he studied the papers.

Was there a connection between the pipeline glitches, the state trooper computers' going down, the false active shooter alert, and the woman's predictions? She'd made a brief comment about the power going out.

Could a hacker actually accomplish that?

From what he knew of all the systems in place, that would be a stretch. And who would do something like that? An attack of that magnitude had the potential to kill tens of thousands of people. *Most* hackers were in it for the money. Not blood.

His gut clenched.

Terrorists.

They could kill more people than 9/11.

Scrambling to the secure and encrypted system that linked him to his office in Anchorage, he checked his email for any alerts. Then he sent an urgent email to his friend at the FBI and another to a friend at CISA. Was there any chatter about terrorists launching cyberattacks?

He hated that his brain had automatically gone this route, but they had to be prepared.

"Jason?"

He jerked around to see Misty at his shoulder.

"Wow. You were deep in thought." She held out her iPad. Pointed to the security video on the screen. "You seem to have a visitor. Should I let him up?"

His stomach plummeted as he looked.

Kirk.

Jason yelled toward the conference room. "Darcie?" He waved a hand at her.

With her brow dipped, she approached. "I saw the security camera. That's your brother, isn't it?"

"Yep. I don't want him in the ops center. Don't think that's a good idea to let him see anything."

"Why don't we use the pressroom?" Darcie suggested with a decisive step in that direction. "He'll feel privileged to be allowed in, just not into the offices. I'm going with you."

"I was going to ask you—thank you. I need someone else's unbiased opinion of what they see."

"Misty, why don't you join us as well. That way it looks official, and it will make him feel important." Darcie headed toward the pressroom.

It was amazing how she had figured out exactly how to handle Kirk. Once again his respect for the woman rose. Her intuition was spot-on.

Misty used the tablet to give Kirk entrance and spoke to the screen. "Take the elevator to the fourth floor. When you exit, the door across the hall in front of you will allow you to enter."

Jason opened the door to the pressroom and held it for the two women.

"Thank you."

"Thank you." Their voices were in unison.

Darcie scratched the back of her neck. "Do you have any idea why he would be here?"

He shook his head. "No. I haven't heard from him since the night you had to come verify my identity." With long strides, he paced back and forth. "This isn't a casual visit. He's got something up his sleeve."

"Alright. Then let's be on alert."

Misty set up her iPad and keyboard and placed her notebook on one of the tables. "I'll take notes."

The door opened, and Kirk entered with a smirk on his face. "Good to see you, Jason." He turned to Darcie. "I believe we've met. You're in charge of all this, aren't you?"

"Yes." Her voice was firm.

"Who's that?" Kirk pointed to Misty.

"She's my assistant." Darcie lifted her chin just a hair.

"Can your assistant turn the TV on?" Kirk's voice dripped with derision.

Misty reached for a remote and did as he requested. "Any particular station?"

"Local news?" His brother sounded all too jovial about the prospect.

"Kirk, what is this about? I haven't heard a word from you since you conveniently asked me to come help you . . . and set me up to be arrested." What he really wanted to do was punch the smirk right off Kirk's face.

His brother put a hand to his chest. "Me? Now why would you think I did that?" The grin on his face widened.

Jason stepped forward, his fist clenched at his side.

A tug on his arm stopped him. Darcie. She engaged his brother. "Let's skip ahead to the real reason you're here, shall we?"

Kirk narrowed his eyes. "Fine. I'm here to give you fair warning." He looked over to Misty. "Turn that up, will you, hon?"

The noon news was in full swing. The meteorologist was talking about the cold front that had settled over their area and stalled. It would stay for a while. Without anything to push it along, it was settling in for a nice visit.

Then the screen changed. Words scrolled across.

But they weren't in English. What language was that?

All of a sudden it went back to the news. As if nothing happened. He glanced at Darcie to confirm that she'd seen the blip too. Her face was blank of emotion, but her hand had a death grip on her fountain pen.

"I'm giving you a heads-up. Since you're my brother and all. My group has big plans. And you can't stop us. But rest assured, we're just getting started." He stepped closer until his face was inches from Jason's. "It's time you listened to me, big brother. Took me seriously. I'm not messing around. We are responsible for all this." With that, Kirk spun and waved a hand over his shoulder.

Jason opened his mouth to say something and then clamped it shut. It was no use.

When the door closed, Darcie turned to Misty. "Did you get all that?"

"Yep. Videoed the whole thing."

* * *

17 Below Zero
November 13—8:49 a.m.
Somewhere Along the Chena River

Cold. So cold. And cold was bad. Very, very bad.

Wait. Why was it bad? She loved the snow.

Placing her hands on the sides of her head, she squeezed. Remember! Why couldn't she remember?

Natalie huddled under the blanket, voices echoing so they came at her from every direction.

"She's smarter than we gave her credit."

Who was?

"An accident needs to shut her up. Permanently."

They weren't talking about *her* . . . were they?

"The clock is ticking."

"Get rid of her. I don't care how."

She gasped and closed her eyes, hoping for clarity. Did they know where she was hiding? They couldn't get rid of her! No!

She covered her mouth with the blanket so she wouldn't scream. Couldn't let them know she was here. But she had to get away. How?

Closing her eyes, she saw Tito. *"Hush, love. It'll be alright."* The voice in her mind was clear and calm.

Natalie turned to embrace him, to inhale his courage into her fear. But dirt filled her nostrils. Tito disappeared as though never there. "Don't go . . ." She whispered against the blanket, the words muffled.

"Quiet! Don't move!"

Natalie obeyed and held her breath.

"Did you hear that?"

Footsteps clomped above her. "Just a moose outside."

Exhaling, she squeezed her eyes tight. *Tito . . . come back . . . please.* She needed him like never before.

Hot tears escaped and burned trails down her cheeks. But she refused to open her eyes. If she did, the bad men might see her. They already wanted to get rid of her. Fear crept up her back and made her spine tingle.

Go away . . . She tried to will the bad men away with her mind. *You're not real, are you? Go away. Leave me in peace.*

But everything was black. And the voices and footsteps and thuds above her continued. What if they *were* real?

"I'll get Julian to hack the traffic lights. Should be easy enough to cause an accident in this ice and snow."

The traffic lights? What would they do to her? She couldn't leave her hiding spot. They would kill her for sure. Natalie curled into a tight ball and gripped the blanket as close as she could. Her foot knocked over her cup. She winced against the sound.

Everything above her stilled.

She was caught. They were going to kill her. Then footsteps. Lots of footsteps. Closer. Overhead and all around her. Fear clawed up her belly and into her throat, where it lodged. She couldn't breathe. *No! No! Don't kill me!* Her screams never made it past the ball of fear clogging her windpipe. A door slammed.

Tito . . . help me.

Even with her eyes closed, she could see the boards and walls above her crumble. Burying her alive.

CHAPTER SIXTEEN

18 Below Zero
November 14—6:30 a.m.
Undisclosed Location

EVERY MAN IN FRONT OF him had vowed allegiance. To their cause. To him.

Now that they'd gotten rid of a lot of deadweight, things could move forward.

To the *real* plan of action. Overthrowing the powers that hindered their freedom.

First things first. "For everything to go smoothly, we have a few more *hindrances* to eliminate."

The old woman in the streets had gotten her information from someone. Thankfully, she looked like a crazed lunatic in the media, but she'd still riled up a lot of people. They could use that to their advantage. But the woman still needed to go. And whoever had tipped her off.

"Is everything set up for today?" He narrowed his gaze at his new right-hand man.

"Yep. Julian and Nick are on it."

"Good." Getting rid of that emergency center—now that he knew what they were up to—was paramount. It would make everything else run without incident. He'd just have to start at the top and work his way down. "Let the games begin."

* * *

18 Below Zero
November 14—3:00 p.m.
Emergency Operations Center

Ever since Jason's brother had shown up at their offices, every agency at Darcie's disposal had been working on the message that had scrolled across the screen during the midday news. No one could find Kirk. And once the authorities saw the video, a warrant had been issued for his arrest.

She'd downed six cups of coffee today before noon and had popped more antacids than should probably be consumed in a month.

She lapped the conference room table again. Chewed on her thumbnail. All the information swirling in her brain needed to be focused.

All right. So it was time to go over everything one more time. She picked up her notebook and tried to make sense of all the scribbles.

Nope. New sheet. New list. Focus.

When the blip had first happened, the majority of the public just thought it was an error from the local station. But those who were more skeptical kept the chatter going.

Then there were the people behind the scenes. The authorities had done their best to keep the weird interruption quiet while they started a manhunt, but the media was having a field day. Of course the local station didn't want to admit that they'd been hacked. But everyone else said it.

The odd thing about the message was that the letters were from three different alphabets. Greek, Hebrew, and Aramaic. No one had been able to figure out a pattern yet.

Jason and Misty both mentioned those were the three languages of the original biblical texts, but what did that mean for them today? How was it relevant?

Ever since they'd mentioned, it though, it had been like a thorn in her side. Bringing up all kinds of memories she'd hoped to keep suppressed. Memories of church and the wonderful times with her family. When things had been perfect. Before it all fell apart.

That's when she'd buried her faith as well. Because if God couldn't keep her family together, then what good was believing?

But that wasn't holding as much weight as an argument in her mind anymore. Why? Why couldn't she just blame God and leave it at that?

Deep down, she wanted it to be real. Faith. Wished she could call out for help like she used to as a little girl.

But He wouldn't answer. Especially not since she'd turned her back.

These thoughts were getting her nowhere. These *feelings* weren't helping.

Wait. How long had it been? No. With a shake of her head, she focused back on the page in front of her.

They had a serious crisis on their hands.

The conference room had been her makeshift office for a while, but she needed a change of scenery.

Grabbing her laptop, she went back to her private office and closed the door.

After cleaning up her desk and transcribing all her scribbled notes into a cleaner, legible list, she sat back in her chair and analyzed it. Was there something she'd missed?

The two threatening notes she'd received sat to the side of her planner. Stupidly, she hadn't given them to the police. She should have. But at the time she hadn't wanted anyone to think she was weak or scared. Which was ridiculous. Especially now.

So the notes were going into her bag. She'd bring them to the police this evening. After she told her team about them as well.

Tapping her fingers on her desk, she tried to will the whirling in her mind to cooperate and get into some sort of order.

Jason had said that Kirk in previous years had been involved with an extreme environmental group. People who wouldn't hurt a fly. Or a person.

Now it seemed, everything had changed. These weren't environmentalists. Every environmental group had come forward saying they didn't have anything to do with the attacks. Especially once word got out there were murders involved and the false active shooter warning seemed to be connected. No one wanted to be associated with either of those events. The group that had given her such a hard time her first day had even sent a letter on official letterhead denouncing the actions of whoever was behind all this. With an apology to her specifically. If things hadn't been so serious, she would have laughed at that.

But who were the terrorists? What was their purpose?

A BOLO and all-points bulletin had gone out for Kirk Myers. But there wasn't a trace of him anywhere. No cell phone. No residence. No bank accounts. No credit cards. No vehicle registered in his name. Nothing.

They were flying blind.

They hadn't had any luck finding the responsible party to the false emergency alert, and Jason had spent every waking moment securing their *new* system. Since their secure portal had failed when they needed it most, he'd taken it upon himself to do something different. A new WebEOC software. He said it was the only way for them to be ready for whatever came next.

She hated the thought that there would be a next time. But that was her job—to be prepared for that next time. And the time after that. And the time after that.

Her thoughts went back to Kirk. He'd seemed awfully sure of himself. Enjoying the power that he presumed was at his fingertips. Enjoying the power over his brother.

But Jason didn't think there was any way his addict brother was the mastermind behind all this. Was he right? Or was he blinded by the fact that it was family?

That was assuming *if* all of it was truly connected. At this point it seemed ludicrous to lump it all together and give one terrorist group credit. As much as they wanted to put a face behind the crises. Slap a bad-guy label on them and be done with it. But then again, were they being ignorant by not seeing that all these so-called coincidences were connected?

Problem was, they had to consider every scenario until they had more concrete information. Kirk's visit could have simply been a smokescreen to distract them from what was really going on.

The issues with Kirk had to weigh on Jason. How could they not? But he hadn't stopped. Hadn't tried to make excuses. Maybe she wasn't the only one who tried to pretend nothing was wrong. Wrapped herself up in her numb cocoon to escape the pain.

Shaking off the thoughts, she glanced at her watch and grabbed her notes and laptop and headed toward the conference room. As soon as her team saw she was on the move, they gathered their things and followed.

Settling into her chair, she opened her notebook while the others situated themselves. Pulled out the two notes. "First, I need to share these with you guys and apologize for not showing them to you sooner." She passed the notes to Misty.

As they rounded the table, no one said a word. But every eyebrow raised.

"I know. It was not the smartest thing to keep these hidden from you. I'm bringing them to the police this afternoon."

A ding on the security system made Misty glance at her iPad. "I'll be right back. It's the messenger service."

Something inside Darcie made her twinge. Yes, they received important documents through a messenger service all the time. But that was also how the first note had arrived. Misty had sent out memos to every agency and informed them after that incident that only official communications through one of the approved services would be accepted.

Jason leaned over the table. "I know you don't need a scolding from us now, but I wish you would have told us." His tone conveyed his hurt. Not that she blamed him.

The numbness that had been her companion for so long evaporated. She wanted to make it better. But how?

Chaz shook his head. "I don't like this, Darcie. Do you think we're in danger?" He tapped the table. Usually easygoing and the jokester among them, his brow was dipped in a deep crease and a sober expression filled his face.

The need to protect these people she'd come to care about overwhelmed her. "These came before you guys were on board. They're directed at me." But what if they got caught in the crossfire?

Was there any chance that the notes and the attacks were connected? If so, was *she* the target?

Misty returned and handed Darcie an envelope.

An eerie sensation traveled her arms as adrenaline pumped through her veins and she took it. What was wrong with her?

She ripped it open and let out a huff as she read that she was being requested to join a task force the mayor was putting together. Another ridiculous group, all to do what? Save face with the public? Why couldn't the politicians just let them do their jobs?

She tossed the message to the side, willed her heart to slow down, and shook her head. It was her job to keep things on track. "Alright. Let's get to it. Jason, how's the new WebEOC?"

"Up and running."

"Great."

Another ding on the security cameras. Misty's eyes went wide. "Quick! It's our mystery woman."

Everyone grabbed coats and raced toward the doors. The echoes of their footsteps in the stairwell made it sound like a stampede.

Jason was the first one to the main entrance. He opened the door for the woman. "Please come in. We've been hoping to see you."

But she shook her head violently.

Then she pointed to Darcie. "You. Come out."

Darcie held up her hands and took slow steps, afraid she would spook the woman like a frightened animal. "I'm here." She felt the presence of her team behind her.

The woman kept stepping backward. "Tell them to stay back."

"Okay." She looked over her shoulder. "Please stay back." Turning back to the woman, she smiled. "But these are good people. I trust them. They are my friends."

The air was so cold it was wreaking havoc on her lungs as she breathed. This was not the kind of weather to stand outside for a chat. She wrapped her coat tighter. "Come inside. It's too cold to talk out here."

"No!" The woman put both hands on the sides of her head. "Don't you understand? There's going to be an accident. With the traffic lights. They're going to hurt me!"

Darcie furrowed her brow. "Traffic lights? How are they going to hurt you? I will do everything in my power to stop them." She tempted fate and slid one foot a bit closer. And then the other. Her lungs burned. Why hadn't she grabbed her scarf?

Tears flowed from the woman's eyes now and froze on her cheeks. "They want to shut me up. To get rid of me. But don't you see? You have to help! You have to save people! They're going to kill everyone. When it's twenty-six below—it's all going to end." The woman lunged for Darcie and grabbed hold of her. "We can't let that happen! We can't!" She collapsed.

Darcie went down with the woman, trying desperately to keep her from falling and breaking anything. She was so thin. Fragile.

In less than a second, multiple hands and arms were around the two of them, dragging them inside.

Once the door was closed. Darcie knelt over the woman to make sure she was still breathing. She couldn't lose her now. The one person—as weird as it was—that had made her start to feel. Drew her in.

"Yes, we need an ambulance at the Emergency Operations Center." Misty rattled off the address. "A woman has collapsed."

Jason's voice retreated up the stairs as he called someone else. Moments later he returned with a bottle of water and a blanket. Their eyes connected as he wrapped the woman up.

Taking this position had changed her life. It hadn't just been their mystery woman and her passionate pleas. Darcie had wanted to start fresh and hoped for something . . . anything . . . to drown out the dead feeling inside. Then she'd watched the video with this woman and looked into her eyes. Over and over.

Something had sparked to life within Darcie again. Then she'd met Jason. Formed bonds with her little team.

Looking down at the woman, her eyes stung with tears and her hands trembled.

The EMTs were let into the building, and Darcie released custody of the frail woman, who seemed stronger than steel and larger than life. In a haze, she headed up the stairs to her office.

Jason and Misty both tried to talk to her, but she waved them off, shook her head, and closed the door.

When the silence engulfed her, she sat down, placed her face in her hands, and cried.

An hour later, after a trip to the ladies' room, Darcie emerged and headed back to her office. Tears dried and face washed.

The ambulance had taken the woman to the hospital, and two state troopers escorted her. Said they would keep the woman under guard and inform the Emergency Operations Center immediately if she became conscious.

Nothing could have prepared Darcie for the emotions that swirled inside. Not only was she concerned for the woman, but the fear inside her had grown that something serious was about to happen. And she had no power to stop it.

That's what frightened her the most. Everyone was relying on her. The woman was relying on her. Had trusted her with her message.

What she wouldn't give for a bit of the numbness to return. It was easier to face crises that way.

The hecklers from the first day repeated in her mind.

Then Mr. Oliver's voice. *"Darcie is not one of the gifted people."*

Then Darrell's comments.

"You ready to go?" Jason stood in front of her desk.

When did he get there? She blinked and looked down at her things. Then lifted her gaze to him.

"To the police station?"

That's right. They'd planned to go to the police station with the threatening notes. "Sure. Let me just get my things together."

"I thought we should swing by the hospital. Visit our friend, just in case she wakes up. We could ask her some questions."

His compassion toward the older woman stirred her. "Yeah, that sounds great. I'm sorry I lost track of time." She hurried to put everything in her bag and then bundled up.

"I'll pull my truck up to the front door. We can come back for yours later."

"Sure." Now where did she put her notebook? Oh, the conference room. Throwing her purse over her shoulder, she hauled her computer bag to the conference room and grabbed the threats and her notebook.

She waved at Misty as she headed out. "See you in the morning. Six?"

"You got it, Boss." Her young assistant munched on a granola bar as she typed with one hand. The girl was a wonder.

Maybe she should pick up a surprise gift for each member of the team tonight. Darcie headed for the elevator—there just wasn't enough energy for the stairs—and waited in the silence of the building.

Their offices were on the fourth floor of the new building. It was nice to be at the top. But the other floors weren't occupied yet. Whether the government had other plans or intended for her office to grow enough to fill them was beyond her.

Her nerves were raw. A self-admitted control freak, she didn't like it when things didn't go by her itinerary. And right now her entire job was that way. Like a tornado had come through and tossed every bit of her plans around the room.

What was taking the elevator so long? She glanced at her watch. She'd give it ten more seconds and then would take the stairs. Jason was surely waiting on her by now.

When the elevator hadn't arrived by the time she counted to ten, she huffed and walked down the hall toward the stairwell.

Jogging down the stairs in her winter gear with all her things made her quite toasty by the time she reached the bottom. She exited the building, winced at the bitter cold, and hopped into Jason's waiting truck. "Sorry. The elevator never came. I should've just taken the stairs in the first place." She set her bags at her feet and buckled her seat belt.

"Not a problem. I've already called the police station and let the captain know we're coming."

"Perfect. Let's get this over with." Leaning back against the warm seat, she smiled. Seat warmers were the best invention ever. "I hate to say it, but I think your truck might be nicer than mine."

His soft chuckle eased the tension. "You should see my little hybrid SUV I just bought. An impulse purchase really, something to get around in and save money on gas when I don't need this beast." He patted the dash. "But it has *all* the bells and whistles."

"Don't even get me started on the price of gas." She let the conversation drop. Silence was just fine with her.

Rush hour was her least favorite time of day. Thankfully, it was only a few blocks to the station. Because she needed to get this over with. The urgent need to talk to the old woman was more pressing anyway.

As they approached Cushman Street, she closed her eyes for a moment. Thankfully, Jason didn't seem to have the need for chitchat.

She opened her eyes and looked over at him. The firm set of his jaw was the only giveaway that he was feeling the same stress of their situation.

The green light ahead was a welcome sight, and they headed through the intersection.

But bright lights barreled toward them from the left.

She grabbed his arm. "Jason!"

Her scream tore through the truck right before the other car slammed into them.

CHAPTER SEVENTEEN

12 Below Zero
November 15—10:08 a.m.
Fairbanks Memorial Hospital

BEEPING BROUGHT HIM AWAKE. WHERE was that horrid sound coming from?

Jason's head pounded. He forced himself to open his eyes fully. But that was harder than he'd anticipated.

Then it all came back.

The crash.

The fire department cutting them out of his truck.

Darcie! Where was she?

He tried to sit up, but the room tilted.

"Whoa there . . ." A nurse entered the room. "Mr. Myers, I'm Jackie. Do you remember what happened?" She pulled the stethoscope from around her neck.

"Where's my friend? The woman in the truck with me?"

"Right here." Darcie's voice came from the door. Then her. With a cup in her hands. "You *would* choose to wake up the minute I leave the room."

Her light laughter did wondrous things to his thudding heart, but he could tell it was forced.

"You alright?" He winced as the nurse poked and prodded on him.

"A few cuts and bruises, but thanks to your truck's superior safety features, I'm alive and kicking." Several bandages covered her face, neck, and arms. A large bruise had formed on her cheek. She pointed to it. "The airbag and I had a fight. But I'm glad it won."

His laugh was squashed with the pain that radiated through his middle as soon as he did.

In an instant she was at his side. With a grimace, she scrunched up her nose at him. "I'm sorry. That was my fault. I shouldn't try to make you laugh."

The warmth that spread through him helped the pain reside. How cute. She was concerned about him. If he wasn't laid up and all fuzzy in his head, he was sure that would mean more. But he couldn't keep his head up, so he leaned it back against the bed.

She walked to the chair at his side and took a seat, groaning as she did. "They tell me the soreness will go away with time. Not sure I believe them yet." She took a sip from her cup. "Jackie, how's he doing?"

"His numbers are good. Especially now that he's awake. How do you feel, Jason?" The nurse raised her eyebrows. "Be honest. Understanding that I *know* about all your injuries already. And you don't."

The woman had pluck. He'd give her that. And right now he really didn't have the energy to argue with her. "I feel like I've been hit by a car. How's that for an answer?"

"Good enough." She adjusted something on the IV pole. "The doctor said once you were awake, we could take you off this one." Lifting the bag off the pole, she replaced it with another. "You were quite a bear when we brought you in. Fighting off everyone and everything while you hollered about this one." She tipped her head in Darcie's direction with a grin. "You'll need to stay on the pain meds for today."

"You're keeping me?" He didn't like where this was going.

"Yep." She typed up something on the mobile medical computer station.

He tried to sit up, and searing pain shot through his left shoulder.

"You had surgery a few hours ago, Jason. Clavicle fracture open reduction and internal fixation. You're not going anywhere. Especially not with the concussion and the amount of blood you lost." Darcie stared him down.

"From a broken collarbone?" He did *not* like people telling him what to do. Or not to do something.

"No. From wounds in your head and thigh." She pointed. "All in all you have over one hundred stitches. That's a lot." She took another sip. Looking a bit too happy about his predicament.

He turned his stare to Jackie.

She licked her lips and smiled. "Don't look at me. She's right. I'll be back to check on you when it's time for more meds." The nurse looked to Darcie. "Good luck. Enjoy the heat wave."

Good luck? Good luck with what? "Wait a sec . . . heat wave?"

"It's a whopping twelve below right now. After the past two weeks of constant dipping lower and lower, everyone is rejoicing at the slight rise in temp."

"Wow, let's have a party." Sarcasm dripped from his words. "Now seriously, what is it you're not telling me?"

Her curly hair covered her face for a moment as she looked down at her hands. When she looked up at him, those blue eyes were filled with humor. "Let's just say you made a mess of the ER when they brought us in." Another sip. Another suppressed giggle.

He lowered his eyebrows. "I don't remember that."

"You have a pretty impressive concussion. The doctor told me that your adrenaline must have really cranked up because you reminded him of Chris Hemsworth in the first *Thor* movie."

His eyes widened at that. "I didn't."

"Yep." She smiled over her cup. "You did. I had a front-row seat."

"What was I so fired up about?"

"They'd moved you from the ambulance gurney onto one of the ER gurneys. Your eyes were wild, and you jumped up yelling for everyone to leave you alone until they rescued me."

Uh-oh. Yeah, he could see it now. Normally he wasn't a violent person, but apparently a head injury caused him to go all kinds of crazy on those poor people in the ER. Heat crept up his neck as the memories tumbled in. He'd shoved two pretty big guys. Tossed over a triage tray. And then grabbed the doc by the shoulders and shook him. "Oh man. That was pretty ugly, wasn't it?" He'd have to do something extra special for everyone who was on call last night. And apologize. A lot. He swiped his right hand down his face. Ouch. He must have a lot of bruises.

"My favorite part was when you finally caught sight of me. I was lying on the gurney from the ambulance the whole time. Every time I said your name, you were yelling or making a racket, so you didn't hear me. But you looked at me and relaxed and said 'Oh, there you are' right as the doc stabbed you with a shot." She covered her laugh with her hand. "Sorry. I don't mean to laugh, but it was so comical to watch. Just like the movie. You wilted like Thor."

He couldn't help but laugh along with her. It was great that she didn't seem uncomfortable with his display. "Glad I could bring you some entertainment."

"It was actually sweet that you were so concerned about me. I know that it was just the adrenaline pumping, but it was still sweet." Her eyes shadowed, and she looked away. "I've gone to see Natalie."

That was a weird change of subject. But the protective walls were back up. He wouldn't push. Getting to see behind the curtain for a few minutes was better than nothing. "Who's Natalie?"

"Our mystery woman. She's here in the hospital. She's been under evaluation ever since they brought her in."

"And?" Rather than making the mistake of trying to sit up again, he reached for the bed controls and raised the head. Listening to the motor whir, he closed his eyes against the dizziness that threatened. He must have conked his head pretty good.

"She's dehydrated and malnourished. Keeps talking in her sleep about the bad men and that they have to be stopped."

"Did you find out anything else? Like where these bad men are?"

She shook her head. "She's scared, Jason." Something in her eyes told him there was more to the story.

"What do her docs have to say?"

Darcie tipped her head. Looked away. "They say she's been diagnosed with Alzheimer's already."

He deflated. "Great. So does that mean her predictions are just the ramblings of a woman suffering from a mental disease?"

"No." She turned her head back to face him. "The trooper I spoke with was the lead on the investigation into the murders of the two men they found after she told them where to look. Obviously, they don't believe she had anything to do with it, but since she was correct in that, and then after our accident last night that was due to someone messing with the traffic lights . . . they've instructed our office to take her predictions into consideration."

"Wait a minute. Our accident was due to what?" He really needed to be back in the office. Back at his computers.

She put a hand on his arm. "You're not going anywhere, Jason. So don't even get that look in your eyes."

How did she know? He squinted at her. "But I thought—what did you say the old lady's name was?"

"Natalie."

"I thought Natalie said they were going to get rid of *her* with an accident."

"With the traffic lights." Darcie raised both her brows. "It's not a coincidence, Jason. Chaz and Simon are already tearing apart the code that was used to hack into the Department of Transportation."

He took in a deep breath and winced at the pain that shot through his left shoulder. That would teach him. Ouch. "You've been busy."

"The doctors wanted to observe me for another day, so I asked if I could work from your room. That way they could keep an eye on both of us."

"So you haven't been discharged?"

"Not officially, no." She pointed to the door. "And I have an escort as well. So do you."

"They've got guards on us?"

"Yep. But they're not guards. They're protection. That's one of the many jobs the troopers do. And I wouldn't mess with them, either. You don't exactly have a great track record." The look she shot him out of the corner of her eye would have been funny had their circumstances been different.

"For how long?"

"Let's just say the foreseeable future." A familiar female voice came from the doorway. Two hulking forms were behind her. Did the mayor of Fairbanks usually need bodyguards? "On my orders."

"Madam Mayor." He swallowed.

"Ms. Phillips. I need to speak with you." The elegant woman had a fierce expression.

Jason wouldn't want to tangle with her in a debate, that's for sure.

"Is in here good enough for you?" Darcie asked from her chair.

"Of course." The mayor closed the door, the two men still visible through the small window. "The governor and I have had some lengthy conversations about our . . . situation."

"Yes, ma'am?" Darcie sat up a little taller.

"The press have had a field day with the events of the past few weeks. Last night a volunteer with the hospital was cornered by a reporter. This volunteer had helped with Ms. Natalie's care."

Oh boy. He hated to even hear what was coming next.

"I assume you haven't seen the news this morning?" The mayor's eyes went from Darcie to him.

"No, ma'am. I was told not to look at screens and to keep them off in here for Mr. Myers's concussion symptoms."

"Good. I'm glad you haven't had to endure it, but let's just say they've played up Natalie's words about the bodies found at Diversion Dike and then your accident last night. So we've got people protesting outside city hall, outside the hospital here, outside the police station and fire station. And probably outside your office too. Her predictions have been all too close." The mayor clasped her hands in front of her.

"We need to nip this in the bud, Ms. Phillips. Tomorrow—as long as you are up for it—I'd like you to hold a press conference. As of right now, my team reports the data shows that people trust you. I'll have my speechwriter send a statement over for you since you are still not discharged. No need for you to have to put anything into words. We'll take care of that. The most important thing is to make sure that we calm everyone down. That people know Natalie—as wonderful of a woman as she is—has dementia and isn't a prophetess. She's simply watched too many movies, or she's been in the wrong place at the right time, or"—she waved her hand in the air—"my people will come up with something."

Jason watched Darcie's brows dip. But she didn't say anything.

The mayor turned and opened the door. "Is noon a good time for you?" she threw over her shoulder.

"Yes, ma'am."

"Good. I appreciate your cooperation." The woman walked out, and her two groupies followed.

Jason caught a glimpse of the trooper outside his door. "Would you mind closing the door?"

The man nodded and did as he was asked.

Darcie leaned her head back against the chair and closed her eyes. "Ugh."

"I hear ya. Talk about being steamrolled. I guess that's why she's the mayor."

"I don't believe I'm going to like what her speechwriter sends over."

He laughed. "You're not a fan of the mayor's speeches?"

"It's not that . . ." She leaned forward. "It's the fact that . . . well, I don't think Natalie is some wacko. I still believe she knows something. Just wish I knew where she heard it." Staring into his face, she squinted at him. "You think I've lost my mind now too, don't you?"

"No. I don't. My gut tells me the same thing. I just don't know what that means."

The door swung open. The trooper was holding the radio attached to his shoulder. "Copy that." He spoke into it and then turned to them. "Natalie is missing. We're asking for your assistance, Ms. Phillips. You're the 'nice lady' she talked about and who seems to be the only one she'll come to."

CHAPTER EIGHTEEN

15 Below Zero
November 16—9:32 a.m.
Emergency Operations Center

DARCIE PACED IN FRONT OF the window in her office. Every last inch of her body felt like a giant bruise. Add to that the sad fact that there'd been no sign of Natalie, and her mood had done nothing but plummet even after three cups of her favorite coffee.

Then there was the speech for the press conference. A bunch of flowery words and hooey that Darcie would never say. For one, she wasn't a politician and didn't take kindly to the mayor's office forcing her to try to schmooze people.

Two, she didn't believe the statement was true.

Three, this was not how she would handle the situation. And she was the Emergency Operations director. The mayor had nothing to do with her job. Couldn't fire her.

The governor had put her in this job.

She hated the thought of going over the mayor's head, which would likely cause a good deal of ugliness between them, but the more she thought about it, the more she resolved it was the right thing to do. With a glance to Misty, she said, "I'm going to call the governor."

"You got it, Boss." Her assistant gave a thumbs-up.

Striding back to her desk, Darcie practiced what she would say, then put in the call. Told the operator who she was and that it was urgent.

Several minutes passed as she listened to the canned classical music, so she rehearsed her words over and over.

A tap at her door brought her attention up. Misty stood there with a notepad and a sharpie. She scribbled something and held up the pad.

Natalie is HERE.

Darcie waved Misty closer and put her hand over the mouthpiece of the phone. "Can you ask her to sit in the conference room for a few minutes? I'm waiting for the governor. I'll be right there."

With a nod, her assistant left.

Her heart raced. Maybe Natalie could give her some information that could change the press conference.

"Ms. Phillips." The governor's voice. "I only have a moment, but let me commend you for the work you've done in the midst of this craziness."

Commend her? Did the man even truly know what was going on? "Thank you, sir."

"Are you alright? I'm being told you were in an accident."

"Yes, sir. But I need to get right to the point, sir. The mayor has asked me to give a press conference today, and had her speechwriter—"

"Stop right there, Ms. Phillips. You don't work for the mayor. You work for me. I trust you can put your own words and thoughts together."

"Yes, sir, I can."

"Good. A press conference is a good idea. It will allow everyone to see that you've got things under control. Frankly, I'm tired of seeing that woman they're calling the Prophetess all over the national news. People are beginning to believe that Alaska is full of superstitious and crazy people."

"She's not crazy, sir."

"Well, I hear she is in the hospital and sick." His voice had lost a good bit of his congeniality. "I trust you to handle this, Ms. Phillips." The line clicked.

Why oh why hadn't she simply kept her mouth shut?

No matter now. She hurried from her office to the conference room.

Natalie sat in a chair, her long hair a mess, a blanket wrapped around her.

"Natalie. I'm glad you came here."

"You're the only one who listens to me. You have to do something." She got up out of her chair and wobbled a bit.

Darcie caught her by the shoulders and eased her back down. She turned to Misty. "Would you get her some food and water, please?"

"Of course."

Her attention back to Natalie, Darcie studied the woman's eyes. "Can you tell me why you think bad things will happen when the temperature reaches twenty-six below zero?"

Natalie put a hand to her forehead. "I have these . . . these horrible dreams. The bad men are very specific. They laugh about hurting people. About having control. Please . . ." she wailed, "please believe me. Please do something!" Her eyes searched Darcie's. Frantic. Haunted. Desperate.

"I will do everything I can. I promise. Can you give me any hint as to who these bad men are?"

The woman's stare became blank. Her head drooped.

Misty set a plate of cheese and crackers and a bottle of water on the table.

"Please, Natalie. Stay with me. You need nourishment. And then you need to tell me all that you know."

With shaky hands, the woman who had reached down into Darcie's chest and jump-started something back to life took the bottle of water and took several sips. Her body sank into the chair even more. "I'm so tired. You'll take care of everyone?"

"Yes."

"Good." Natalie grabbed Darcie's hand and squeezed. "I know you will. Thank you for listening." Then she placed her arms on the table, laid her head on top, and closed her eyes. "The bad men . . . at the cabin . . ."

"Natalie?"

No response.

Darcie checked the woman's pulse. It was faint, but at least it was there and she was still breathing. "Misty." She kept her voice hushed. "Call an ambulance, please. This poor woman needs medical attention."

Her assistant nodded as she held her cell up to her ear.

Darcie patted Natalie's cheek. "Natalie? Can you hear me?"

The woman moaned and turned her face toward her. Eyes mere slits. "At the cabin . . . they make their plans." She closed her eyes again, and her body went limp.

Darcie wrapped an arm around the woman, hoping that it would provide comfort, even in her unconscious state.

The EMTs made it in record time and rushed the gurney over to Natalie.

"Please. Be gentle. She's quite frail."

One of the men gave her a single dip of his chin. "Yes, ma'am."

With quick steps, Darcie headed back to her office. She closed the door. How many cabins could there be in the Fairbanks area?

More than anyone actually knew. There were so many off the grid. Without Natalie coherent and alert, they'd never be able to find a cabin. What if it wasn't true anyway? The doctor was clear yesterday that Natalie suffered from Alzheimer's.

Were the dreams she was having just part of her imagination, perhaps hallucinations, or were they real?

The only thing Darcie knew for sure was that she believed the woman thought she was telling the truth. Thought there was some real danger.

But there was no proof.

Not of something happening when the temperature dropped. But there'd been plenty of proof about what had already happened.

A knock at her door stopped her pacing. "Come in."

The door opened, and there stood Jason. Bruised, his left arm in a sling, and a smile on his face. Her heart picked up its pace.

"Hey. I know I don't look all that great, but I'm here to help."

Actually, he looked better than she cared to admit. Something had shifted in her after the accident. It had been a long time since anyone had wanted to protect her. Since *she'd* wanted anyone to protect her. Of course she hadn't needed it. But still, it was nice. "You sure you're okay?"

"Everything hurts, but they discharged me. I'm supposed to 'take it easy,' but you and I both know that's not going to happen. Not when we have all of this going on." He sat in one of the chairs by her desk. "How's the speech from the mayor's office?"

"Horrid." She took her seat as well and tossed the stapled print-out to him. "Read it yourself. I put in a call to the governor, and he told me that I don't work for the mayor. I work for him. Pretty much gave me free rein, although . . ." She grimaced. "He's not too happy about Natalie getting all the press either. Says that the whole country thinks we are superstitious crazies." Rolling her eyes, she shrugged. "You know, I would love to just do this job and not have to deal with the press."

He glanced down at his watch. "Sorry to be the bearer of bad news, but you have a press conference in an hour." One side of his mouth tipped up in a grin. It made him look a lot younger than the crinkles at the corners of his eyes portrayed.

"I know." She groaned and leaned back in her chair.

"Any idea what you're going to say?"

"Nope. Not yet."

"So . . . the trooper who's been my shadow drove me over here and told me that the bullets from the bodies at the dike match the other victims as well." He drummed his fingers on the other side of her desk. "To me that sounds like all of this is related. I told him that."

She studied him. "Talk me through what you're thinking."

"When the governor asked my boss to call me in and help at TAPS—the pipeline—they were having trouble with the computers."

"Right. I already knew that."

"Well, there were multiple glitches that showed faulty valves when there weren't any. To replace a major valve, the entire pipeline has to schedule a maintenance shutdown. It took me two weeks to reprogram a new system I installed after the other proved faulty. Don't forget that's where the first body showed up."

She jotted down notes. "Okay. I'm with you so far."

"Next, I get a call from Kirk that he needs help. I go out to the salvage yard, and there's been a murder. I'm arrested. The trooper tells us at their offices that they've been having computer problems."

She scribbled as fast as she could. "Ah, I see it now. *You're* the problem."

"Wait, what?" He looked at her funny.

With a laugh, she waved her hands back and forth. "Sorry. I'm terrible at humor. I was just pointing out that you were there for both computer issues and dead bodies."

He didn't laugh. "That's not a nice thought." With a dramatic shiver, he winked and continued. "Then we have the Emergency Alert System hacked and the news hacked. Two more dead bodies. All shot with the same gun."

Tapping her notebook with her pen, she let it all sink in. "Surely the investigators must have put all this together as well."

"It's an ongoing investigation, and the trooper couldn't share anything else, but if they hadn't put all that together before, they have to now. The bullets all match."

"My question is this . . ." She bit her lip, and thoughts swirled. "Do you think your brother knows what's going on?"

Jason winced. Then his face hardened. "Sadly, I think he's involved somehow. As much as I hate to admit that. But I also told the police and the state troopers the same thing. They've been looking for Kirk for a while now. I gave them his whole sordid history of mental illness and drug abuse. Which isn't encouraging."

She leaned over her desk and rested her elbows down. "If you were to guess right here and now about what the 'bad men'—as Natalie calls them—are up to, what would be your first thought?"

"A cyberattack."

"On what?"

"The power grid? Didn't Natalie say something about the power going out? That's really our only clue, right?"

"Yeah—"

The phone on her desk rang, and she lifted the receiver to her ear. "Darcie Phillips."

"Ms. Phillips," a man cleared his throat. "Marshall Willis. Hospital Administrator."

She straightened a little in her chair. "Yes, sir. How may I help you?"

"I'm sorry to give you this news, but I wanted to personally be the one to inform you that Natalie has gone missing again."

Her heart plummeted to her feet. No. Not again. "When?"

"The nurse just sent in the alert."

"How could this happen? She's not in any condition to be in the streets." As soon as the words were out, she regretted them. It wasn't her place to scold the hospital administrator.

Another clearing of the throat. "Ms. Phillips, Natalie was given a full hydration drip along with steroids for her lungs. She completed the hydration and somehow managed to evade anyone seeing her as she left. I'm sorry, but I wanted you to be the first to know."

"Thank you, Mr. Willis. I appreciate it."

The call ended and she let out a groan.

Jason leaned forward. "Natalie?"

Her phone rang again as she nodded and held up a finger. "Darcie Phillips."

"Darcie, hey, it's Melinda." Her counselor from Juneau.

"Hey there. Hang on just a minute." She covered the mouthpiece and looked at Jason. "Do you mind?"

"Not at all." He left her office, closing the door behind him.

"Hey, Melinda. How can I help you?"

"I know this is a tough day for you. And every year we have a special session. I hadn't heard from you since you moved, and I had a little break, so I thought I'd call and check up on you."

All the air seemed to be sucked out of the room. Darcie closed her eyes. No. That wasn't today. No.

"Darcie?"

"I'm here." She swallowed and kept her breathing as steady as possible. "You know, Melinda, I have to give a press conference in just a little bit, so could we talk later?"

"I'm sorry to bother you. Of course." Melinda sighed. "You sure you're okay?"

"Yep. I appreciate you calling." She hung up before she lost it.

Tears rushed to her eyes.

November 16. She'd been so caught up in the drama around her that she'd blocked it.

The day when she was nine. Dad told her that he no longer loved Mom. When Darcie asked him why, he'd just shrugged and said he loved someone else. She'd kicked him and cried and screamed. But it didn't change anything. He still left. Even after she asked if he still loved *her*.

He never answered.

Then five years later, on the very day, her best friend committed suicide. Darcie found the body.

Once again, she wasn't enough.

To be loved.

To be a friend.

Then in college. November 16. Her mom left her too.

Darcie wasn't good enough for anything.

CHAPTER NINETEEN

16 Below Zero
November 16—12:00 p.m.
Pressroom

EVER SINCE DARCIE RECEIVED THE phone call, she'd been pale. It worried Jason. But he couldn't do anything about it now. All he could do was watch as she stood just beyond the threshold of the door between their offices and the pressroom. Her shoulders slumped. She clenched and unclenched her hands.

He'd taken up residence at the front of the pressroom with his trooper friend, and her trooper friend stood on the other side. Since someone had tried to kill them, they couldn't take any chances. Although Jason didn't think whoever tried it would be so stupid as to attack them in the open.

Hopefully, he wasn't wrong.

Misty went to the podium and introduced the Emergency Operations director.

Darcie lifted her chin and walked to the podium, the door making a solid click behind her. Her red fleece vest over a long-sleeved white shirt, jeans, and snow boots gave off the calming persona of a strong Alaskan woman. But her face was ashen. Void of expression.

She cleared her throat. "Good afternoon, everyone. This will be short and sweet. Our borough has been through some challenges lately, but rest assured, this office, the governor's office, the mayor's office, the FPD, and the state troopers are all doing their very best to get to the root of the problem. As the Emergency Operations director, I ask that everyone stay calm. Protesting in the streets isn't safe, especially at these temperatures." She paused.

Which proved to be a huge mistake.

"And what if the Prophetess is right and we lose power? How are you going to keep the public safe 'at these temperatures'?" The voice mocked from the back.

Jason wanted to punch the guy.

Hands raised all over the room, and people shouted over one another to be heard.

No matter what Darcie said, they cut her off and threw more questions at her.

Not only was she still ashen faced, but she now looked defeated.

Jason couldn't deal with another second of it. He charged the podium and stood next to Darcie.

The room quieted.

"I'm Jason Myers." He spoke so loud into the microphone that it squealed with feedback and they had to shut up. "Cybersecurity specialist and part of the team here at the Emergency Operations Center. We are well acquainted with what has been said about when the temperature reaches twenty-six below zero. We are asking for everyone to stay in their homes when it's too cold to be outside. Go to work. Stock up on staples in case there's a storm. If you have a backup generator, test it. Make sure it has fuel, and let your neighbors know they have a safe place to come to. None of this is rocket science, people. We are Alaskans. This is what we do. We help one another, and we prepare for the weather, because we have weather like no one in the lower forty-eight can understand."

Chuckles filled the room. But Darcie abruptly left through the door to their offices, the trooper on her heels.

"As you can tell, our director is very busy. We all have a lot on our plates. We appreciate your time today." With that he left the podium as well and hoped Misty wouldn't kill him for abandoning her.

The roar of the press crowd dimmed as soon as he closed the door.

"Dude." Chaz lifted a hand in a high five as Jason passed his desk. "Nicely done." He pointed to the computer screen. So they'd watched.

Jason gave him a halfhearted grin and made a beeline for Darcie's office. The door was closed.

He knocked.

No answer.

He tried the handle.

It was locked. He glanced at the trooper standing a few feet away. "Is she in there?"

"Yes."

Guess she didn't want to talk. Alrighty then.

What was going on with her? Bolting from the press floor was exactly when and where the press could chew someone up and spit them out.

He went back to his desk and attempted to focus on his work, but he failed.

Thirty minutes later he headed to her office and knocked again.

Still no answer.

Guess she wanted to be left alone.

His head throbbed. His heart twinged.

He didn't have time for this.

Turning to his own protective escort, he tipped his head toward the door. "I'm not supposed to drive. Will you take me home?"

An hour later, Jason stretched out on his couch. He'd left three voicemails for Darcie. Two emails. And a message with Misty. But not a peep in return.

Since he'd messed up everyone's schedule by going into the office and then his abrupt departure home, he told Trooper Mitchell that he really didn't need protection at home today. The complex was gated and had security. He'd call if he was planning on going anywhere else. He promised.

The man had left, but only because Jason assured him that Simon and Chaz were coming by in a few minutes to grab their things since they'd found their own apartment to rent.

He was exhausted. Draping his good arm over his forehead, he shut his eyes.

God, I don't even know where to start. But You know everything that's going on. Please help Darcie through whatever is happening. Help her to see that she has all of us to lean on. That she's not in this all by herself. And, Lord, give me the right words to say. Or tell me to shut up if I need to be quiet.

His doorbell rang, and he groaned as he rose from the couch. The aches and pains from the accident were more than he wanted to admit out loud, but right now he'd like nothing more than to swallow a pain pill and take a nap. Why were the guys ringing the doorbell? They had a key.

Opening the door to his apartment, he breathed deep. He didn't have the energy to help them. "Hey—"

"Hey, big brother. How are you doing? I heard you were in an accident?" Kirk squeezed Jason's bad shoulder.

Dots danced before his eyes. He really should've taken that pain pill. "Yeah, so nice of you to drop by. Now, get out." He tried to close the door, but Kirk stopped it with his foot.

"Not so fast." His brother grinned. But the look in his eyes was pure evil. "I can't have you messing up our plans." With lightning speed, he lifted a syringe and plunged the needle into Jason's neck.

*   *   *

18 Below Zero
November 16—4:51 p.m.
Somewhere Along the Chena River

Natalie wandered through the fireweed, their blooms full at the tips and withering at the bottom. Winter would arrive any day. She looked up. Even now clouds threatening snow circled the sun. Once winter came—once it got too cold—it would be too late.

Harsh words above her made the scenery change. The beautiful outdoors crumbled into the dark walls of her shelter.

Wrapped in five blankets, it still wasn't enough to take the chill away.

Tito had encouraged her to find another place, but it was so hard. She closed her eyes. Wishing Tito back. Wanting to just sleep . . . forever.

Two loud crashes and a thump made her open her eyes.

What were the bad men doing now?

She tried to focus, but it was dark. What time was it?

Someone groaned. Then a voice. A voice she knew. A good voice. Who was that?

She crept closer to the hatch, trying to understand what they were saying.

"He can't give us any trouble from here." Followed by a mean laugh.

Several scuffs and footsteps. A door closing. Then motors revving. Diminishing in the distance.

Natalie peered through a small slit. Were they gone? No. A man was on the floor. Moaning. The good man? Then someone else walked past.

But there were no more words.

She waited and watched. It only seemed like one bad man was left.

A surge of energy rushed through her. She was needed. No one else could help.

She couldn't let them hurt the good man any more. Grabbing her flashlight, she sneaked out the other small hatch that came out under a shrub. Stalking to the door, she flung it open and whacked the man there on the back of the head with her flashlight. After he fell to the floor, she hit him one more time just to make sure he was down. Blood oozed from the wound.

Rushing to the other man's side, she recognized him. Darcie's friend. He was a good man.

But now what should she do? She couldn't come back here. They'd know it was her. They already wanted her dead.

Untying Darcie's friend, she used the same rope to tie up the bad man. Then she opened the inside hatch and grabbed her sled that she dragged her supplies on, her blankets, and the few trinkets that were her only reminders of who she had been. The only other things were the papers and pencil. She shoved those into the deep pocket of her coat, closed the hatch, and rolled the good man onto the sled. Piled him high with her blankets and things.

Now she just had to rouse up enough strength to get this man to the hospital. It was a long, long way on foot. Her eyes roamed the cabin, and she found a stash of protein bars in the corner cabinet along with a few bottles of water. She tore into one of the bars ravenously and tossed the others onto the sled.

She put on her gloves and then a pair of fur mittens over them. Tugged a hat down over her hair, wrapped her scarf over her nose and mouth, pulled up her fur-lined hood, and said goodbye to the place that had been home for a short while. It didn't matter now. She needed to rescue the good man.

Using every ounce of her strength, she pulled the sled behind her. Hopefully, none of the men returned, because she couldn't cover her tracks like she usually did. She'd just stay away from the roads. She knew some shortcuts anyway.

With each slow step, she had to force her mind to focus straight ahead. Kept repeating to herself over and over, "Hospital." That's where she was going. She couldn't forget.

The starry sky morphed into the blue of summer.

Tito gripped her hand. *"You can do this, love,"* he whispered, almost as though his voice was inside her head instead of beside her. *"Be brave, my love."*

Brave. Yes. As Tito had always been. She owed it to him to do what was right.

Do what was right. Do what was right. The hospital. She was taking this man to the hospital.

Do what was right. *God, help me to do what is right. Help me to save this man. Help me remember where I need to go.*

The notes. Where had she put her notes?

Her pocket. They were in her pocket.

One step in front of the other, she pushed on. Dreaming of Tito. Their children. A lifetime of memories.

Do what was right.

By the time she reached town, her legs and arms were numb. But she had to keep going. To the hospital.

"To the hospital," she said against her scarf. Again and again.

But she was lost. Why couldn't she find it?

She stopped. Completely wiped of all energy, she fell to her knees. Where had her feet taken her?

The sky changed again. To terrible-looking clouds. The fireweed field with strangely moving aspen trees wavered and blurred. She closed her eyes and opened them again, seeing a familiar building. The aspen trees morphed into people running toward her. Tito's hand appeared again. *"You did it, my love. Now tell them."*

He disappeared and in his place were the notes she'd painstakingly recorded from snatches of memory the last time the fog of dementia cleared.

"You can do this, love," Tito's voice whispered again. This time she recognized it as a precious memory from when their first child was born.

"Be brave," she whispered in answer, fully aware that this could be her last chance. Who knew when—or if—she'd ever have another spell of clarity. Or if the men intent on silencing her would succeed. Fear filled her chest. Every face became an enemy ready to pounce.

But she owed it to Tito to be brave and good.

The familiar woman with the piercing eyes reached her. "Natalie!"

Praise God. She was safe. She made it. "I had to save him." Her teeth chattered.

"Who?"

The others gathered around the sled. "Someone call an ambulance!" Voices echoed around her.

But Natalie grabbed the woman in front of her and shoved the notes into her hands. "This is everything." She gripped the sides of her head. "I tried to remember . . ."

"Oh, Natalie. You did a wonderful thing." The woman wrapped her in a hug, and they knelt in the snow together.

In her mind, the sky was blue, she was young, and the fireweed was just beginning to bloom.

Walking barefoot with her hand in Tito's, all was right again.

CHAPTER TWENTY

Zero Degrees
November 18—4:39 a.m.
Fairbanks Memorial Hospital

MORE BEEPING. WHAT WAS UP with all the beeping?

"Sorry, Mr. Myers." Someone next to him spoke. "Looks like your IV is out. I'll just change that and you can get back to sleep." A woman. Someone he didn't know.

IV? That meant he was back in the hospital. "I don't want to sleep." He looked over at the chair.

Empty.

"Don't worry—visiting hours are in just a few hours. I'm sure you'll have a slew of people in and out. Won't they be excited to see you awake today?" The woman kept talking about the weather and wasn't it nice that they'd had another warm spell.

"How warm?"

"It's a whopping zero degrees. But don't go breaking out your swim trunks yet. We're supposed to get hit with a severe cold snap in a couple days." Her words were cheery, but she had no idea what they were doing to him.

"What happened?" He punched the button on the control of his bed to raise his upper body.

"You had to have surgery on your clavicle again. You have a bruised rib and a lot of other contusions. But other than that, you're doing pretty well." Again with the cheeriness. She finished with the IV. "Let's get your vitals and I'll be out of your hair so you can rest."

She placed the blood pressure cuff on his good arm.

Another surgery. Why? Then it came back. The press conference. Going home. Kirk.

Everything else was fuzzy. What a nightmare. But exhaustion seeped into every corner of his being. He couldn't keep his eyes open. Perhaps sleep was the only cure.

"Knock knock!" Misty's voice was even more cheerful than the nurse's earlier. "Can you handle a few visitors?"

He blinked away the dream he'd been having and watched her peek around the door. "Sure." He sent her a smile. Was it visiting hours already?

Chaz and Simon followed her in. And then Darcie stood in the doorway. He wished he could ask her how she was doing, because the last time he saw her, she was hightailing it out of a press conference. The distance between them felt like a chasm. He wanted to bridge that more than anything.

"Dude!" Chaz shook his head. "You gotta stop making this a regular occurrence."

Polite laughter filled the room.

Jason took a deep breath. "Okay, so who wants to tell me what happened? How did I get here?"

He watched as they looked at one another. The two boys shoved their boss forward.

Darcie rolled her eyes. "Very mature." She breathed deep. "Apparently you were drugged and kidnapped. The doctor said it is out of your system now, but they've been flushing you like crazy." Her face was still devoid of emotion. What had happened to her that day? "Natalie was the one who found you. She dragged you into town on a sled, of all things."

"What! Is she okay?" He wanted to sit bolt upright, but the pain stopped him.

More looks between his team.

"She hasn't woken back up. She's in the hospital as well. But she had been writing some things down when she had moments of clarity. Trying to help us after we met. She brought you to our building. At first she thought it was the hospital and thought she was lost, but I think subconsciously she knew we could help."

"Did you get any info from the notes?"

Darcie nodded. "The police have them now. She's the only one who knows where they took you. It seems she'd been living in the cellar of the cabin. That's where her 'dreams' came from. She overheard them talking."

Whoever the *them* was, it had to include Kirk. "I need to make a statement to the police. I know who kidnapped me."

All the eyes in the room widened.

"My brother."

"What?" Darcie's jaw dropped, clearly incredulous. "Kirk did this?"

"I don't know if he did all the injuries, but he was the one at my door, and he was the one who stabbed me with a syringe. So yeah, I know that Kirk was the one who kidnapped me."

Misty left the room and then came right back with the state trooper, who must have been outside his door.

Trooper Mitchell raised his eyebrows.

Jason gave the man what he hoped was an apologetic look. "Don't say anything. I won't send any of you home again. I promise."

After he gave a statement to Mitchell, who called it in to the police department and his boss, Darcie and Misty came closer.

Darcie gave him a half smile. "Good to see that you're alive."

"It's definitely better than the alternative." Simon laughed at his own joke.

Jason groaned. The guys had lived with him for how long? Yeah, he hadn't kept his faith hidden in front of them, but he hadn't exactly shared openly. Always thinking there was time for that down the road. Well, with as many close calls as he'd had lately, it was about time to have a serious conversation with those two and invite them to church. Of course, he should probably go himself. Rather than working around the clock like he had been. Once all this was over.

"We're going to head back to the office, but we have our cells and obviously email." Darcie waved her phone.

The expression on her face was too forced. How long would it take before the weight of all this crushed her? The thought made him wince. He couldn't allow that to happen.

"The guys are going to stay with you, and if you're up for it, run some ideas by you. I'm assuming you heard we had a bit of reprieve with the weather?"

"Yeah. But it's supposed to plummet pretty soon, right?"

She nodded. "We haven't let the public know yet about what Natalie shared with us. The mayor and governor think it will bring about panic. We're the only ones who can stop whatever is coming."

"Don't they realize that if her predictions come true, the public will panic anyway? There's no guarantee we can stop it. We don't even know what *it* is."

"I tried to tell them that, but you know how it goes." She nudged Misty. "Let us know if you need anything."

Misty waved at him. "Don't get too comfortable in here. We kinda need you."

And then they were gone. Jason shoved down the urge to jump out of the bed and chase Darcie down. Talk to her. Make sure she was okay. But he wouldn't do it. Couldn't, if he were honest.

Chaz and Simon nodded to each other and started rearranging the whole room.

In a matter of minutes, they had chairs with makeshift footrests and their laptops set up.

Chaz rubbed his hands together. "Okay, Jas . . . run us through a scenario of a power grid hack." Then narrowed his eyes. "Unless, of course, you need your rest, old man?"

Jason didn't miss the challenge in his voice. "Old man. Yeah, right. I'm ready for whatever you can dish out. See if you can keep up, kid." He launched into the intricacies of what would have to be done to pull off a hack of that magnitude. Especially since he'd spent a good deal of time studying the power grid up here since Natalie's predictions.

It was nice to think about work. Kept his mind off the pain. But after running through three different scenarios, he couldn't figure out what the motivation could be behind it. All the best work he'd done in cybersecurity involved understanding the mind of the hacker. There was always a motivation. Most of the time, money.

"Alright, let me get this straight." Simon munched on an apple. "Power gets shut down. The BESS takes over. We have fifteen minutes, relatively speaking, to shut down the hacker. Which should be more than enough time. Right?"

Jason mulled that one over. "If we had plenty of help from the FBI, CISA, and all the cyber guys in my office back in Anchorage working on it—yeah, that might be doable."

"If all the power is out. The BESS can handle it for at *least* fifteen minutes, so we might have more time." Chaz. Always the optimist.

"There's a chance, but we shouldn't plan on it." Jason rubbed his head. "Did one of you bring a laptop for me to use?"

"Hey, dude, you're not supposed to use a screen today because of another concussion. Tell me what you need, and I'll do it." Chaz wiggled his eyebrows.

"I want to run diagnostics on the secure emergency WebEOC again. We need to do it twice a day until we get past this. Also, call Misty and make sure that the maintenance guy has ensured that the backup generator at the office is tested and run regularly. It's run by natural gas, so we should be good on fuel. We don't want to take any risks."

"You got it."

"And I could seriously use a cheeseburger. A real one. Not a hospital one. Who wants to make a run for lunch?" Jason tried to keep his voice light, to convince the guys he was all right, but he secretly hoped they would both leave so he could beg the nurse for more pain meds.

"We'll go." Simon jumped to his feet. "I'm starved." He closed his laptop.

"Hold that thought, dude." Chaz studied his screen. The smile from his face gone as he brought his laptop to Jason.

There it was. What he hoped he wouldn't see.

A generalized warning from CISA about cyberterrorists. In Alaska.

* * *

4 Below Zero
November 19—3:37 p.m.
Emergency Operations Center

Nothing had gone right for her today. Nothing.

Darcie's coffee maker at home had died. Her garage door opener hadn't worked. Then she saw Darrell Collins on another morning talk show.

Why was he so popular? Did the man not have a life other than making hers miserable? Obviously, since she refused to hire him, the answer was no.

And the authorities still hadn't found the cabin where Natalie had overheard the plot. Which meant they weren't any closer to finding the bad guys. But now that everyone believed her words about something happening when the temp hit twenty-six below, nerves were frazzled and senses were on high alert.

Darcie hoped for Natalie to wake up and have some clarity. But the sweet woman who'd done her best to warn people had woken up and tried to run away again, only to fall in the hospital stairwell. The doctor had to sedate her. Then discovered she had internal bleeding from tumbling down the stairs. It wasn't looking good. The doctor said they needed to keep her in a medically induced coma for now.

Which was probably for the best. The press had been asking where their mystery woman was. And with the weather reports showing that the temperature would most definitely dip below the dreaded predicted number, people were scrambling. Panicking. Some had even left town.

Darcie's thoughts were all over the map, and she was tired of it. Tired of not being in control. She was the one responsible for stopping whatever was about to happen. Oh, her boss would try to tell her that her job was to get everyone through the crisis. But since she knew the crisis was coming, wasn't it better to stop it before it ever hurt anyone?

The elevator dinged, and Darcie looked at the security camera.

Jason.

Her heart thrummed. What was he doing here? Her mind went from fury that he hadn't stayed at the hospital to concern that he was injured and overdoing it. Then all the feelings from the other night when she found out he'd been drugged and kidnapped . . . she bit her lip.

This was more than just being worried about a coworker.

She was afraid. To care. To be hurt.

No. No no no.

There was no time for this. No room for it in her mind or heart. Clamping her lips shut, she willed every emotion clawing at her throat to go back inside her carefully constructed walls.

When he walked into the office, Misty, Chaz, and Simon all clapped for him. His steps were slow, his face pale, but he was smiling.

And headed straight for her office.

Of course.

Spine stiff, she planted herself at her desk and crossed her arms over her chest.

"Hey." He stopped in her doorway. "May I come in?"

She nodded.

Jason stepped in and closed the door. "Any news on Natalie?"

"No."

"Well . . ." He smiled. "I'm here. Put me to work."

"Should you be here, Jason?" She stared him down.

"Doc discharged me. Said he sent you an email." He pointed toward her laptop.

She clicked open her email account—yep, there it was.

"I thought you'd be glad to see me. I figured you needed all hands on deck."

"I do." She needed him, and admitting that made her even more irritated.

"Darcie?"

Raising her eyebrows, she pressed her lips together and refused to answer.

"What happened the other day? One minute you were fine, and then right before the press conference it was apparent you were *not* fine. I've been praying for you, but if you need someone to talk to, I'm here."

Why did he have to sound so understanding?

Closing her eyes against the questions, she shook her head. "I don't need to talk."

"You look like you're about to explode." His voice was calm, soothing. The look on his face at peace. Even after all he'd been through.

And yet she hated that. "I'm fine, Jason."

"No. You're not."

Pushing her chair back, she stood up. Grabbed all six darts. Aimed at the dartboard on her door.

She threw a dart with every ounce of power she had. "Why is it"—inner bull's-eye—"that people"—another flew, outer bull's-eye—"don't believe me"—one more outer bull's-eye—"when I say"—triple twenty—"I'm fine?"—bull's-eye.

Jason stood. His face clouded with . . . disappointment? That muscle in his jaw tensed. "Point taken. I'll leave you alone."

CHAPTER TWENTY-ONE

24 Below Zero
November 20—9:00 a.m.
Undisclosed Location

WALKING INTO WHAT HE LIKED to think of as his computer arena, he couldn't help but smile. The plan was coming together nicely. Even if they'd had a little setback. Jason Myers couldn't stop them.

No one could.

Because no one knew everything. Only him.

He'd kept it all compartmentalized on purpose. And it had worked like a charm.

Stepping behind Julian, he put a hand on the young guy's shoulder. "You've got the message ready to go out?"

"Yep." The kid showed his straight, white teeth. "Have to say, this is probably the most brilliant code I've ever written."

"Let's hope so." He walked around the room and looked at all the screens.

"And you're sure they haven't discovered your little backdoor?"

A smug grin, then a laugh. "Positive. I've been five steps ahead of them this whole time."

"Good." Now all he had to do was wait.

* * *

25 Below Zero
November 20—10:00 a.m.
Emergency Operations Center

Jason had avoided Darcie all morning. She'd stayed holed up in her office after their first briefing in the conference room.

Misty was concerned. So were the guys. But no one knew what to do, and no one wanted to talk about their boss behind her back. The solution? They all stayed at their desks, hunkered down, doing everything they could to prepare as the thermometer dipped dangerously close to that fateful number.

Lord, I need divine help here. And not just with the job. Darcie has come to mean a lot to me. But I can tell she's wounded. I don't think any of us can help her. But You can.

After double-checking the WebEOC and all their emergency protocols, he stood and stretched. They weren't even close to having everything Darcie had planned online and in place, but they had miraculously done way more than a team of five should have been able to accomplish in less than a month.

Grabbing a fresh cup of coffee, he felt the urge to go talk to her. Right now.

Following the prodding, he filled another cup and then walked to her office.

Knocking on the door with his boot, he was surprised when she answered his taps with a soft "Come in."

"Um . . ." He leaned close to the door. "My hands are full."

A few seconds passed, and he wasn't sure if he should try again or wait it out. But then the door opened. He walked in and closed the door with his foot. As she walked to the small couch under the window, he noticed her swiping at her cheeks.

"I brought you a cup of coffee." He held it out. Like a kindergarten boy holding out a daisy for his favorite girl.

"Thanks." She at least took it.

He sipped.

She sipped.

"You probably want me to leave you alone, but I can't do that." He took a risk and sat next to her.

Another sip. Another swipe at her cheeks. She grabbed a tissue. He lifted her chin with his finger and turned her to face him.

"You're hurting, Darcie. And that just kills me. I don't have any right to ask you about it, but I'm here. Asking."

She stared at him with those big blue eyes.

Time stood still as he held his breath. Then she leaned into him and rested her head on his shoulder.

Afraid he might scare her away, he counted to ten before wrapping his good arm around her shoulders. Then counted to twenty, relishing the feel of her against him. "Look, we're facing the biggest crisis any of us have ever faced. With both hands tied behind our backs. My brother is involved somehow. I'm injured. Natalie is in a coma. The temperature is dropping. I want to help you." He was rambling and he knew it, but somehow he had to get her talking. "I don't have any idea how—"

"Are you finished?" She sat up but stayed under his arm.

"Um, yeah." He leaned back against the couch.

"I'm sorry for lashing out at you."

That was unexpected. "You don't need to apologize, but I do think you need to talk."

"You sound like my counselor." With a shake of her head, her curls fell over her eyes. She pushed them back with her hand.

The silence stretched again. But this time he was hopeful. So he waited.

"You want to know what happened on November sixteenth?"

He let his arm fall so it was around her waist. "Was that the day of the accident? Or the day of the press conference?"

She leaned her elbows on her knees. "On November sixteenth, my dad came into my room and said, 'Hey honey, I don't love your mom anymore. I'm running off with my physical therapist, and we're going to live in Italy. Wish me luck.'" The horrible mocking tone she used for her dad sliced through him.

"Oh, Darc."

"I asked him—no begged him—to stay. Begged him to love me still. But he never responded. I wasn't enough." She stood up and grabbed her computer off her desk. When she faced him, tears shimmered in her eyes. Sitting back down, she leaned against his arm and opened her laptop. A video was paused on the screen. She tapped the Play button.

A young Darcie and another young girl with dark hair were hiking together. Someone behind them caught their antics on camera as they climbed, sang silly songs, and laughed a lot. The video ended.

"That was my best friend. Amy." She pulled the computer toward her and closed the screen.

"Was?"

"On November sixteenth, when I was fourteen, she committed suicide. Knowing that I was coming over because every year on that date, we skipped school, and watched movies, and did something crazy to get my mind off what had happened. I found her body."

Inside, Jason felt like a knife had stabbed him. But he tried not to react. Just listened.

"She left a note saying that she didn't want me to have to endure two sad days every year—that's why she chose the same date." More tears pooled in her eyes.

The anguish there nearly broke him. "Why . . ." But he couldn't finish the thought. Wished he could pull it back.

Darcie shifted sideways so she was facing him, her back against the armrest, her knee bent. "I don't know. I never knew she was depressed. But her mom blamed me. Said I was always dragging her down with all my sad stories. Told me after the funeral that I should just get over the fact that my dad didn't love me and left and move on."

"When people are hurting, they lash out—"

"I know, Jason." She held up a hand. "I found out Amy had been treated for depression and an eating disorder for two years. Her mom refused to let anyone know because it was embarrassing for the family. But don't you see? Once again I wasn't enough to keep my friend from killing herself. I had no clue what she was going through because I was caught up in my own pain. My friendship should have been encouraging and a lifeline to her. But it wasn't. And then . . ." She choked up a bit.

The thought that there was more just about did him in. He couldn't believe all that she'd endured.

"On November sixteenth, my freshman year of college, my mother moved to Hawaii. I haven't seen her since. She sends me a card on my birthday. Doesn't that just take the cake?" She forced a laugh through her tears. "My own mother doesn't want me."

It all made sense. Had no one ever poured into her? "Darcie, I'm amazed. You are such an incredibly strong, intelligent, and capable woman. How you managed to survive even after all of . . ." He hesitated and then barreled ahead. ". . . the people you cared about most abandoning you and hurting you."

Mopping up her face, she gave him a sad smile. "I've been in counseling ever since. Through college, through my time in the Air Force, through graduate school. But nothing ever works when November sixteenth rolls around. This year I actually hadn't even *thought* about it, we were so busy. Then my counselor from Juneau called to check in."

Realization hit him hard. The phone call. The day of the press conference. No wonder she'd been ashen. Why hadn't he put two and two together? "I'm so sorry. We should have called it off . . ." Then he remembered how he had jumped in. "I never should have taken over." He winced.

"No, I'm glad you did. You saved my bacon. Although at the time, I was pretty mad at you for it. Only because I couldn't admit the truth." She smoothed a hand over her laptop and then set it on the desk with the green leather notebook she took with her everywhere.

"I noticed you use that a lot." He dipped his head toward it.

This time a real smile filled her face. The first one he'd seen in a while. "My friend Amanda gave it to me."

"That's your friend who's an emergency manager down in South Carolina, right?"

"One and the same. We were in the Air Force together. She's brilliant, and she's the first person to understand me in a long time. We both pour ourselves into our work, which doesn't leave us a lot of room for other relationships. She's the one who got me through when Greg . . . well, you know what happened there."

That guy was a real winner. Jason hoped he never met him in person.

"There you have it. All the pathetic stories of Darcie Phillips." She pulled both her legs up onto the couch and hunched over her bent knees, her eyes clearer now. "You're right. Talking about it made me feel better. Now how about you? Are you just one big bruise now?"

"Pretty much." The fact that she'd opened up and allowed him to hold her gave him hope. Because it was hard to deny his feelings for her any longer.

"I can only imagine. I'm still sore, and I don't have near as many injuries as you." Another shake of her head. This time she tucked her hair behind her ear. "I'm sorry about what Kirk did."

It was clear that she needed the subject off her. At least for now. She'd taken the first step of opening up, and he'd take it. "I want to throttle him and try to protect him all at the same time. Which I can't do. It's pretty hard to not be in control of the situation."

"Tell me about it!" She lifted her hands in the air. "From one control freak to another, I feel your pain."

Their phones both wailed at the same time an emergency warning blared over the TV.

What on earth? The screen was black.

But then a message started to scroll.

The US government can't be trusted. They can't save you. They can't help you.

Jason looked at his phone. The same message was there—on an emergency alert.

He jumped up from the chair and opened the door. All the monitors in the room said the same thing. The rest of the team held up their phones, showing the same.

Oh no. He whipped his gaze back to Darcie. "What's the temperature?"

She glanced at the portable indoor/outdoor weather station sitting on her desk.

"Twenty-six below." The words came out on a hushed breath.

Then the power went out.

CHAPTER TWENTY-TWO

26 Below Zero
November 20—11:15 a.m.

"EMERGENCY OPS CENTER TO ANY and all emergency services. Please respond." Darcie spoke into the two-way radio.

Static was the only reply. On every one of their channels.

The open room was quiet. Too quiet.

Misty stepped to her side. "All our landline phones are down."

"Cells too." Chaz tossed his onto his desk. "No signal."

So it happened. They'd succeeded. Whoever *they* were.

Everyone in her office had done exactly what they were supposed to. It wasn't chaos. It was calm. Why couldn't she pull her thoughts together?

Darcie closed her eyes and took a deep breath. The backup generator should kick on at any moment.

But it didn't.

"I'm going to go find out what's going on with the generator." Jason left the room hollering for Chaz and Simon to follow him as he went.

Her mind whirled in a million different directions. This was what she was hired to do. It was her job to save people's lives now. That weight on her shoulders felt like five tons.

She opened her notebook and ran down the list of protocols for an emergency situation.

"Just tell me what to do, Boss." Misty stood in her doorway. Calm. With a fierce expression on her face.

They were in the trenches now. "No one is responding on the radios. So the first thing I have to do is log in to the secure WebEOC and get a message to all emergency services." Since the generator wasn't running yet to give them access to the internet, she'd have to use her phone.

Unlocking her home screen, she winced. No service. Chaz had said that. But it hadn't registered. "Do you have service?" They were so used to being connected all the time.

Misty tried on her phone. "No."

"Alright, plan B."

She grabbed her winter gear and prepared to go outside. "Misty, stay in here and keep trying. Maybe the cell towers will come back online. It might take a bit for all of them to switch to backup power so we can get a strong signal."

Bundled up as best as she could be, she raced outside to where the guys were. "Any luck?"

Jason growled. "Someone cut the line to the generator."

"What!" The backup generator for their building was state of the art. Ran on natural gas.

"I have to turn off the gas at the main valve." He shook his head. Then stepped closer to her. "I've got a generator in my truck. I'll get the guys to help me bring it in. Don't worry. We'll get things up and running."

With a nod, she shivered and ran back inside. Time was of the essence. Plan C it was.

She tried the radio again, but the only sounds were crackling and static. Lots of static. Jason and the guys arrived huffing and grunting in record time. Impressive. Jason's generator was a Titan solar. One they could use indoors without the threat of carbon monoxide poisoning. Darcie had looked into purchasing one herself.

Grabbing her laptop, she raced to the center of the main room, where he'd set up the generator. They both had their computers plugged in within seconds. Then Jason plugged in the backup power source for the hard-wired secure satellite internet for the building.

As soon as the light glowed green, Darcie allowed her fingers to fly over the keyboard and logged into the WebEOC. Prayerfully, others had as well. They had to be able to communicate with one another. Panic was sure to be throughout the entire area by now. Especially after Natalie's dire prediction came true.

As soon as she was in, relief flooded her. Her protocols were working. But then a black screen with red script overtook everything.

"Shut it down!" Jason yelled. He unplugged everything from the generator.

But her laptop screen still showed the awful message.

If you want access to help your people, the ransom is twenty-five million US dollars. To turn the power back on, you better pay up.

"What happened?" Misty looked over her shoulder.

"Ransomware." The fury on Jason's face couldn't be missed. He swiped a hand down his jaw. "On the secure WebEOC."

*   *   *

Eight Minutes Since the Blackout
26 Below Zero
November 20—11:22 a.m.

"I thought I specifically told *both of you* to reinforce the firewalls." Jason stared down Chaz and Simon. "To keep an eye out for anything like this!" He hated losing his temper, but this was unacceptable. This meant he had failed.

"I did. We did." Chaz was the only one to respond. He gulped.

Simon appeared to be catatonic.

Jason paced. "The first protocol for everyone is to log into the WebEOC for communications. Which means, every office—if successful—has been infected."

He walked around and read the screen on Darcie's laptop. It couldn't do any more harm since it wasn't connected anymore, but thankfully, she'd left it open, so he could examine it. They were asking $25 million for the ransom. Quite a chunk of change. But somehow they'd gotten into the secure portal, and whoever they were knew the value of what they held hostage.

Darcie looked at him.

"You know what this means, right?"

"It's not good—I know that." She dropped her pen on the desk but seemed to be keeping her cool for now.

Which was better than he could say of himself. His insides were roiling. He needed to calm down. Anger wouldn't get the power back on. Wouldn't save people's lives. "This means they've already gotten everything they wanted. They're not just holding the WebEOC hostage—they extracted every bit of valuable information."

"They know our playbook." She slammed her open palm down onto the tabletop.

"Does this mean if the ransom gets paid, the power will come back on?" Misty's brow was deeply creased.

"Yeah, right." Chaz's sarcastic words were accompanied with a short laugh. "They'll probably charge another ransom once we have communications up and running."

Darcie paced around their huddled group. She chewed on her lip.

"What are you thinking, Darc?"

"The message that came in right before the power went out. It was all about the government. So whoever is behind this is trying to get the people to distrust us or to turn against us by keeping us from doing our jobs. Understanding that will help us to play their little game of chess a bit better." She narrowed her gaze and pinched the bridge of her nose. "It's not our job to investigate. Let's leave that to the professionals. It *is* our job to keep the continuity of operations—which means we do whatever it takes to get the power back on, to make sure that people are safe."

She pointed at him. "Jason, I need you to drive as far and fast as you can until you get a cell signal. If that means going all the way to Anchorage—do it. You need to get in touch with the governor's office. Tell them what's going on. It takes hours to get the National Guard mobilized, but I have a bad feeling about this and am pretty sure we're going to need them. Ask him to declare a state of emergency. They have access to the portal—so maybe their guys can do something about it. They can get in touch with the FBI or whoever will handle this."

"If they log on, they'll get the ransomware too." He stated the obvious.

"I know. Just make sure they know what's going on *here*." Darcie turned to Chaz. "Drive out to GVEA. They're going to be scrambling to get the power back on. Get whatever information you can. Tell them we are here to help. Find out why BESS isn't working or if it *will* work. Use every bit of knowledge you have." Then she glanced at Misty. "I will go to the hospital and make sure their backup generator is running and see how much fuel they have, then head to the troopers' HQ. I need *you* to go to the fire department and the police. We've got to figure out how to communicate. How to get an account of people and who needs help. There's got to be some reason why the radios aren't working." She tried her radio again and the static was louder than before.

Simon cleared his throat. "Jammers." His voice cracked.

All eyes shot to him.

The young guy held up his backpack, his face pale, his breathing labored. "I just found this." He pulled out the device. "I . . . I needed my inhaler."

"How'd that get in there?" Jason marched over and grabbed it.

"I don't know." Simon held his hands up. "I promise."

He studied the younger team member's eyes. Got in his face. "It's a violation of federal law to use this—you know that, right?" Jason smashed the jammer against his desk. Plastic and metal shards fell to the floor. He stomped it for good measure.

"I didn't have anything to do with it." Simon stepped back, his face white, eyes wide. He used the inhaler. Once. Twice. "But if they've planted these things in every office, that might be why we can't use the radios."

"The static." Jason shook his head. Sneaky move. "I should have known."

Darcie stepped closer. "Tell me what's going through that mind of yours."

"They went old school on us. Low-tech. Otherwise we'd be hearing canned music, tones, gibberish, or whatever they wanted us to hear." He clenched his jaw. "But they were clever. Didn't want to announce that they were jamming communications."

"Alright, then. What do we do?" Her gaze was fierce.

"They can't jam transmitters, only receivers. So everyone keep trying the radios. Keep transmitting. Tell everyone to be on the lookout for portable jammers. Hidden. Their motive has got to be to keep the dispatchers from being heard. To create chaos."

She nodded. "Makes sense. Realistically, how many jammers could be out there?"

Jason narrowed his eyes. "I hate to say it, but if I were the one planning this massive of an attack, I'd plant one in every emergency services office—police, trooper, fire, hospital, utilities . . . anywhere I could think of."

"Then that's what we have to assume. When we all go our separate directions, take the radios and inform everyone to be on the lookout for a jamming device. We've got to shut down as many as we can and get the radios working."

"What about me, Darcie? What can I do?" Simon stepped forward.

"You get the lovely responsibility of going to the mayor's office. In this situation, our office overrules hers. Tell her staff to be on the lookout for jamming equipment and remind them of the emergency protocol." With a glance down at her watch, Darcie sighed. "It's now been twelve minutes since the power went out. Everyone check in on the radios every quarter hour. Assuming that we eliminate the hindrances, we should be able to make contact. Keep transmitting. No matter what." She tested the radio again.

At least they could hear each other. For now. Until they got beyond their building. Jason shot a prayer heavenward, and they bundled up to face the bitter cold outside.

But when they reached the parking lot, all five of their vehicles sat low. Too low. Jason ran toward his truck. The tires were all slashed.

CHAPTER TWENTY-THREE

Fifteen Minutes Since Blackout
26 Below Zero
November 20—11:29 a.m.

SOMEONE HAD GONE TO A lot of trouble to keep them from getting out. Darcie let the anger boil inside her. They wouldn't succeed. She *would* find a way to do her job. Lives were on the line. "Why didn't we see this on the cameras?"

Misty shivered. "Because they probably did it as soon as the power went out. Then took off."

Who was behind this? And why such an elaborate plan? Were people just . . . evil? "Inside. Now." She marched toward the entrance and unlocked the door. Once her team was all inside, she shook her head. "At this point, I don't know where it's even safe to talk. So I need each and every one of you to keep your guard up. We've got four snowmachines in the maintenance shed behind us. I don't know if there's extra gas tanks, but let's hope. We still need to split up, but we'll need to get gas first. I don't think there's very much in each one because they don't want to risk the gas going bad."

"But there's only four snowmachines and five of us." Jason had his good hand on his hip and looked like he was ready to throttle someone. Anyone.

"Every second is precious. Simon, the mayor's office can wait. You stay here and keep trying the radios, phones, and cell. As soon as any of them work, get the message out about the jammers and find out who needs help. Critical first and then on down the line. Misty, you go to the mayor's after the police and fire departments."

Her assistant nodded.

"Jason, get gas. And lots of it. I hate to ask you to face this weather on a snowmachine, but maybe you'll find a vehicle along the way. I still need you to get ahold of the governor's office. Do whatever you have to do to make contact."

He dipped his chin. "If I have to go all the way to Anchorage, I will."

"You know, we should all get gas. I think it would be wise to have an extra tank to be safe. We don't know how long this will last and what our resources will be. So plan ahead." She ran to her desk, unlocked the safe, and pulled out cash. Dashing back, she counted out bills. "Here's some cash to pay for gas since they probably can't take cards."

"There's two gas stations that are close that I know for sure have transfer switches and generators." Jason led them over to the large map of Fairbanks that hung on the wall. "Here and here." He pointed. "These other two are closer, but I don't know if they'll have power to pump. I'd check the app on my phone, but we know that won't work. It's probably best to head straight to the ones we know will have gas accessible. Chaz and I will head here"—he tapped the map—"Misty and Darcie, you can take the closest one."

If things weren't so critical, she would take the time to appreciate the fact that she and Jason worked so well together in crisis. But there wasn't time. Darcie went to the lockbox by Misty's desk and grabbed the keys to the snowmachines. "Alright, let's go."

Back out in the bitter cold, she opened the maintenance shed, and they made quick work of firing up the snowmachines and headed out from the operations center. Twenty-six below zero was brutal to simply stand in. But on the back of a snowmachine traveling twenty-five miles an hour, she wasn't sure how long she'd be able to endure. Her face was protected by her scarf, but her eyes stung and watered so much she could barely see.

An avid snowmachiner, she knew how to dress. But that hadn't exactly been on her list for today. Jason was the only one who had a pair of ski goggles in his truck. The rest of them would just have to suck it up.

Traffic was backed up on all the streets. Rather than staying put, apparently people thought it would be a good idea to head home from work or go who knew where. It didn't appear to be a panic. Not yet. But horns blared as the backups worsened. At least it was light out and they had a few hours of daylight to go.

Thankfully, the snowmachines could get around the traffic since there was plenty of snow pack on the roads. Which only made people madder, but if they knew what was at stake, they'd get over it. Hopefully.

At the gas station, the line was several vehicles deep on each pump. So she raced to the door and pounded. A man came and unlocked it, and she told him she was the Emergency Operations director and needed assistance. He ended up being the owner, who didn't want to abandon his store since there were so many people coming to get gas. He had a generator to run the pumps and a small one that kept a portable electric heater running by his cash register. She paid cash for two gas cans—every last one he had—and went back to her snowmachine and waited for Misty to arrive.

The only thing that seemed to save her at the moment was the hand warmers on the machine. And since the engine was warm, at least sitting on it gave her a bit of warmth. Misty showed up, and Darcie waved her over.

"Ugh. I forgot straps." Darcie handed her a fifty. "Go knock on the door and tell the owner you work for me. He should let you inside. Get what you can to secure these. I'll keep our place in line."

Misty nodded. Ice all over her face. Poor thing would probably relish the tiny bit of warmth inside the store.

Twenty excruciating minutes later, they headed their separate ways. But the roads were even more crazy. People's patience had apparently worn thin. Wouldn't take long for panic to set in.

Feeling frozen to her very bones, she headed to the hospital first. Hoping the entire way that there was calm there.

Everyone would know the weight of the situation. The homes without power at these temperatures could be death traps once night fell.

One thing at a time. She couldn't allow her thoughts to go there yet.

Hopefully, she could get an emergency vehicle somewhere, but for now she'd be thankful for the snowmachine, especially since traffic was easier to manage with the smaller, maneuverable vehicle.

What she wouldn't do to be in her nice warm truck with the heat at full blast and her seat warmer on high.

That wasn't an option. There were one hundred thousand people needing her to do her job. Darcie called out on the radio. "Com check."

After everyone answered, relief filled her. If they could just keep communications up, they could weather this.

This was one of the times she wished she still had some sort of relationship with God. So she could pray and not feel like an idiot doing it. She wasn't so prideful to know that she needed every bit of help she could get.

As she pulled into the hospital parking lot, she zoomed toward the front and parked her snowmachine in a space by the ER. Glancing down at her watch as she rushed toward the doors, she cringed. It had now been fifty-six minutes since the power went out.

* * *

One Hour Thirteen Minutes Since Blackout
26 Below Zero
November 20—12:27 p.m.

Jason was thankful he hadn't gotten pulled over by a cop since he'd driven that snowmachine back to his apartment topping speeds of eighty miles an hour. It was only after he pulled out of the parking lot of the ops center that he remembered his smaller SUV. With gas prices soaring the way they were, he'd wanted to save some money. Thank God he'd had the foresight to do that.

Once he ran up the three flights of stairs to his tiny abode and retrieved the keys, he'd raced to a gas station, filled up the tank, and drove like a maniac out of town. He'd blared his horn constantly and put on his flashers to get through the worst of it, not that many people had cooperated, but he was thankful for the few who let him by. Now that he was out on one of the back roads, he prayed that the Richardson Highway wouldn't be jammed once he got there. Not as fast as the Parks Highway if he had to go all the way to Anchorage, but he needed less traffic and hoped the outage couldn't be that far widespread.

The way things had looked in town, he wouldn't be surprised if there was a mass exodus out of Fairbanks. And there were only two ways in and out. The Parks Highway and Richardson Highway.

Richardson would take him out to Delta Junction and then on to Tok, where he could take the Glenn Highway back toward Anchorage if he had to.

But he sure hoped he didn't have to.

The roads were packed with snow like they usually were after a snowstorm—and sometimes all winter long. But he sped along anyway.

Lord, keep the troopers off my tail. Now that he was out of town, the last thing he needed was to get himself pulled over for speeding.

When the road was straight enough, he'd get the little hybrid up to ninety miles an hour.

North Pole was coming up. He checked his phone. Still no signal.

What lengths had these guys gone to—to make *this* happen? More importantly, how many people were involved and was there any way to stop them?

What he really needed to do was get back to the office and get his computer hooked up to the generator and satellite internet so he could see if he could trace the hackers in any way.

But his laptop was locked down with the ransomware.

Good thing he hadn't tried to log in on the big desktop. At least he could still use it. But first he had to make contact with the governor's office and then make it back.

All of which took time.

He was almost to Moose Creek when he realized he wasn't far from Eielson Air Force Base.

He slammed a hand on the steering wheel. Why hadn't he thought of the military installations? They were sure to have secure communications, weren't they?

Flying past Moose Creek, he took the exit for Eielson and headed for the gate. Now he just had to pray that he could get through.

At the gate, the guard motioned him forward.

Jason rolled down his window.

The guard held out his hand. "ID?"

He handed over his driver's license.

"You don't have a pass?"

"No, sir. But this is an emergency."

The man held up a hand. "Your purpose for coming to Eielson Air Force Base?" The man didn't look accommodating. In fact, his frown was deep.

"My name is Jason Myers. I work for the Emergency Operations Center in Fairbanks, and there's a huge blackout. A terrorist attack. All communications are down, and I have got to get in touch with the governor's office immediately."

The guard eyed him. "Wait here."

He went into his little guard station and used the phone. While he was still on the phone, two Security Force vehicles pulled up, blocking Jason's path.

Great. They thought he was a lunatic. He did not have time for this.

Debating whether to crank it into reverse and speed away or to sit and wait, Jason's decision was taken away from him when the guard returned. "These two vehicles will accompany you." He handed his license back.

No smile.

Nothing.

But Jason would take it.

The first SF vehicle pulled forward, and the other one waved him on. Jason followed the lead vehicle and watched as the second one followed closely behind *him*. They probably wanted to make sure that he wasn't planning to take off and do something stupid.

They pulled in front of a building that was obviously for the Security Forces. He'd take it. As long as they had working phone lines, he was good.

He jumped out of his SUV and followed the armed men to the door.

After a lengthy explanation to the Security Forces officer in charge, Jason was finally led to a small room.

"This is a secure line. We've confirmed the situation in Fairbanks, and the colonel is being briefed as we speak. Please tell the governor that we are coordinating with Fort Wainwright and Greely to be on call." The man dipped his chin to him.

"Thank you, sir." Jason picked up the phone and watched as the man went to stand outside the door. At least they had the military behind them. With close to 7,500 men and women stationed at Fort Wainwright, and over 9,000 at Eielson, the military bases were secure. Each with their own coal plant to provide the electricity needs.

The call with the governor's office made him jump through every hoop imaginable until they figured out he was telling the truth and had seen the ransomware for themselves. Then the governor's assistant actually jumped on the line. Things began to move at that point. Finally.

At least the higher powers were taking control. Now he just had to get back to Fairbanks and figure out how to stop this. He had to help Darcie.

He'd seen her master list when he first started. And several items on the list included making the necessary connections with the military bases in the area. He should have thought of this sooner, because Fort Wainwright was just outside of Fairbanks. But the military was its own entity and had their own protocols in place. So the EOC's first priorities had been for the civilians in the area.

He glanced down at his watch—1:39 p.m.

Only a couple more hours before the sun went down.

CHAPTER TWENTY-FOUR

Two Hours Thirty-One Minutes Since Blackout
28 Below Zero
November 20—1:45 p.m.

NATALIE'S EYES FLEW OPEN. WHAT was that? Where was she?

She looked around the room. A hospital room. She had tubes taped to her arm. Using the other arm, she reached up to her face. There was some kind of a tube up in her nose as well.

What was going on?

A woman opened the door and rolled a cart in. She was dressed in dark-blue clothing. What were those called? Scrubs?

It made her smile to think of the word.

"You're awake." The woman left her cart with some sort of computer on it and walked toward her. "I'm going to check your vitals now, alright?"

Natalie nodded. The woman was so kind. The bed was warm. For the first time in a long time, she felt secure. Safe. Why?

"You probably noticed that the power went out. But our backup generator will keep this place running for days, so don't you worry about that." The woman pulled a contraption from around her neck, placed two ends of it in her ears, and then placed the round part on Natalie's chest. "Try to take a deep breath for me."

Natalie took as big a breath as she could. But her chest felt weird. Heavy. Weighted down.

The power had gone out. The bad men. Tears squeezed out of her eyes. She'd failed. Was it all her fault?

"It's alright, Natalie. Calm down. I won't hurt you. Just another deep breath please."

"Where is the nice lady?"

The woman studied her. "I'm sorry—I don't understand. What nice lady?"

"The one with the blue eyes?"

A soft smile lifted the lady's lips. "I'll see if I can find her, alright?"

"Thank you." She relaxed against the pillows. The lady with the curly hair, she could fix all this. Natalie knew it.

Her chest felt so heavy. Maybe she could just close her eyes for a few more minutes before she had to go out into the snow. The bed was so warm.

Warm was good.

Soft was good.

Even the beeps were good.

* * *

Two Hours Thirty-Eight Minutes Since Blackout
28 Below Zero
November 20—1:52 p.m.
Fairbanks Memorial Hospital

For what seemed like forever, Darcie had helped the security at the hospital search for the jammers. Once they knew what they were dealing with, it seemed like it would be easy. But they hadn't found one portable jammer, and none of the radios in the hospital were working. Which meant they weren't hearing anything from the ambulances as they came in, dispatch's hands were tied, and they were unprepared.

At least they had power. The massive generators at the hospital were equipped with enough fuel to last a week in Fairbanks's brutal winters. Which was truly a lifesaver, but if they didn't get communications back up and running, the risk of losing lives could skyrocket.

Darcie also hadn't heard from her team and whether they had any success. Which made her heart want to explode out of her chest. But she took deep breaths and forced herself to calm down. The hospital was running. That was a huge plus in their favor.

Racking her mind, she went back to the security office, where all the security personnel were gathered. She was greeted with shrugs and the shaking of heads. "Why can't we find it?"

"Ma'am, we've searched every inch of this hospital. It's not here." The head of security pulled out a battery-operated AM radio. He turned it on. "The closer you get to a jammer, the louder the static will be. But it's the same throughout the building. It's simply not in the hospital."

Darcie went to the window and smacked her palm against her forehead. The static. Of course. Why hadn't she thought of it sooner? Especially after Jason's explanation. "I'm going to check the parking lot. Some of you guys need to check the dumpsters and any smaller buildings on the campus. May I borrow this?" She pointed to the AM radio.

"You got it."

Bundling back up in her winter gear, Darcie made a mad dash for the parking lot. But there were multiple buildings as well as dumpsters. This was going to take even more of her precious time. But the hospital was a priority. She had to get communications back up.

Looking out at the emergency room parking lot, she stopped. If she were planting a jammer, where would she put it?

The ER parking lot was too easy. She changed directions and headed toward the south entrance. There were several parking lots over there. One across Nineteenth Avenue. Maybe she should start heading that direction and see if her radio could help her find it.

The fierce cold hit her in the face as she walked out, and she pulled up her scarf. The temperature had dropped even more. Meteorologists had predicted they would hit thirty-five below tonight.

The static and crackling continued in her radio, so she ran up and down each row of vehicles trying to keep warm and hoping to find the source of the jamming as soon as possible.

When she crossed Nineteenth Avenue, she continued her search, and within seconds the static grew louder. She must be getting close.

By the time she reached the fourth row, she stopped and looked at all the vehicles in front of her. Was it inside one of them?

Then she spotted a truck with lights mounted up top. She marched toward it, and the sound about blew her eardrums. She turned her radio off and climbed into the bed of the truck. Something was mounted behind the lights. It had to be it. But it was so much larger than the portable one they'd found in Simon's backpack.

Shoving her radio into her pocket, she used both hands to tug and pull at the massive radio-looking apparatus. But it wouldn't budge. So she searched her surroundings. No rocks or anything of substance that could damage the dumb thing.

She spotted a dumpster across the parking lot, but then one of the security guards caught her eye. "Over here!" She cupped her hands to get her yell to him.

He turned and ran toward her.

"Give me your flashlight." She jumped up and down in the bed of the truck.

He handed it over. "You found the jammer?"

"I sure hope so." With all her might, she swung the large flashlight and smashed the object. Over and over again. Until she'd put several large dents into the top of the pickup. With the flashlight in one hand, she pulled the radio out of her pocket and turned it back on.

Words washed over her.

Yes! She'd gotten rid of it!

"Good job, ma'am." The security guard offered an arm to her as she hopped down. "But you could have simply turned it off."

Huh. There was that. His statement helped to lighten the moment. She handed his flashlight back. "Hopefully I didn't damage it."

"You put it to good use. Now let's get back inside and see if they are hearing from dispatch."

They ran across the parking lot, crossed the road, and raced toward the doors of the hospital.

Several staff were speaking into the radios as Darcie entered.

It worked. Thank goodness.

A few pounds of the two-ton weight on her shoulders fell away.

A nurse in blue scrubs ran toward her. "Do you know Natalie?"

She yanked her scarf down. "Yes."

"Oh good. She's been asking for the nice lady and then finally remembered that you ran the Emergency Operations Center. Do you have time to come with me?"

Logic told her that she needed to contact her team, but her heart drew her to the older woman. "Please take me to her."

On the way through the hospital corridors, she used her radio to reach her team. Everyone answered, including Jason, who was on his way back to the office now. She asked for a report from each of them in fifteen minutes. That should give her enough time to see the woman who drew her like a magnet.

When they reached the room, Darcie took a second to collect her thoughts. But Natalie glanced over and saw her. "Come in. Come in." The smile that lit her face made the woman beautiful and radiant.

The nurse grabbed her elbow and whispered into her ear. "She's got fluid on her lungs and internal bleeding. She doesn't have a lot of time left."

Darcie whirled around. "What? How did this happen?"

The nurse let out a long sigh. "I'm sorry. That's all I know."

"Come in. Please." Natalie called to her.

Darcie took off her coat, scarf, and gloves and laid them in the chair beside the bed. "How are you feeling?"

"I'm glad you came. You were able to stop the bad men?" Her eyes were so hopeful.

What could she say? "Not yet. But your help has been invaluable."

The woman's face fell. "I had hoped. Prayed that I had done enough."

"You helped us a lot, Natalie. Thank you. Now you just need to focus on resting. Getting well." She stepped to the side of the bed and gripped the woman's hand. It was worn by years of hard work.

"You remind me of one of my daughters." Natalie's voice was breathy.

"What's her name?"

"Ivy. My Tito named her." Her gaze was drawn to the window. "I haven't seen her in such a long time."

"Maybe I could find her for you. Do you know where she lives?"

A small shake of her head and then her gaze connected with Darcie's again. "When their father died, I was beside myself with grief. I told all of them to leave and never come back."

"All of them? All of who?"

"My children. They wanted me to move in with one of them, and I refused."

"How many children do you have, Natalie?" While the woman seemed clear and not confused, Darcie wanted to spend as much time with her as she could.

"Six." Her gaze drifted to the window again. She closed her eyes. Raspy breaths were the only sound.

Unsure what to do, Darcie stood there holding the woman's hand.

"I love my children. I didn't really want them to go away. But I couldn't deal with the grief. It took me months to crawl out of the black cloud that had surrounded me."

"Let me help you find them. I bet they would love to see you."

"My Tito found God right before he died. Asked me to go to church with him. But I refused. Because I was too busy. Too concerned with my own things. It was my greatest regret after he died. That I didn't even give him the time I should have. But God didn't mind." Tears slipped out of her eyes. "I wish I'd told my children."

"Once we get past this crisis, I will find them. I promise." Why she was promising such a thing to this woman she didn't even know was beyond her, but Darcie felt her own eyes well up with tears. "Can you write down their names for me?"

Natalie nodded. Her hand shook when Darcie handed her a pen and paper. But she managed it.

"You did good. You listened. You helped. But your eyes are hollow, dear girl. You need Jesus." She closed her eyes and winced. Then coughed several times.

There was no response she could give to that. At one time she'd had Jesus. Or so she'd thought. What difference could that make now?

"I need to rest. You . . . go help people." Natalie's eyelids raised to half-mast as she patted Darcie's hand and then closed her eyes again. "You are loved. Remember that."

Darcie grabbed her things and stepped quietly out of the room. She pulled the door closed behind her and put her coat and scarf back on so she could brave the elements for the snowmachine ride back to the ops center. But Natalie's words rolled over and over in her mind.

So weird. The woman had appeared like a crazed lunatic on national television for all to see.

Why should Darcie let it affect her? She had work to do. People to help.

Shaking her head of the thoughts, she marched out of the hospital.

Before she could think about anything else, she had to keep one hundred thousand people from dying in the cold.

CHAPTER TWENTY-FIVE

Three Hours Forty-Eight Minutes Since Blackout
29 Below Zero
November 20—3:18 p.m.
Emergency Operations Center

THE OFFICE WAS FRIGID EVEN with Jason's generator running two small space heaters. He stared at his team members. Every fiber of his being wanted to fix this. Right here. Right now. But it was out of his power.

Fury burned at Kirk. What had he gotten involved in? At this point Jason didn't see much hope for his younger brother coming out of this unscathed.

Movement brought him out of his thoughts. Little brother didn't matter right now. Misty, Chaz, and Simon still all wore their winter gear as they rushed around and gathered in the center of the room with pads of paper, pens, and their handheld radios.

Constant talk and crackle of radio chatter made him at least breathe a sigh of relief. They didn't have full communications yet, but they were working on it.

Misty plugged a set of earbuds into her radio and popped one into her ear. "I'll keep an ear out for anything that needs your attention, Darc."

Jason gave her a thumbs-up. "Old school. Love it. I always keep a set of wired ones in my bag too. Just in case."

"Thanks, Misty. Everyone else turn the radios down for a few minutes. Just so we can regroup." Darcie slid a chair up, and it scraped along the floor. She still wore her gloves and scarf, though her coat was tossed across a desk. "Okay, thank you all for the hard work. But now I need to assess where we're at. Thanks to Jason and his quick thinking, the governor's office knows what is going on. We have the three military bases in our area on alert. They have all since locked down just in case this is a bigger terrorist threat than we know." Her lips pursed, and she tapped her fingers on her notebook in her lap. "I can tell you that the hospital is up and running just fine. It took us more than two hours to find a huge jammer mounted on a vehicle in the parking lot, but once we eliminated that, all the ambulance, dispatchers, and EMTs could communicate." She went to the whiteboard and started making lists and notes. "They have enough fuel to run for a week." After writing these things down, she looked at Chaz. "What'd you find out?"

"It's not good. The governor's office paid the ransom. Since they have cyber insurance—which is a must for all governments to procure nowadays—and they didn't want a panic or uprising in the citizens saying that the government didn't take care of them. If there is a major loss of life because of this, we all know there will be massive protests against any and every person in government. The public will want someone to blame."

Jason leaned forward. "And if the perpetrators behind this remain anonymous and aren't caught, people will be even more inclined to point fingers."

Darcie cringed and stared at him. "At us." She let out a long breath, and her marker flew over the board.

Simon pointed to his laptop screen. "We can access the WebEOC now. A statement was posted there as soon as it was unlocked and freed from the ransomware. Apparently the governor also had a live press conference that the rest of the state was able to see, so people know what is going on. There's information here about other agencies coming to help." He looked thoughtful. "Will anyone use the

WebEOC now? I'm not seeing much of anything, and I can't blame them." Negativity dripped from the young guy's voice.

Jason nudged him. "How about we work on a solution then?" Things were pretty bleak if the two young optimists in the group couldn't keep a positive vibe going.

Chaz ran a hand through his hair, which was already spiked in every imaginable direction. "You're right, Jas. It's our job to find a solution."

Darcie wrote on the board. "Keep morale up. You guys work on securing the system from allowing this to happen again. We've got to build up everyone's trust again. Work the problem, people. Lives are at stake."

Misty lifted her hand, looking uncomfortable. "If the governor paid the ransom, why isn't the power back on?"

Jason mulled that over. He reached for the paper with the verbiage of the ransomware attack, which he'd thrown on his desk. He read it out loud. "'If you want access to help your people, the ransom is twenty-five million US dollars. To turn the power back on, you better pay up.'" Shaking his head, he slammed his palm on the desk beside him. "The ransom was for the WebEOC." Standing up, he swiped a hand down his scruffy face. How had they missed it? "Shutting down our communications system was a big problem, yes, but it was just a distraction. They want us scrambling. Since they'd already made a backdoor into the system, they acquired all the information they needed long before the actual cyberattack." He pointed to the paper. "Read the wording. Paying the ransom wasn't ever about the power. But shutting the power down is what got everyone's attention."

"And could be what kills the most people." Darcie's eyes were wide, but the anger on her face couldn't be missed. She looked at Chaz. "What did you find out at the power company?"

He shook his head. "Not enough. The only thing we could figure out is that there's some kind of hack on the system. Malware maybe? But the BESS is a totally different story—there were small explosions throughout that disabled the large battery system. They're working on the repairs, but they said it could take weeks."

"We don't have weeks. So scratch the BESS." Darcie wrote on the whiteboard. "We'll come back to that. But you guys have to focus on helping GVEA find the issue." She pointed at Chaz, Simon, and Jason and then capped the marker. "Misty, how about you?"

"The police department had already found the jammer by the time I got there. And the fire department found the one there pretty quick once I told them the problem. They are in great shape, other than the fact that there is massive looting going on and several crowds of panicked protesters. Seems they took Natalie's words and the emergency message right before the blackout quite seriously. They're calling for defunding of not just the police and our office, but the entire government." She grimaced. "But once the radios were back up, the police had things under control. The chief said it was a bit like boxing with one hand tied behind his back, but they were doing their best and said to let them know if anything changes and we need anything else. Several churches in the area with backup generators opened their doors to the public who don't have their own sources of power. They are working at getting that information broadcast out via radio, but they suspect there are still jammers around town, because lots of people are reporting the static. It might take days for all of them to be found." She glanced down at her notes. "The chief said that most officers who weren't on duty voluntarily headed to the station to help as soon as the power went out. Troopers said the same thing. Gotta love our guys in blue. But even if they used all their manpower to find the jammers, we'd be in a heap of trouble because there's chaos in the streets."

"We don't have days. *People* won't have days. Not in this cold." The marker squeaked as Darcie updated the board. She looked back to Misty, her voice resigned. "And the mayor's office?"

"Her chief of staff was there with a radio, and thankfully, we found the jammer. But the mayor hasn't been seen or heard from."

"Ouch. That could be a real problem. Do the police and state troopers know?"

Misty nodded. "Yep. I went back by and let both HQs know." She held up a finger and then placed that hand over her ear and listened.

"More jammers have been found, so there's a lot more communication. I'll take this into the conference room and see what's needed."

"Good." Darcie turned her blue eyes to him. "Jason, I know you have a lot to share. I can see it on your face."

He sat on the corner of his desk. His thoughts raced, and he scrambled for them to be in decipherable order. "First, I found another vehicle to use and drove out the Richardson Highway. As I was almost to Moose Creek, I realized I was right by Eielson, so I stopped at the gate in hopes they had communications up."

"Brilliant idea." Darcie sank into her chair with an exasperated sigh. "That's right. I should have thought of that. The bases have their own power plants." She rolled her eyes and hopped back up to write on the board. "I need to add that to our emergency situations action list."

"I wouldn't have thought of it either had I not been driving by. They almost didn't let me in." Jason tried to lighten the moment with a strangled laugh. It didn't work. "But I was able to get through to the governor's office. Like Chaz said, they paid the ransom after I gave them all the pertinent information. The governor called in the National Guard, which might take a few hours. He also said he would loop in the Department of Defense for Defense Support to Civil Authorities. What they need from us is, we've got to do our best and keep them in the loop of what is transpiring. Whether you want to attempt the WebEOC or not, we've got to do something to update them. Phones are down because there was an explosion at Pioneer Telephone. There were also small detonations at all the major cell towers for the entire Fairbanks area, taking out the backup power sources. The towers are still intact, but without power there's no cell signal. We can thank the amazing folks at Fort Wainwright and Eielson Air Force Base for getting us all this information. They've sent word to get people out to repair or replace the backup power systems. But the guys have to come from Anchorage."

Darcie looked at her watch. "Which in winter driving conditions could take up to nine hours."

"Yep." Jason waited for her to look at him again. Their eyes connected. Before the blackout, he'd had hopes for something deeper. But the pain and doubt in her gaze made him realize the weight that she now bore. Where would they be—relationship-wise—when all this was over? It seemed like a year had passed in the last few hours. Would she shut him out?

"Jason?"

"Yeah?" What had he missed?

"Was there anything else?" She pinned him with her gaze.

With a deep sigh, he let out his breath. The worst part he didn't particularly want to share. "I heard on my radio as I was coming back into town that there were explosions at the pipeline viewpoint on the Steese Highway and at the Alaska Range Overlook on campus at the university."

"Was anyone hurt?" Darcie's voice cracked at the end.

"I heard there were casualties, but with communications the way they are, I don't know how many. It cut out again, and I lost the rest of the transmission."

"It doesn't make sense." Darcie studied the board. "If the whole point was that the government can't save people, why all the senseless explosions?"

The silence seeped into Jason. If he thought too much about all that happened and all the people who were at risk and in danger, rage would consume him. And right now the only true hope he had was faith in Almighty God to guide them and give them the wisdom of what to do next. Because they'd depleted all their own ideas and resources. The face of his brother flashed through his mind.

If Kirk had anything to do with this . . . No. He couldn't go there. Not now. Their main objective had to be to get the power back on before people froze to death.

"Simple." Simon's voice behind Jason broke the quiet. "Just like Jas said earlier. It's all been a distraction." He stood and lifted his laptop. "Look, if I want to keep the resources taxed, I'm going to create as much chaos as possible while I'm working at my real plan.

That keeps the good guys from being able to home in on what I'm doing." He looked at Jason. "Which is keeping the power off. So that people panic and blame the government and emergency services and everyone else they can think of. Whoever is doing this is pretty brilliant. They've cut a major life-sustaining utility. The power. Which people need when it's cold to survive. They've kept us from communicating effectively and kept the public from being able to tell us they need help. Add to that the distractions. Which are horrible in and of themselves, but it steals resources from the fire department, police, and troopers. *Chaos*."

The kid was right. But who planned something like this? What kind of demented genius did this?

"All to make a point? I just don't get what makes people like this tick . . ." Darcie huffed and wiped a gloved hand over her hair.

It hit him in the gut. Kirk's words bounced around in his head. *"Oh yes we can. And we will. We have power."* Why didn't he see it before? He and his parents had even gone to counseling to understand the mind of an addict. One of the personalities that was drawn to an addictive lifestyle was one who wanted control. He hoped Kirk wasn't behind this, but that didn't matter now.

"Power." Jason stood up. "And not the electricity kind. Whoever this is wants to show that they're powerful. More powerful than us. More powerful than the police and state troopers. More powerful than the government." He shivered and not from the air temperature.

Simon showed him his laptop screen.

Jason studied it. "Wait . . . did you figure out where they hacked into the power grid?"

"I'm not sure. But maybe I'm close?" He shrugged. "I could be wrong though. I definitely don't want it to be like what was planned in Ukraine in 2016. You know, the plan was for when everything got turned back on, it would all blow up. Thankfully, they goofed. But this reminds me a bit too much of that. And the thought of blowing up a power grid that could put us without power for weeks in the winter isn't something I want to even consider."

Jason squinted and followed the trail Simon had marked.

Darcie stepped closer. "Please tell me you can figure it out?"

"I don't know." He looked at his watch. Already after 4:00 p.m. The sun was down, and that meant the temperature would continue to drop. "Let me work on this on my desktop. It's a more robust system, and I can search multiple places at once on the separate monitors."

"Okay." Darcie put her hands on her hips. "Crucial elements. One is the power, two is BESS, three is the jammers, and four is the population. Then there's the mayor, but we can assume that the police are handling that one." She crossed *Mayor* off the list. "We *can* help with number one." Circling it, she looked over her shoulder. "Simon, you do whatever you can to help Jason figure this out. Number two is out of our hands, but there are experts working on it." She crossed that one off. "Three is something else we can tackle. Chaz, you get on the radio and keep testing it. Drive around town if you have to and figure out where there's no signal. That brings us to number four."

She drew a big red circle around it. "Misty and I will handle incoming requests for help. Which I'm sure will be constant. I've got to find out how many people are missing in this weather. How many were lost in the explosions. How many homes have backup generators. How many citizens are over sixty-five years of age and might need transportation to an emergency location like one of the churches. Somehow we need to coordinate all this and get people moved to safety without causing traffic jams or panic."

* * *

Six Hours Eighteen Minutes Since Blackout
30 Below Zero
November 20—5:32 p.m.

The large warehouse had obviously been empty for some time. Griz's footsteps echoed on the cheap tile floor.

"I finally get to meet the guy in charge, and you come in here wearing a ski mask?" Collins laughed. "A little cliché, isn't it? We're not robbing a bank."

Griz let out a huff. Some people could be so dense. "What did you need, Mr. Collins? I didn't drive across town during a blackout for the fun of it."

"Look. You did a great job. What I paid you to do. You hacked the power grid. But I don't see why it's necessary for all the other things you have going on. I just want to get it straight right now that I'm not responsible for anyone's death. I only wanted to prove Darcie Phillips wasn't cut out for the job."

It was his turn to laugh as he shoved his hands into his pockets. The imbecile. "You're in over your head, Collins. We didn't do this for you. You're not in charge."

"Now wait just a minute. I paid you a lot of money to get this done, and you assured me you would do what I wanted."

The sleazy idiot had no clue. "No, you paid a *small* amount of money because you were jealous and greedy and wanted your way." He lifted the Glock out of its holster. "You're a spoiled rich kid who didn't get the job you wanted, so you thought you'd buy your way in." He stepped closer.

Collins's hands were in the air. His eyes wide. "Hey now, wait just a minute. There's no need to get violent. You and I . . . we're businessmen. I'm sure we can come up with some sort of agreement. I have money." The more he talked, the more desperate he sounded.

"I don't care about your money." He aimed at the guy's kneecap and fired.

The other man screamed, doubled over, and collapsed to the ground. "You shot me!"

"Keep your mouth shut and I might not do it again." He picked up the casing and shoved it into his pocket as he walked out the door.

Collins was the perfect guy to take the fall.

CHAPTER TWENTY-SIX

Seven Hours Forty-One Minutes Since Blackout
31 Below Zero
November 20—6:55 p.m.

THEIR RADIOS HAD BEEN FILLED with constant requests for help for a couple hours now. Hopefully, most of the jammers had been found so people could communicate via radio, which most Alaskans had in their homes or in their emergency kits in their vehicles. Darcie had sent Chaz on one run after another picking up those who didn't have transportation and taking them to one of the shelters. A few calls had even sent him out to check on those whom family or friends hadn't heard from.

One eighty-nine-year-old man was found snoring, but alive—albeit a bit chilled—in his recliner. Apparently he hadn't slept well the night before and sat down with a blanket to take a nap around 11:00 a.m. Right before the blackout. His daughter was in a senior center and hadn't been able to get ahold of him.

He'd slept right through it until Chaz busted down the man's door and woke him up. It was one of the cheerier stories their young teammate shared. People were angry, disgruntled, and scared.

Of course, he was most proud of himself for kicking in a door. Not that he would try it again. He kept rubbing his leg when he thought no one was looking.

The constant barrage had prevented Darcie from tackling anything else, but this was what she needed to do. The fire and police departments were also overrun with calls and lots of furious people outside their stations. But one thing they could thank the cold for—protesters couldn't stay out in it for too long. So they retreated to their cars, warmed up, and started in again every twenty minutes or so.

They even had several protesters in their parking lot. But a few had already left. A news crew had come and gone with their mobile unit. Not that they would be able to broadcast until the power came back on. But Darcie had watched out the window as the reporter talked for several minutes and pointed to their building. Hopefully, talking about what the job of the Emergency Operations Center was and how this was the first test of the office's strength. But more likely it was asking why the EOC didn't have the power back up and running already. Even though it was the power company's job and she was supposed to simply coordinate with them, at the end of the day? She would be blamed.

Darcie shook her head. She would deal with the media later. All their guessing would get them nowhere. Besides, only a few people even knew about the ransomware. Which was a good thing, because if people found out what happened and that the governor's office paid the ransom and they still didn't have power? Who knows what kind of rampage they'd have on their hands.

She checked the working map they were using to show where services had been called out to. A lot of the troopers had been summoned out to the highways. With all the people leaving Fairbanks, traffic was slow going. Especially with no end to the blackout in sight, she couldn't blame them. But she worried about all those people. Did they have a plan? Had they made hotel reservations? Were there even enough rooms? Did they have enough fuel? At one point she'd been briefed that there were roughly twenty-five thousand hotel rooms in the state.

But her job wasn't to worry about everyone leaving. She had to focus on those who stayed. Her area was huge, but the more remote people were, the better they were equipped to handle power outages.

Thankfully, everyone she'd heard from so far was hunkered down and riding it out. Many people were off the grid anyway, but when cell and internet service were interrupted, that could be a problem for those who were farther out.

She scribbled on another piece of paper as she took a call on one of the four channels open for citizens. The radio stations with large enough back-up generators were broadcasting the information every fifteen minutes about how to contact emergency services and which frequencies and channels to use for those with two-way radios. Most Alaskans were great at being prepared. Darcie just hoped that everyone kept fresh batteries in their radios since they weren't used often.

After another call to Chaz for where he needed to go next, she stood and stretched. Then headed to the bathroom to splash some water on her face. Using a flashlight to guide her way, she shook off the eerie feelings the dark hallway sent up her spine.

What would people think of her after this disaster? Would they even appreciate what the ops center had done? The office was barely up and running. And nothing had been set up for full operation yet. But would people understand that and give her a break?

Not if lots of people died.

That would rest on *her* shoulders.

Where would she go after that? She had nothing else. This job was everything. It kept her sane. What would Jason think of her after all this was over?

Placing her hands on the bathroom counter, she dipped her head. Thoughts like this weren't healthy. What her counselor called destructive.

Her mind took her back to her office, on the couch, right before the blackout. Her face burned. Sitting next to Jason had seemed normal and made her feel alive and human again. With hope. She'd shared her deepest pain, and then everything went crazy. Was he regretting asking what was wrong with her? Did he despise her as much as her parents did? As much as she despised herself sometimes? She couldn't worry about her own future. Right now there were lives on the line. And she didn't even know how many.

Turning the faucet on, she wondered how much more water was in the pipes and quickly turned it off. With the electricity down, the pump couldn't pull more water into the building. Their generator was running necessary equipment. Best to ration the water as much as they could. They needed the toilets to function for as long as possible. Of course, if the pipes froze in the frigid temperatures, it would all be a moot point.

Good thing they had plenty of Clorox wipes and hand sanitizer stashed in the supply closet to at least keep their hands clean. With a new mission, she went to grab those supplies and desperately wished she could simply snap her fingers and all of this would be fixed.

If she lived in a make-believe world, maybe that could happen.

She delivered a bottle of hand sanitizer and container of wipes to each person there and then headed back to her desk. The radios were a constant hum.

Misty handled it all like a pro. When all this was over, Darcie needed to buy her something special. A gift that showed her appreciation.

She turned to her laptop and checked her email. Thank goodness for Jason's generator and their satellite internet. Although, she refused to log back into the WebEOC. Whatever these hackers—well, best to call them what they were . . . cyberterrorists—were after, they'd done a good job of creating havoc.

A message from Amanda popped up. Darcie opened it and read:

Hey friend. It's all over the national news what you guys are facing up there. It's unfathomable the evil that people are capable of, but remember that you are strong and are trained for this. I am here. Cheering you on. Sending thoughts and prayers. You've got this, Darcie.
Amanda

PS—
I am an American airman.
I am a warrior.
I have answered my nation's call.
I am an American airman.
My mission is to fly, fight, and win.
I am faithful to a proud heritage,
A tradition of honor,
And a legacy of valor.
I am an American airman.
Guardian of freedom and justice,
My nation's sword and shield,
Its sentry and avenger.
I defend my country with my life.
I am an American airman.
Wingman, leader, warrior.
I will never leave an airman behind,
I will never falter,
And I will not fail.

Darcie repeated the words in her mind as she read them. She'd recited the Airman's Creed over and over again during her years in the Air Force. And she loved the poem. It had boosted her confidence and morale more than once.

If only it had the power to do that now.

But even as she repeated it in her mind again, the last line got to her. She'd already failed.

She hadn't stopped this from happening.

Hadn't fixed it.

Hadn't really done much of anything to help.

Tears burned at the corners of her eyes.

She had to *do* something.

Turning to Misty, she closed her laptop. "I'm headed to the hospital. I should be back in an hour. Let me know if you need me."

A puzzled look crossed Misty's face. "Has something happened?"

"No. I just want to check on things in person."

No sense in letting any of the others know the mess that she was. It would all come out soon enough. Even though Amanda's email had encouraged her, she realized she wasn't anything like her strong, amazing friend. The woman had handled multiple hurricanes and disasters with grace and ease. Her community not only depended on her but loved her. Because she'd earned their trust.

What had Darcie done?

That was another destructive thought. She pushed the negativity away and tried to feel anything else. Even anger at whoever had done this would be welcome. But the numbness seeped into her bones again with the cold.

Right now she wanted to see Natalie. The woman might be old and Alzheimer's had done a number on her mind, but at least with her, Darcie had begun to thaw.

And she was desperate to fan the feeble flame the woman had lit inside her. Because she couldn't handle the numb anymore.

She craved something more.

What she'd seen in Natalie.

In Misty.

In . . . Jason.

*   *   *

Eight Hours Forty-Seven Minutes Since Blackout
32 Below Zero
November 20—8:01 p.m.

The computers in the room hummed along with the generator.

"You've done a great job." Griz pulled the trigger of the Glock twice toward Nick's chest.

The kid dropped to the floor, a pool of blood seeping out around him.

Then he pointed the barrel toward Julian. "That gives you a chance to tell me where your allegiance lies. Have you talked to anyone about any of the work you've done for me?"

Pushing his glasses up his nose, the usually smiling Julian stared at the body on the floor. Then jerked his gaze up toward the gun. "Uh . . . no. Of course not. I'm smarter than that." A grin split his lips.

Then two bullets hit the kid's chest, and he fell to the floor next to his buddy.

With a sigh, Griz fired at each of the computers, picked up his brass, and then walked out of the room.

Two more places to visit to eliminate the nonessential personnel. And drop off a present. He'd gotten what he needed out of them. And proved his point quite magnificently, if he did say so himself.

Everything was going according to plan.

CHAPTER TWENTY-SEVEN

Eight Hours Fifty-One Minutes Since Blackout
32 Below Zero
November 20—8:05 p.m.
Fairbanks Memorial Hospital

THE HOSPITAL WAS A WARM and welcoming sight. But the chaos inside overwhelmed Darcie. People were crowded into what seemed like every crack and crevice of open space. Whether they actually needed medical attention was questionable, as a good number of people stood around and chatted. But there were many who appeared incapacitated. Covered in blood.

The protests and looting had increased in violence. That was to be expected at a time like this. But the foolishness of people made her shake her head.

Why couldn't human beings simply follow the rules and guidelines? Weren't people good anymore? Or was the world simply filled with a bunch of messed-up, selfish, evil-doing criminals?

Was that the level where humanity had sunk?

Pushing through the crowd, she wound her way to the security officer guarding the door that accessed the hallway and elevators. Showing her emergency director ID badge, she asked to be allowed through.

With a nod, he opened the door and she slipped in, knowing the poor man would have to fight off a crowd of people who watched her. And if he told them who she was when he explained why *she* was allowed to go through, she'd probably have a riot when she came back down. Which meant she needed to leave a different way.

Taking the elevator up to Natalie's floor, she leaned against the wall and let out a long sigh. Maybe the older woman had some great words of wisdom or insight that would help her. Or maybe just seeing her would give Darcie's heart a jump start to feel *something*.

With a ding, the elevator doors opened. She removed her coat and walked to the room. But the trooper outside looked grim, and the chaos inside the room didn't bode well.

"What's going on?"

"Natalie was trying to give me information about the cabin's location when she coded." He shook his head. "It doesn't look good."

"No!" The cry tore out of her mouth, and she lunged for the room. But the trooper's arms held her back.

Deep anguish in the pit of her stomach surged. Nausea threatened as bile rose in her throat. She covered her mouth and swallowed it back down. But she couldn't stop it.

The trooper was fast. While holding her with one arm, he grabbed a trash can and placed it under her chin just in time.

When her system had expelled everything in her stomach, the heaving finally halted and she wilted in the arms of the stranger.

A nurse raced to her side. As shorthanded as they were, it only made Darcie feel worse. "Please. Save Natalie."

"Ma'am, they are doing everything they can."

But as Darcie watched the staff in the room, in her heart she knew. It was bad.

They weren't going to save the woman.

Darcie wouldn't be able to have one more conversation. She wouldn't be able to figure out what it was about Natalie that drew her. Couldn't look into the deep, feeling eyes one more time.

The solid tone that came from the room devastated her.

No heartbeat. No matter how many times they used the paddles to shock her. Nothing happened.

Then the sobs started. Great big, huge wailing sobs that she couldn't stop.

Natalie was gone.

*　*　*

Nine Hours Twenty-One Minutes Since Blackout
32 Below Zero
November 20—8:35 p.m.

The code in front of him practically leapt off the screen. Jason jumped up from his chair and surveyed the room. Where was Darcie? He had to share this with her. Right now. It was just what they all needed to lift the somber mood.

But a sudden urge to stop and pray for her overtook him. Jason sat at his desk and closed his eyes. *God, I don't know what's going on, but You've obviously placed this on my heart. Please protect Darcie wherever she is.*

Not knowing what else to pray, he opened his eyes and looked back at the screen in front of him. This was it. It wasn't going to be easy, but they could get the power back on. "Simon"—he hollered across his desk—"get over here and check this out."

The young guy ran over. "Whatcha find?"

"This." He pointed to one of his monitors. "I need a second set of eyes to make sure I've found the source."

For several minutes, they both scrolled and read. Line by line.

"Dude. That's it." Simon held up a hand for a high five.

Jason didn't hesitate in granting it. "That's what I hoped." He quickly plugged in the printer and then hit Print for the cheat sheet he'd made. They'd been charging their laptops on the generator as well, but they couldn't rely on technology to work with all of this. He wanted paper. Just in case.

He made twenty copies and then took a picture with his phone too.

Praise God.

It would take time. But they could do this.

With Darcie gone, he went to her assistant in the conference room. "Hey, Misty?"

Bundled up, she held up a gloved finger as she finished a call on the radio. "What's up?"

"We figured it out." He couldn't help the smile.

"You mean you can get the power back on?"

"Yep."

Misty jumped up from the chair and rushed him with a hug. "Awesome! How long will it take?"

He held out the schematic.

She leaned over and studied it. "I have no idea what I'm looking at."

"The hackers got in through the RTUs—the Remote Terminal Units—and shut the power down. Then they wiped the software and the entire system on each one. Which means there was no way for GVEA to get the power back online until they found this."

"How hard will it be?"

Jason shrugged. "I don't know, but Simon and I will head out there right away. I have a feeling that their engineers will have to replace every RTU. So each breaker system will have to manually be turned back on. It's going to take time."

"But you figured it out!" Misty reached up and kissed his cheek. "God bless you, Jason Myers." She pumped her fist in the air as the radio crackled to life with another call. "I gotta get this. Wait until Darcie hears!"

"Hears what?"

Jason spun around to see the head of their team. "Our fearless leader!" He couldn't contain his enthusiasm and hugged her.

But she was stiff and gazed at him with blank eyes. "What's going on?"

"We've found the solution." He explained the whole process again, but her eyes still didn't change. "What's wrong? I thought you would be overjoyed to hear this?"

Darcie's eyes pooled with tears. Her shoulders lifted and then sagged. "Natalie's dead."

*　*　*

Ten Hours Thirty-Two Minutes Since Blackout
32 Below Zero
November 20—9:46 p.m.

Darcie walked into her office and closed the door. It was freezing in here, but that didn't matter. She needed some space. Some quiet from all the mayhem.

Jason and Simon had left an hour ago to work with GVEA. Now that there was a solution to their biggest problem, she should feel relieved, but the deep sorrow stayed with her.

Chaz was shuttling people around and had helped to find three more vehicle-mounted jammers and shut them down.

Misty was handling the radio like a pro. Calm, confident, and steady.

The operations center was doing exactly what it was supposed to do. So why did she still feel like a complete and utter failure?

This whole disaster had been the perfect storm.

And had brought out every one of her weaknesses. At least in her mind. Had the rest of the world seen them too?

Resting her arms on her desk, she gazed out at the dark sky. Then lowered her head to her arms. What was wrong with her?

A knock at her door and then Misty's voice brought her head up. "Hey, Boss."

"Do you need me?" She heard the exhaustion in her own voice but didn't have the energy to fake it.

Her assistant's eyebrows shot up as she crossed her arms over her chest. "Nope. In fact, I was coming in here to say that we should probably take turns resting when we can. I'd say you clearly need to go first." Without allowing her to answer, Misty walked away and then returned with the smaller of the two portable heaters. "Here. This should help warm up the room a bit. Since it's just me in the other room, I'm fine with one." Glancing down at her watch, she clucked her tongue. "I'll come wake you in an hour?"

"Half an hour." That's what a good leader would say, right? "A power nap is all I need." Saying it didn't make it true, but it was worth a try.

"You got it." Misty sent her a soft, concerned smile but left and closed the door.

Laying her head back down, Darcie closed her eyes. Another wave of sorrow hit. But this one was different.

The room around her was cold. Almost sterile.

Student desks sat in neat little rows.

A long chalkboard at the front was empty.

The windows looked out to gray, cloudy skies.

There was nothing on the drab, concrete block walls.

"Darcie doesn't belong here." The voice of Mr. Oliver.

What was he doing here? Oh, how she despised that man.

From the corner of the room, Darcie watched her mom sit across from the teacher and nod.

"Mom!" How could her own mother agree with him? But her shout did nothing. She couldn't move her feet and get closer.

"She's not smart enough. She doesn't belong with the gifted kids." The man droned on.

Another nod from Mom. "You're right. She never has belonged here."

The weird room changed to their home in Juneau. But it was all black and white. No color anywhere.

Dad stood in the middle of the kitchen with his arms wrapped around Mom.

"I don't want you to go." Her mother cried into his shoulder.

"You know I have to." He pulled away. "If we didn't have Darcie, I could stay. When she came"—he shrugged—"she ruined us. She didn't belong here."

As he walked toward the door, Mom chased after him. "No. We can send her away. Get rid of her."

But then he was gone.

The room changed again. It was the hospital. She was the one in the bed. Hooked up to countless machines.

Jason stood over her, his face devoid of emotion, his eyes black. "It's time to pull the plug. It's best this way."

Darrell stepped into the room, a sneer on his face. "Yeah, she didn't belong here anyway."

The long tone of a flatline made her want to cry. But she couldn't. She was dead.

A crowd of faces stood over her. Jason, Misty, Chaz, Simon, Darrell, cowboy hat dude, wire-rimmed steel eyes, large lady, the mayor, the governor, Trooper Mitchell, and . . . Natalie.

She was the one who spoke. "You should have listened. It's your fault I'm dead."

CHAPTER TWENTY-EIGHT

Eleven Hours Since Blackout
33 Below Zero
November 20—10:14 p.m.

WITH A JOLT, DARCIE SAT up at her desk, her heart racing. She put a hand to her forehead. It was just a dream. A hideous one. But a dream.

She had to get out of here. Clear her head. She was no good to anyone like this. Grabbing her gear, she tried to shake the elements of the dream from her mind.

It didn't work, so she layered up for the cold outside and brought the other heater back to Misty. She forced her mind to the details of their crisis. "I'm going to check on the shelters. Any news on the National Guard?" They were supposed to be bringing extra generators, water, supplies, and lots of heaters and blankets.

Misty stopped talking into the radio and looked to her. "Three hours out."

Darcie nodded and headed for the door as Misty went back to the radio. That would put them getting in at roughly the coldest time of the night. The question was, how did they help the ones who needed it most? Her mind couldn't even grasp what it would take to make it all happen.

Which was unlike her. She was a master at organization and delegation. This was where she thrived. And yet her mind felt locked up. Unable to process.

Whether it was lack of sleep or food, it shouldn't matter. She. Needed. To. Do. Her. Job.

But she couldn't.

Darcie climbed back aboard the snowmachine, started the engine, and headed toward the heart of town.

There was no rhyme or reason for where she went. The streets were chaos. Looting and fires.

More cars on the road than normal. Probably because many people didn't want to try to make it through a night with no power when the temperature was so extreme.

Were the shelters all full?

Chaz had reported they weren't at capacity yet, but by now they were probably getting overrun with all the people who acknowledged at the last minute they were unprepared—whether by their own choice, financial reasons, or whatever. People without generators who hadn't prepared and had gone through all their wood during the day—if they had a woodburning fireplace or stove. People who had insisted that they were Alaskans and could soldier their way through, until they couldn't. And the people who had tried everything else and failed.

Darcie could relate.

Last week she would have wanted to scold those people. But now? She realized how unprepared *she* had been too. That no matter how much planning and research she did, bad people still did bad things.

Driving from one shelter to another, she checked in with each one. Only the numbness inside her grew along with the numbness in her limbs from the cold. Each place had encouraging stories and shared how many people found shelter and warmth. One man even told her that the Alaskan community had come together like a family.

Which should have made her feel better. But instead, her heart sank.

Natalie was gone. Was that her fault?

A small chapel on the corner drew her attention. A warm glow from inside told her people were gathered there. But it wasn't on the list as a shelter. Without a second thought, she pulled the snowmachine over and parked it.

Darcie ran up the steps to the door and opened it. The soothing music of a guitar filled the air.

Several people sat in the ten or so wooden pews. The room was small and intimate. Lots of candles burned for the light, and a small heater up at the front must be running by a generator.

She slid into the back pew. A woman walked over and handed her a blanket.

"No, but thank you. Save it for someone else who needs it." Darcie was warm enough with her coat on. At least for now.

The woman didn't say anything, but the sweet smile in her eyes as she touched Darcie's shoulder made her want to cry.

Which sounded sad to her own mind, but was also welcome. Crying was better than numb.

Then it hit her. The sparkle in that woman's expression matched that of Natalie's. And Jason's. Now that she thought about it.

The guitarist stopped and shifted some music on the stand in front of him. He began to fingerpick a beautiful accompaniment. An older woman stepped forward. She spoke as the man played. "My grandmother used to sing this old hymn for me. I doubt many of you have ever heard it. We've changed up the tempo a bit, but the original tune and words are just as powerful now as they were when they were penned. I think some of you might need this right now."

The guitar played a little louder and then the sweet soprano voice lifted to the vaulted ceiling.

> O safe to the Rock that is higher than I,
> My soul in its conflicts and sorrows would fly;
> So sinful, so weary, Thine, Thine would I be;
> Thou blest Rock of Ages, I'm hiding in Thee.

Looking into the woman's face made Darcie wilt.

The passion in her voice conveyed she believed those words. Had faith in those words.

Darcie longed for a place of rest. A place to hide in shelter and comfort.

All her life, every time she got comfortable, it seemed like the proverbial rug had been yanked out from under her.

> How oft in the conflict, when pressed by the foe,
> I have fled to my Refuge and breathed out my woe;
> How often when trials like sea billows roll,
> Have I hidden in Thee, O Thou Rock of my soul.

The guitarist played it even slower for a few measures, and the woman sang that last verse again.

Darcie wiggled on the pew, the words reverberating in her mind. When she was a kid in church, she remembered the pastor talking about God being their refuge. After church, she'd asked him what that meant. He'd knelt down in front of her and told her that it was like having a secret hideout with God the Father. A place where He would always keep her safe. No matter what happened.

But she'd tried to find that refuge when Dad left. It hadn't worked. She'd been just as abandoned and hurt as ever.

Someone cleared their throat. Darcie watched as a different person was up there now. Sitting on a stool. The man looked straight at her. "We're going through a rough patch right now as a community."

Several people around the room nodded and said yes.

She looked away from the man's piercing gaze.

"Well, God never told us it was going to be easy here on this earth. But He did tell us He would always be with us. That no matter what, He would always find us. Always love us. Always walk beside us in the darkest times.

"You know"—the man laughed—"I remember a bumper sticker from when I was young. It said something like, 'If God seems far away, who moved?'" He stepped a few paces back. "As cheesy as that might sound to your twenty-first-century ears, it's a great illustration for us today. You see, God is omnipresent. He's always here. Ready with open arms. For you. For me. He doesn't leave us. He doesn't move away. That's what *we're* good at."

Light laughter from around the room echoed off the beams above her head.

"I wasn't going to say a lot, but I'm feeling the nudge."

"Go ahead, George. It's not like we can binge our TV shows right now." One of the guys up front waved him on.

Darcie couldn't help but laugh. The attitude of these people in the middle of what was happening around them made her pause and think.

George—or at least, she assumed that was his name—got up from the stool. "I'm a recovering alcoholic. A bad one. My liver is damaged because of it, and I'm not an old man."

Yeah, he looked younger than Darcie. More chuckles from the room.

"My sweet Mama led me to the Lord when I was six years old. I was so eager to know Jesus. So happy that He was my very own superhero. But then my parents were killed in a car accident caused by a drunk driver. My grandparents took me in, and one died of a heart attack that first year. The other died of a stroke the next. I got tossed into the system. Had loving foster parents. They even wanted to adopt my teenage-angry self. But by that point I had no friends. Got introduced to the wrong crowd. Discovered that alcohol dulled the pain. I ruined that poor couple's lives. Put them into serious debt. And I walked away without ever saying goodbye."

Darcie leaned forward. The man was so sincere. And when he caught her eye, she saw that same look Natalie had.

She shook her head and looked down at her feet.

"Years later I was sitting in my own filth. Rotting in a jail cell in Mexico. How I got there? I couldn't even tell ya. But the man in the next cell starting praying out loud one night and then started singing.

"He sang the same song over and over and over again. Until I found myself on the floor, facedown, crying out to God, begging Him to take me back."

Sniffles were heard from the woman a few rows ahead of her. But Darcie only wanted to hear what came next.

"And you know what? I didn't hear God's voice audibly, but I felt Him imprint on my heart that all was forgiven—Jesus had already paid the penalty for me—and that He rejoiced in my return." Tears glistened on the man's cheeks in the candlelight. "You see, I knew instantly that God didn't leave me. He'd never abandoned me. *I* was the one who did that. Because He lovingly gives us the free will to do so. But He had been patiently waiting for me with open arms."

The guitar player started the familiar tune. Then George sang, his tone raw and gut wrenching.

> Amazing grace! How sweet the sound
> That saved a wretch like me!
> I once was lost, but now am found;
> Was blind, but now I see.

The familiar words rang out in her mind. It had been her favorite song to sing as a little girl. Darcie closed her eyes and bit her lip. But then George stopped for a moment. The guitarist kept playing, but George prayed.

The passionate plea from the man's lips was so heartfelt that she tucked her chin to her chest and squeezed her hands between her knees.

Then he started to sing again. Words she hadn't heard in a long time.

> Yea, when this flesh and heart shall fail,
> And mortal life shall cease,
> I shall possess, within the veil,
> A life of joy and peace.

As the last verse was sung, the emotions building inside her spilled out in her tears. Darcie jumped up from the pew, fled the little chapel, and hopped on the snowmachine. It wasn't the smartest idea to head out into the freezing cold while tears streamed down her cheeks. Her eyelashes and cheeks froze. But she couldn't deal with this in front of anyone else. She couldn't.

Every moment of hurt and abandonment fell away as she cried out to God. How much had she ached to feel loved and to know that she belonged? To realize that He had always been there filled her heart with warmth. She wished she could go back and tell her young self not to abandon her faith. That yes, life could deal horrible blows and be harder than she ever imagined, but He was still there.

Looking back she saw how many people God had placed in her path to bring her back into His arms. Even though she kept running, God kept pursuing her.

She pulled into the parking lot of the Emergency Operations Center and couldn't wait to talk to Jason. In the midst of this crisis, she was seeing everything clearer.

Racing into the building, she didn't bother to knock the snow off her boots or anything. By the time she reached the top of the stairs, she was out of breath and the tears on her face had thawed out and dripped into her scarf. It couldn't keep her from smiling.

Entering the code for the secure door, she couldn't get "Amazing Grace" out of her head. The way George sang it would stick with her for the rest of her life.

As she opened the door, a figure dashed out of sight. Who was that?

She stepped forward and looked at all the papers strewn across the floor. What was going on? "Misty? Everything okay?" Then she rounded the corner into the conference room and saw her friend tied to a chair with duct tape over her mouth. "Oh my goodness. What happened?" She dropped to her friend's side and pulled off the tape.

Misty shook her head. "Darcie, run!"

CHAPTER TWENTY-NINE

Twelve Hours Fifty Minutes Since Blackout
35 Below Zero
November 21—12:04 a.m.

THE DRIVE BACK FROM THE last power plant showed Jason how all his muscles were tied up in knots. There wasn't a way to get his back, shoulders, and arms comfortable.

Of course, some of that could still be residual from the accident. Or his brother kidnapping him. But he'd rather attribute it to stress.

Praise God that he and Simon had been able to talk to each man in charge at the power plants and give them the necessary info on what had to be done to restore power. Simon volunteered to stay and help bring everything back online at the main offices once the engineers manually replaced all the RTUs. It would take some time, but hope was on the horizon.

Jason hadn't been able to get ahold of Darcie, so he'd made the decision to send the information to the radio station so they could broadcast the good news. Letting people know there was a solution and the techs were working on it would help them to make it through—to endure for a little longer.

Prayerfully, by tomorrow afternoon they could have all the power restored. He'd seen the National Guard roll in just a few minutes ago, and that gave him another boost. At least knowing there would be more generators, blankets, heaters, and frankly plain ol' manpower to help with the crisis. Perhaps the looting and violence would stop once people knew help was here.

The familiar streets passed in the glow from his headlights. Funny how everything looked different without streetlights or traffic lights. He turned into the parking lot for the ops center. A place he'd come to think of as home.

Which meant what exactly? Was he willing and ready to give up his life back in Anchorage? His church? Band of accountability brothers? Friends?

The thought was hard to swallow. And yet . . .

The more he thought about it, the more he felt called to work here. And the idea of spending time with Darcie made him smile. But that was selfish to allow his mind to go there. His company definitely needed an office up here. Most law enforcement stations were under-staffed and underfunded when it came to cyber. Wouldn't it be great to be able to volunteer his time and help?

Not that he could have stopped something like this. He doubted anyone could have.

As he exited his SUV, his thoughts once again turned to his brother.

Kirk obviously wasn't involved with what Jason had come to think of as a "little environmentalist group." He'd gotten involved with people who had much more sinister intentions.

Was his brother too far gone to reach?

What would his mom and dad have to say?

Punching in the code for the door to their secure building, he tried to push the thoughts aside. But he couldn't. He'd put his whole life on hold for his brother. Yeah, he'd gone through school and worked hard—but it had all been to help him find his brother.

Well, he'd found him all right.

Not how he'd hoped.

The building felt like a giant walk-in freezer as he ran up the stairs. He let the hood of his coat fall back but left his hat on for the warmth. *Father God, please let people get to one of the shelters or have access to a generator tonight. Please.*

There wasn't any way people could survive without some form of a heat source when it was this cold.

His radio crackled. "Myers?"

"Yeah." He stopped at the third-floor landing. "This is Myers."

"Trooper Mitchell. I've been asked to inform you that the two casualties out at the pipeline viewpoint today were friends of yours. Sarah and Beth McPherson."

He swallowed hard. The news punched him in the gut. No.

Mac's family. His boss—David McPherson—had been one of the greatest mentors and influences in his life. That man loved his wife and daughter more than anything. "Oh man. Are you certain? What were they even doing up here? David wasn't with them?"

"Yes, we're certain. They were here for a school project Beth had chosen to do on TAPS. When we spoke with David, he'd stayed behind because of the CISA warning." The trooper went silent. "I'm sorry for your loss."

"Me too." Jason released the Talk button and climbed the last flight, his heart heavy. How long had it been since he'd called Mac?

"Myers"—the trooper's voice was serious—"I know it's late, but we've received a tip about the location of the cabin I think you were held in. Would you be willing to meet me out there and verify whether it is the place?"

"I don't know anything about the location, but I can guarantee you if I am inside it, I can tell you if it's the same place."

"Got some paper?"

"Let me get into the office." He unlocked the door and opened it, then pulled his flashlight out of his pocket. "All ri—" His heart dropped. "Trooper Mitchell, I've got a problem."

"What is it?"

"The Emergency Operations Center has been ransacked." Jason took long strides to Darcie's office. No sign of her. He headed to the conference room. Found a chair knocked over with Darcie's scarf on the ground and a strip of duct tape. "I also think our director and possibly her assistant are missing."

247

"Tell me what you see."

As Jason described everything in detail, he was convinced the women were in danger.

"It could very well be that it's just been looted. Both women have been helping with support all over the city. They could be at one of the shelters. Or perhaps they met the National Guard as they came in. I'll send someone over to check it out. But, Jason, I still need you to meet me out at the cabin."

Jason didn't like it. "I don't know."

"Write down the directions." The command couldn't be ignored.

As he scribbled himself a note with the vague directions, he shook his head. He should be out looking for Darcie and Misty.

"Look, it will take me an hour to finish up what I'm doing and then drive out there. So find out what you can about Ms. Phillips and her assistant and then meet me at the cabin as soon as you can." The trooper signed off.

Jason tucked the radio in his coat pocket and surveyed the room. Where should he even start? He wasn't an investigator. Finding someone on the computer he could do, but this?

Something cold and metallic pressed against the back of his neck. "I think we should follow your friend's advice and head out to the cabin as soon as we can."

His brother. Jason closed his eyes against the pain that started in his gut. How had his brother fallen this far? "Kirk. I should have known."

"Yep." His brother jerked him around to face him. "You should have. Now empty your pockets. All of them."

Jason did as he was told, except for the radio.

"Now take off your coat."

"What! If you haven't noticed, it's just a little cold."

"I can't risk you doing anything stupid. Take. Off. The. Coat."

Again, he did what he was told.

"Good. Now grab the car keys, and let's head out to the little SUV I've been watching you zip around town in. Like everyone's big hero."

The mocking tone cut Jason to the core.

They went down the stairs, and Jason braced for the cold to hit him. But he couldn't let Kirk know how much it affected him. So he took a deep breath before exiting the building and walked briskly to the vehicle. He'd already pushed the auto-start, and it hadn't been long since he'd arrived . . . so the vehicle should be at least a little warm.

"Don't even think about trying something. Keep your hands up until I get in the vehicle. Got it?"

"Fine." By the time Jason opened the driver's-side door, his skin already burned from the exposure. His long sleeve sweatshirt over a T-shirt was no match for thirty-stinking-degrees-below-zero. He climbed in and slammed the door shut. Buckled up. Then placed his hands on the wheel and waited for his brother to give him instructions.

"Alright, Jason. No theatrics or heroics. Drive under the speed limit. Don't attract attention and do what you're told. Then there's a chance I'll let you live."

* * *

Thirteen Hours Forty-Five Minutes Since Blackout
35 Below Zero
November 21—12:59 a.m.

Darcie wriggled her left fingers from the rope. Finally. One hand was free.

She and Misty had been at it for what felt like forever.

Darrell Collins had broken into their office apparently looking for something. Whether he found it or not, Misty hadn't known, but as soon as she walked in on him, he'd attacked. Tied her up.

Then he'd hit Darcie over the head with something. It had knocked her out for a while. By the time she came to, her hands were tied up behind her back. Darrell had hauled them outside and pushed them down into the back of his big SUV and driven away.

When they got to the cabin, he'd shoved them onto the floor and tied their hands together.

Darcie tried to kick him in the knee when she saw the blood-soaked shirt wrapping whatever wound he had there, but he had jumped out of her reach just in time. The crazed look in his eyes scared her. Then Darrell had passed out in a chair. Probably from loss of blood.

So she and Misty had scooted themselves on their backsides closer to the fire burning in the small fireplace. Their numb fingers couldn't untie knots. And she'd prayed for a way to escape.

Misty too. In fact, her friend hadn't stopped whispering her prayers since they got here.

Darcie glanced at Darrell to make sure he was still out. Then turned quietly to examine the knots that were left.

Good grief, this guy had used enough rope for five people. It was a good thing she had small hands and fingers. From the looks of it, she hadn't actually untied anything but somehow had maneuvered the one hand out.

"Can you get it?" Misty's whisper was low.

But as Darcie peered into her friend's eyes, she saw the panic there. "I don't know."

"My arms are asleep. That's why I haven't been able to help. My fingers are all pins and needles."

"How about you keep praying and I'll keep working on the ropes."

"Okay."

Darrell stirred, and they stilled. But he went right back to snoring. What would make the man kidnap them? Was he behind all this? Why? Just because he didn't get the job? From what Darcie had learned about the man after his little appearance at her first briefing in Fairbanks, he didn't need the job anyway. His family had money. Lots of it.

Working with one hand, she picked at the rope. But there were so many knots tied in the dumb thing, she couldn't make any progress.

"This is infuriating." She kept her tone as quiet as possible, but she wanted to throw something across the room.

"Even if we get untied, how are we going to get out of here?" Tears shimmered in Misty's eyes.

Lord, we need help. Please. It had been a long time since she'd prayed, but the peace that followed filled her with confidence and strength. "He shoved the keys in his coat pocket. If I can get them, we'll race out to the vehicle and drive away."

"But he's got a gun."

That was something she hadn't seen at first. Until he threatened to shoot them when he was dragging them out to his car. "I know. We'll just pray he doesn't wake up."

Darcie kept working at the knots, but the rope was stiff and her fingers cold. The fire was dying down. Another reason to hurry.

Prying another piece of rope free, she was able to slip out her other hand. Now if she could just get Misty untied.

"Please hurry. I'm not feeling too good."

Darcie moved so she could get close to Misty's face. "Take long, slow breaths. Nice and deep. In. Out. That's good. You're going to be fine. *We* are going to be fine."

Taking her own advice, she took deep breaths along with Misty and finally found the knot that would loosen the ropes around her friend's wrists.

Once she had it undone, Misty hugged her. "Thank you," she whispered in her ear.

"Okay. Now . . . I'm going to try to get the keys. You head to the door and get ready to run."

Misty nodded and shivered at the same time.

Darcie crept to Darrell and reached into his coat pocket, moving slow. With her fingers on the keys, she held her breath. Just a few more seconds and they could get out of here.

Wrapping her fingers around the keys so they wouldn't make any noise, she slid her hand out of the down jacket's pocket. When

Darrell didn't move, she risked taking another breath and stepped backward stealthily, keeping her eyes on him the whole way.

She backed into Misty. "Open the door."

Cold air met her back, and she whipped around, crashing into Misty's slight frame.

"And where exactly do you think you're going?" A vaguely familiar man stood there with a gun to Jason's neck. Kirk!

Her gaze connected with Jason's. He was here. While seeing him brought a warmth to her heart, the gun to his head kicked her heart into overdrive. What were they supposed to do now? Kirk was working with Darrell? None of it made sense.

"It looked like a nice day for a stroll." The sarcasm dripped from her mouth.

The man—Jason's brother—laughed. "This one's got spunk. I like her."

Darcie laughed along and crossed her arms over her chest.

"Get back inside." Kirk's voice turned menacing.

She and Misty moved back. And the two men entered. Kirk kicked the door closed with his boot. "Collins. Wake up!"

Darrell moaned and opened his eyes. He bolted from his chair, and despite wincing when he put weight on his injured leg, his gun was out and pointed toward the rest of them.

Now there were two men with guns.

CHAPTER THIRTY

Fourteen Hours Two Minutes Since Blackout
35 Below Zero
November 21—1:16 a.m.

AT THIS POINT, SHE DIDN'T have any brilliant ideas. Kirk had a gun at his brother's head. Darrell looked crazed enough to pull the trigger at anyone at any time.

Darcie stepped a couple inches behind Misty so her hand was out of view and tucked the keys into her coat pocket. Not that they were anywhere close to needing a getaway vehicle, but at least she had them.

Darting her glance between Darrell and Kirk, she hoped the fear she legitimately felt was in her eyes. As long as those two idiots assumed she and her friends were afraid and helpless, that would play in their favor.

Of course, she didn't want to admit the panic that screamed its way through each of her limbs, but it was there.

And poor Misty. The woman was shivering, a look of horror on her face.

"Tie him up." Kirk threw rope at Darcie and then shoved Jason in her direction.

She glanced at Misty and eased her friend behind her. Maybe she could tie Jason's bonds loose enough for him to get out. If they could come up with a plan after that, it would be a miracle.

She wrapped the rope around Jason's wrists and kept it loose with an easy cinch knot. Their eyes connected. His calm yet concerned. Did he have some kind of a plan?

What if she did the wrong thing?

At least she had an advantage right now since she wasn't tied up. But how long would that last?

Kirk shoved his brother into a chair. "Move, and I'll shoot one of them. Got it?"

"There's no need to hurt anyone, Kirk."

"Always trying to tell me what to do, big brother. Well, in case you haven't noticed, that doesn't work anymore." He waved the gun around. "We're going to wait here for your trooper friend and take him hostage as well. Then we'll have plenty of leverage to get what we want."

"What do you want?" Jason's voice was calm.

"Money." His brother sneered.

Darrell sank back into the chair. His arm hung loose at his side.

"That's what all of this has been about? Money? I don't think so. You're not the one in charge—you probably don't even know what all this—"

Kirk reared back his hand and smacked his brother across the face. "Shut up."

"You—" Darcie launched at him, but Misty grabbed her from behind. She bit back the rest of the words.

Kirk's laughter filled the cabin. But the gun was now pointed at her forehead. "That's a good way to get Jason shot." The smile slid from his face. "Or would you rather sacrifice yourself?" Stepping closer, he touched the barrel between her eyes.

Misty clung to her from behind.

Darcie's heart threatened to beat out of her chest, but she took a breath and swallowed.

He glanced out the window. "Right on time." Then he looked at her. "Don't do anything stupid. I won't hesitate to kill every last one of you." He reached into his pocket and popped a pill into his mouth.

A knock sounded at the door. "Jason? You here?"

She held her breath. Everything slowed down.

Kirk stepped behind the door.

The knob turned.

Darcie grabbed a log from the fireplace and charged Kirk.

As the door opened, she tackled him to the floor, and the gun went off. She clobbered him in the head with the log. Again and again. It burned her hands, but she didn't care. When Kirk didn't move beneath her anymore, she stood up.

Trooper Mitchell's eyes were wide as he assessed the room with his gun drawn. "Everyone alright?"

Jason jumped up from the chair. The rope fell to his feet, and he wrapped his arms around Darcie. As he pulled her close, the warmth was wonderful. Except for the fire in her hands.

"Darcie, what were you thinking? You could've been killed!"

She blew on her burned hands and shrugged. "Darrell had passed out again, and I knew it was the only chance we had. I wasn't sure if the troopers would be here or not, but I was hoping it was the cavalry."

Misty lunged for them and made it a group hug. "Let's not ever do that again, okay?"

Darcie laughed against Jason's chest and turned her face to the trooper. "How'd you know where we were?"

"We'd gotten a tip about the cabin. And Jason here had pressed the Talk button on his radio when his brother surprised him. Thanks to his quick thinking, we knew what we were up against."

Several troopers entered the small cabin. Two grabbed Kirk off the floor and handcuffed him. Two others went to Darrell.

"You okay, Jason?" Trooper Mitchell picked up the gun from Kirk's side.

"I am now." He pulled Darcie even closer.

She opened her mouth. Wanting to put into words all that swirled inside her. "Jason—"

"Look at this. A Glock." One of the troopers pulled the gun from

Darrell's hand. "How much you want to bet this gun will be a match to the ones used in our unsolved murders?"

Darrell came to and blinked at the man, shaking his head. "No way. I'm not taking the fall for any of this. I didn't kill anyone. I just hired a guy to hack the emergency WebEOC and put ransomware on there. Who you should be looking for is the mastermind. Kirk knows who he is." He nodded toward Jason's brother as the troopers cuffed him.

Kirk shrugged in response. "I thought you were the boss."

* * *

Twenty-Three Hours Nineteen Minutes Since Blackout
22 Below Zero
November 21—10:33 a.m.

Climbing into his warm SUV, he stashed his Glock in the console and then closed the door and buckled up. Allowed himself one pill. Just to get him through the drive.

His perfect plan had a few kinks in the execution, but it had done exactly what he wanted.

Created chaos. Created panic. Created distrust.

He'd proven that the government couldn't be their savior.

People would clamor for someone to truly help them. But he would show them what they needed was a leader who would take them into the future with their own identity. Alaskans were tough. They could take care of themselves. They were proving that. Right now.

They also had plenty of resources. With the pipeline, the possibilities of ANWR, and the largest state by far, they would do well on their own.

They didn't need the National Guard. They didn't need all the government agencies and Emergency Operations Centers.

The United States government had become corrupt with politicians. Career politicians. With their cushy lifestyles thinking they could speak what was best on behalf of the working man. The ineptitude was embarrassing. Well, they had shown they were all incompetent and a mess.

Alaska could stand on its own two feet and secede. It was best for everyone.

Especially him.

* * *

15 Below Zero
November 24—1:30 p.m.

The power had been completely restored for seventy-four hours, and the town of Fairbanks was still partying. Not that Jason could blame them.

He checked his watch and waited in the doorway of Darcie's office.

"Yes, sir. Thank you, sir." She hung up the phone and wiped her hair from her face. Leaning back in her chair, she smiled up at him. "The governor is coming and wants to present us with medals or something or other to show his appreciation for our quick thinking and recovery. I'm assuming you'll be available?" The smile that lifted her lips caused her eyes to crinkle.

It was so good to see her truly smile, breathtaking really. "Anything for you." He winked. She'd asked to pray together two days ago when they'd come into the office for the first time after their harrowing ordeal. And the words she'd spoken were simple but heartfelt. Something big had changed for her.

Yesterday had been so crazy, they hadn't been able to talk yet, but they would. Today. Because he couldn't wait any longer.

The engineers for the electric co-op had the RTUs replaced in record time, and the power had come back on twenty-four hours and two minutes after the blackout.

"The governor does understand that it will take us months to recover from this, doesn't he? The systems at the electric company alone will have their IT guys working until probably summer. Our office here too."

"Does that mean you'll hang around for a while?" Her eyes were hopeful. They mirrored the hope in his own heart.

"If you'll have me, yes. In fact"—he pulled a sheet out from behind his back—"this is why I came to see you. My company would like to keep me here to help you for the next six months while they build a new facility for a permanent office. There's a big need for cyber-security up here, and, well, I'm going to head up the team." He handed her the paper from the CEO of his company.

Her eyes widened as she read, and she jumped up from her chair and walked straight into his arms and hugged him. "I'm so excited for you!"

She released him, but he kept his hands on her waist. "Thank you. I was hoping you would be in favor of the idea."

She didn't pull away. "I am in full agreement." Lifting her hands, she placed them on his chest.

His pulse picked up speed. He had to ask her before he lost his nerve. "There's something I would like to ask you."

"Alright." The warmth in her eyes gave him all the confidence he needed.

"Would you like to have dinner with me tonight?"

She looked down and then bit her lip. "I'd love to."

EPILOGUE

26 Below Zero
January 1

DARCIE WATCHED THE SNOW FALL outside her office window. The flakes weren't large as they drifted down. The air was so dry, the moisture wouldn't last long. But she loved watching it anyway.

These early morning hours were her favorite. When the sky was still dark but the office was warm and cozy and she could work on her to-do lists for the team.

She'd found a wonderful church home and had been challenged to study the Bible more, so what better way to start the day—and her year—than by reading the Word. Maybe she should do this every day.

Jason had given her a new Bible for Christmas, and she let her hand run over the smooth leather. The perfect gift.

The love she held for Jason overwhelmed her at times and took her breath away. After all they'd been through, they promised to take their time and get to know each other.

But even with all her resolve to take things slow, she'd jumped into his arms last night as they rang in the new year and told him that she loved him.

Her phone vibrated and jolted her out of the warm memory.

A text from Jason. She couldn't help but smile.

God had done a mighty work in her heart and mind. Had helped her through some of the toughest hurdles.

Had opened her heart for love.

She lifted her phone and read.

> Meet me outside?
>> Sure. Let me grab my coat.

Crazy man. It was another brutally cold day. But she would go. Because she loved him.

Bundled up, she shoved her gloved hands into her pockets and took the stairs down to the exit.

But when she ventured into the cold, Misty stood there grinning from ear to ear. Not Jason.

"What's going on?" Darcie tipped her head to the side and eye-balled her assistant.

"I'm just the camera person." Misty shrugged. "Follow me."

"O-kay." She drew the word out. What was Jason up to?

Her friend walked her to Jason's SUV, where she opened the door. "Your chariot, Ms. Phillips."

With a laugh, Darcie slid into the passenger seat. Jason was in the driver's seat facing her, a bouquet of roses in his hand. She shut the door, and the echo of a door shutting behind her made her glance in the back seat. There sat Chaz, Simon, and now Misty. All with goofy grins on their faces.

She raised her eyebrows.

Jason grinned. "I needed witnesses."

"Oh boy. For court?"

His laugh made her insides flip. "Maybe."

She shook her head. Hoping that what she saw in his eyes meant that even for a girl who didn't believe in fairy tales, they could come true. She bit her lip.

"Darcie, life is too short and too unpredictable for me to waste another minute. I love you. Will you marry me?"

She glanced at the faces in the back seat. "Witnesses?" The tone she used to tease him was sure to get a rise out of him.

"Yep. So I can hold you to it even when I do something stupid and you get frustrated with me . . . I don't want you to back out." He pushed the roses toward her. "Well?"

She couldn't stall any longer. Her heart was about to pound out of her chest. "Yes. Yes. Yes."

Reaching over the console, he wrapped her in his arms and kissed her. A long, sweet kiss that made the interior of the vehicle heat up at least ten degrees.

Whistles came from the back seat along with the shutter sound of Misty's camera on her phone.

"Hey, guys, look!" Misty giggled and pointed to the dash. "It's twenty-six below."

Jason hit Play on his phone, and the string introduction to their song made Darcie's pulse skip a beat or two.

He opened his car door. "May I have this dance?"

"Out there? But it's cold."

"I'll keep you warm." He winked. "At least for the length of the song."

She hopped out, and they left the car doors open so they could hear the music. As Etta James belted out the first lines of "At Last," Darcie stepped into his arms and melted against him.

No matter what they faced, this was where she belonged.

* * *

23 Below Zero
January 3—4:42 p.m.
Fairbanks Correctional Center

A long buzz sounded, and then the heavy steel door opened.

"Sit. We'll bring the prisoner to you in a moment." The guard was a hulk of a man with steely eyes.

A minute later, another buzz, and a different door opened.

Kirk Myers sauntered in wearing his orange jumpsuit and a grin.

"Glad to see you're in good spirits."

"Of course." Myers sat in the chair while the guard stood watch. "It's meatloaf day."

"Phase one was such a success that I think it's time for phase two. What do you think?" He leaned back in his chair.

"I can't wait."

ACKNOWLEDGMENTS

EVERY BOOK TAKES A LARGE tribe of people to bring it to the point where it is in your hands. I'd like to thank a few of them here.

Jeremy, you are the most amazing man on the planet. Thank you for loving me. And for your brilliant idea that put this story into motion.

The heroine in this book is named after my dear friend and crit partner, Darcie Gudger. Darc, you've been through thick and thin with me. Thank you for the years of support and encouragement.

Steven Whitham and the ACI—Jack Voltaic Project—thank you for all you've done. Steven, thank you for double-checking the manuscript for accuracy and picking on me as only a good son-in-law can.

Amanda Knight—Emergency Management and Resilience Officer in Mount Pleasant, South Carolina. You are an incredible person. Thank you for assisting on this project. All the emails, texts, and phone calls where you answered my questions. I couldn't have brought the EOC to life without you.

There were several retired Alaska State Troopers who gave me wisdom for *26 Below*. I know you didn't do it for the accolades, but—thank you.

TAPS peeps—thank you for not calling the police when this crazy author called and asked a million questions.

Kayla—my beautiful and brilliant daughter who has always given honest feedback—thank you. Love you more.

Carrie Kintz—you are the best. For all the hours of reading, brainstorming, and sage wisdom . . . I owe you.

Becca Weidel and Kailey Bechtel—thank you for being willing to read even if it was only the first half. LOL—left you hanging!

My Mastermind Group—Jaime Jo Wright, Jocelyn Green, Tracie Peterson, Jana Reidiger, Becca Whitham, Darcie Gudger—you guys are the best.

I couldn't do this without my prayer partners—Tracie Peterson, Karen Witemeyer, and Jocelyn Green. I love you all.

The team at Kregel, editors, design team, marketing, publicity, all of it . . . thank you. Thank you. Thank you.

Karen Ball—lady, you know why this is here. You loved this story idea from the beginning and cheered me on. Thank you for believing in me. Love you bunches.

Tamela Hancock Murray—my wonderful agent. Thank you for all you do.

And to my readers—I know I say this every book. But I couldn't do this without you. You are my team. My cheerleaders. My tribe. THANK YOU.

To God be the glory!

NOTE FROM THE AUTHOR

I'M SO THRILLED THAT YOU joined me for *26 Below*. Thank you so much, readers!

Because of the very real threat of cyberattacks, I changed a few things in the story for protection of our emergency services. I have the deepest respect for our police departments and state agencies. The FPD and Alaska State Troopers had people who assisted me with the story, but I also chose to keep some things vague. This was intentional and not out of a lack of research.

Technology is ever-changing. Sometimes minute by minute.

BESS (Battery Energy Storage System) is an incredible initiative that was completed in 2003. Since there have been talks about updating BESS, to make this book as accurate as possible for future readers, I decided to fictionalize an upgrade (that hasn't happened as of 2022) and call it BESS 2.0.

The JACK VOLTAIC ® project of the ACI, its research, and events inspired much of the behind-the-scenes in this story. My incredible son-in-law—MAJ Steven Whitham—worked on the project as scenario developer, lead facilitator for the exercise, and software designer for the toolkit. I am so proud of the immense amount of energy he poured into it to provide life-saving information for cities, companies, and governments.

Steven taught me a lot about the cyber world, and I have to say there is a lot that scares me about our 24/7-instantaneous-technology-driven world. But I'm thankful we have the good guys like him on our side.

The pipeline in Alaska is a sight to behold. The engineering and magnitude of the project are astounding, and I raise my hand in full kudos to all the people who keep it running. It was a blessing to have several people from TAPS help me with the details.

ANWR (Arctic National Wildlife Refuge) is about nineteen million acres and is a highly controversial subject when it comes to drilling. For decades it has been debated about opening it up for drilling for oil and for a potential gas pipeline. While the wealth of oil and gas seem to be plentiful in the region, the debate is whether to disturb the refuge. It can be a hot topic for Alaska, so I brought it up in the story even though (as of the moment when I'm typing these words) a temporary moratorium has been in place on all oil and gas leases in ANWR.

Alaska is my favorite state and is very near and dear to my heart. I pray that I have honored her with this story and that you—dear reader—now have an insatiable desire to see Alaska with your own eyes. She is unlike any other.

Until next time, I hope you enjoy the journey.
Kimberley

ABOUT THE AUTHOR

KIMBERLEY WOODHOUSE IS AN AWARD-WINNING and best-selling author of more than thirty books. A lover of history and research, she often gets sucked into the past and then her husband has to lure her out with chocolate and the promise of eighteen holes on the golf course. She loves music, kayaking, and her family. Married to the love of her life for three decades, she lives and writes in the Poconos where she's traded in her hat of "Craziest Mom" for "Nana the Great." To find out more about Kim's books, follow her on social media. To sign up for her newsletter/blog, go to kimberley woodhouse.com.

SNEAK PEEK OF
8 DOWN

PROLOGUE

DOWN
8. Six letters. Number 6 on the periodic table.
November 25
Fairbanks, Alaska

NOTHING COULD HAVE PREPARED HER for the dead body at the crime scene. None of her training, classes, or visits to the morgue could have accomplished that feat. The impeccably dressed woman before her had been dead for several days.

Walking a 360-degree perimeter around the deceased, Carrie Kintz took in every detail. As a brand-new major crimes investigator for the Alaska Bureau of Investigation, the need to prove her mettle pushed everything else aside. She used the voice memo function on her phone to record all her observations—but kept to herself the thoughts of the horrible stench that almost made her lose her breakfast.

No blood. No signs of a struggle. No bullet holes, knife wounds, scratches. Nothing.

Was there a chance this woman simply died of natural causes and the only reason they'd called in the ABI was because of who she was?

"Hey, there's the rookie." Kevin—her supervisor and head of the division—pointed his pen at her with a wink. "So . . . have you figured it out yet?"

The veteran investigator had welcomed her like family and answered every one of her questions. Too bad he was retiring soon. She'd felt a camaraderie with him right away and would love to learn from him for as long as she could. "You mean, how she died?"

"Don't you mean, who killed her?" He tapped the pen to his chin.

Okay. So he was certain it was murder. Even before an autopsy. Huh. What did he see that she didn't? "Sure."

"Bet you weren't anticipating your first case to be the murder of the mayor of Fairbanks."

"There's been a lot I hadn't anticipated." She let out a breath. One entire day on the job and she'd already driven from Anchorage to Fairbanks. The Parks Highway was everything she'd read about and more. She'd seen Denali. She'd seen moose. She'd even seen a mama bear and two cubs.

But Carrie would gladly take the nose-hair-freezing weather outside over the stench here in this remote cabin.

With the entire Fairbanks office of the Alaska Bureau of Investigation working the aftermath of the cyberattack that could have killed thousands of people, her boss in Anchorage had sent her up north with a team to handle this delicate case. Said there was no time like the present for her to get her feet wet.

Funny how things worked out. Here she was, a part of the ABI with the Alaska State Troopers. A year ago, she'd been a police officer in her hometown back in North Dakota, dreaming of becoming part of the FBI. But when an old mentor with connections mentioned that the Alaska State Troopers were looking for investigators, she'd jumped at the opportunity to leave her small town behind. Her fascination with the work profilers and investigators did drove her to pursue the intense physical training.

Physical training that was about one hundred times more grueling than anything she'd ever done back at home. But she never gave up. She passed every test with flying colors. Then she'd been recommended for the ABI because of her assessments. Something she'd never expected but hoped to work toward.

With this incredible opportunity, she wanted to soak up every bit of knowledge and experience she could. Because the hope of being a part of the FBI still floated in front of her.

Maybe one day. A girl could dream.

"Why didn't the Fairbanks police move the body?" She faked a nose scratch, just to give her an excuse to breathe behind her hand for a second.

"They didn't find her until this morning and called us first thing. Boss asked them not to move her or touch the crime scene until we arrived. Just in case." Kevin studied her, then clasped one hand over his other wrist and narrowed his eyes. "The medical examiner is waiting on us to release the body, so we need to be thorough."

Alan—the third member of the ABI team from Anchorage— snapped hundreds of pictures around the body and the room, and then went outside to photograph the exterior of the cabin.

"Alright, Kevin." Carrie knelt in front of the woman who'd been powerful and alive a week ago. "What do you see? Teach me."

"My gut is telling me this was no accident. It wasn't because the power was off. She's not layered in blankets. There's a top-of-the-line generator that runs on natural gas capable of running the entire cabin. So we have to rule out the power outage and temperature. The mayor disappeared on the twentieth, in the middle of the crisis. Her security team had looked for her, but all other hands were needed elsewhere. We know that this cabin has been in her family for over a decade. *Why* did she come out here? Especially when she was needed. *How* did she get out here? There's no vehicle. The cabin has the highest security and alarms available. She's sitting on her couch like she was comfortable. We are unaware of any health problems. So . . . I'm thinking carbon monoxide poisoning."

"But I see two carbon monoxide detectors in plain sight right now. Wouldn't she have an alarm for that with the advanced status of her system?"

Kevin smiled. "Smart girl. Yep."

"Then why would you still think it's CO?"

"Because as we are all too familiar with now, cyberterrorism is on the rise. I'm betting someone hacked the system. And"—he stepped to the side and pointed to the window behind him—"it's open."

Only a couple of inches, but enough to feel the frigid temp of the outdoors. "I'm not following you. I thought someone opened it because of the smell."

"Nope. Her security detail sent a file to the office. The mayor hated open windows. Some weird pet peeve of hers." He waved her closer and showed her the file on his iPad. "Look, right here. As soon as the open window was noticed, things changed."

"Hmm. So, what . . . the killer somehow bypassed the alarm system and CO alarms, then opened the window to let the place air out? Why?" But as soon as the question was out, she didn't need him to answer. "Ah . . . they needed time to search for something and didn't want to breathe in the poison themselves."

"Look at this place." Kevin stuck out a hand and made a circle. "It's immaculate. Pristine."

The pieces fell into place in her mind. She could picture it like a movie. "This was cold. Calculated. Well-planned. The victim is untouched. Not only did the killer take the time with the murder, but they also took even more time to search for whatever they were looking for and then clean it all up."

Alan entered through the back door and picked up the conversation without missing a beat. "Yep. Not a single print found on the premises." He poked his thumb over his shoulder. "I can ask them to check again. Just in case?"

"No." Kevin crossed his arms over his chest and stared at the scene. "They're thorough. It's just as I suspected anyway."

Alan's phone rang, interrupting his next question. He tapped his earbud. "Yep. Whatcha got?"

Carrie held her breath and waited.

With a nod, Alan disconnected. "There's some files at the mayor's office that we need to see. Seems like she might have been one of the planners of the cyberattack."

"What?" Carrie frowned. "That's hard to believe, just from my research of her."

Kevin shrugged as he knelt in front of the dead woman. "People are capable of crazy things."

"I know. But it doesn't seem congruent with her public persona." Something wasn't right. But she couldn't put her finger on it. Carrie ran all the information they had so far through her mind. "To me, it doesn't add up."

"These things rarely do." He stood again and wrote on his iPad.

"What if she was framed?" Alan stuck a piece of gum into his mouth, which Carrie was learning was a sure sign his mind was working in overdrive.

"If she was . . . this case just got a lot more interesting."

Kevin strode to a space heater in the middle of the room and narrowed his eyes to examine the box.

Carrie tilted her head to the side. "He's taunting us."

A smile lifted Kevin's lips. "Good observation. Tell me what you see."

"This old decrepit space heater." The excitement of the chase was in full force now. "Why would the mayor even have it when everything else in here is top of the line? Besides, what's the point of it when there's a giant fireplace directly in front of you?"

"Exactly."

"My theory is that the killer left it here. Specifically for us to find. But why? To pin the cause of death on it? Isn't that a bit . . . elementary?" She studied the heater. In the exact center of the room.

"That's it. Your gut instinct was right on, Carrie. Whoever did this? I think he's insinuating we're not smart enough to figure it out. It's brash. The person we're looking for isn't going to be easy to find. They left nothing behind except for the heater—which was obviously intentional." He knelt beside the heater and let out a long sigh. "We're being challenged—dared almost—to get in on the chase and find him."